Marked

An Evergreen Academy Novel

Ruby Vincent

Published by Ruby Vincent, 2019.

Prologue

W ide, terrified eyes gazed at me in the glint of the steel until they disappeared in the gush of the liquid. It flowed down the metal—hot and thick and seeking my fingers.

Someone was screaming. Horrible, piercing shrieks that made it impossible to concentrate. Impossible to understand what was going on.

Why wouldn't they stop? Why wouldn't they—

Oh, wait...

I put my hand to my raw, aching throat and smeared it with blood.

The person screaming was me.

Chapter One

"Ugh. Size zero." Olivia picked up my uniform with two fingers and tossed it over her shoulder. "I used to be a size zero too, little show-off. Before you wreaked havoc on my hips."

My reflection rolled her eyes. "How many times should I apologize for being born?"

"Until I get my figure back!"

I burst into laughter, and after a second, Mom did too. Our giggles filled the room until a soft whine cut through our mirth.

I closed my lips with a snap and looked at Adam in the mirror. *Please don't wake up. Please don't wake up!*

The baby stirred from the comfort of my bed, scrunching up his little face, while I held my breath. After a few tense seconds, his face smoothed out and he settled back into sleep.

I relaxed and reached for my brush. Adam had fought his nap all morning, screaming and wailing so loud the neighbors must have thought we were murdering someone in here. It took so long to get him down that I was in serious danger of being late on my first day to Evergreen Academy.

"That was a close one," said Olivia. She reached over and pulled the blanket up to the baby's chin. She settled back onto the comforter, propping herself up on one arm, and watched me in the mirror.

Olivia, as she insisted I call her whenever we were in public, still looked amazing for her thirty-five years, despite how she complained about me ruining her figure. Mom's chestnut hair fell in soft waves to her shoulders, framing a heart-shaped face, Greek nose, and piercing green eyes with flecks of gold.

That face was my face. We looked so much alike people asked if she was my older sister and that pleased Mom to no end. Gray had yet to touch her brown locks and wrinkles dare not grace her skin. She was still young and in the prime of her life. Just ask her.

"You sure about this, kid?" The hand brushing my hair stilled as I pulled myself out of my musings. I met Olivia's eyes in the glass. "This fancy new school," she clarified. "Things have been different for you at Joe Young High. You've made friends."

"I'll make new friends," I insisted. I smiled at my reflection, drawing my lips across my teeth and grinning widely. The smile trembled as if the muscles had forgotten how to do this. It began to look like a grimace and I dropped it.

It's alright. Things will be different from now on. Soon... all of my smiles will be real.

"This is a great opportunity, Mom," I continued. "This is *the* opportunity. Of course I'm sure about Evergreen."

Olivia sighed. "I just don't want you to think you have to go because of—"

My grip tightened on the brush. "Mom."

"—everything that happened—"

"Mom!"

Adam shifted at my shout, but I didn't pay it any mind as I spun on Mom. She met my glare without flinching. This was Serious Olivia. This side of Mom and I were barely acquainted.

"Don't give me that look," she said calmly. "I only want to make sure you know that you're in control. If you don't want to go, then you don't have to."

The tension leaked out of my shoulders. "I know. I'm sorry." I took a breath and released it. "But I do want this, Mom. Kids from all over the world fight to get into this place. Having a school like Evergreen Academy on your application pretty much guarantees automatic admission to any university in the country. I'll go, graduate, get into a good school, get an even better job, and then"—my eyes swept my room—"I'll get us out of this place."

Olivia studied me for a moment, then she offered me a smile. "Glad to hear it, kid. You get your mom a big house and deck her out in diamonds and pearls. It's the least you can do."

I snorted. "Let me guess, it's the least I can do after messing with your figure?"

She tapped her nose and winked. "Exactly."

I shook my head and took the five steps to the other side of the bed to pick my uniform off the floor. My room was just that small.

I gazed around the space with the royal blue monogrammed fabric dangling from my fingertips. My old life and my new.

The cracks in the plaster greeted my eyes. I had tried to cover the worst with posters, especially the hole made when one of Mom's ex-boyfriends put his fist through the wall, but there was no covering the hideous puke green the landlord refused to let us paint over.

There was no disguising the brown stains dotting the ceiling due to the leaky roof. There was no hiding how cramped the space was, made even smaller by Adam's crib pushed into the corner that used to have my desk. That desk was in the living/ kitchen/dining room now. We had been eating off of it since Mom's last boyfriend broke our former dining table and we couldn't afford to get a new one.

This tiny two-bedroom apartment in the poorest part of Wakefield had been my house for the last twelve years. Living in government housing is as glorious as one would expect, but as I often reminded myself, it was better than moving from one friend's couch to the other after Mom's parents closed the door in their pregnant, college dropout, twenty-year-old daughter's face. And it was certainly better than the street corner we lived on for a time when I was two.

This has been all I've ever known... but now my life was going to change in every way.

I pulled open the door of my wardrobe and ducked behind it. It shielded me as I stripped out of my PJs and into my new uniform.

The top of the dress clung to my curves while the skirt flared at the waist. It was solid blue except for the stiff white collar wrapped around my neck. There was a definite Wednesday Addams vibe coming off this outfit but it was still quite stylish for a school uniform.

"In that case," Mom spoke up while I tugged my long, brown hair out of the dress. "Since you're skipping about going to this place, there's no reason for me not to go out with Marcy and Jeanine tonight. They invited me out to celebrate my kid getting into the best school in the country."

"Um, there is a reason." I poked my head out to give her a look. "Who is going to watch Adam?"

She waved that away. "That's what babysitters are for. There's this new club that opened on Fourth Street. I've been dying to check it out, and if they're buying, I'm all for it."

I shoved the wardrobe closed and hurried back to the vanity to finish my hair. I needed to hurry up. I couldn't be late on my first day.

"Okay, but who are you going to get?" I asked as I pulled my hair back and wrangled it into a scrunchie. "Not Monica. The last time she spent the whole time running up our cable bill and didn't change his diaper all night. And not Dorcas, she—"

Mom heaved herself off my bed. "Relax, relax. Mrs. Potter on the fifth floor is going to watch him. You don't have to worry, Val." She came up behind me and flicked the back of my head.

"Hey!"

"This isn't my first kid. I know what I'm doing."

"That's debatable," I mumbled under my breath, but not low enough.

"What was that?" Mom grabbed me from behind. I shrieked as she wrestled me to the floor. "You watch that sass mouth of yours," she cried as she peppered my face with kisses. "I'm the gold standard of moms. It doesn't get better than me."

I was laughing too hard to answer back. It had been a while since we messed around like this... and even longer since I laughed.

A wail shattered our fun.

"Look what you did now." Mom got to her feet and picked up a crying Adam. "I'll get this one a bottle while you finish getting ready."

She took him out and I scrambled to do as she said. In no time, I was standing at the door of the apartment with my suit-cases at my feet. This was it.

There was a sense of finality in the rickety elevator ride down. I knew I would be back at the close of the semester, but still, I couldn't fight the feeling that everything would change.

Good. I want everything to change. I gave a smile another try. *Evergreen Academy is going to be the best thing that ever happened to me.*

Chapter Two

Mom turned onto the final street and made a face. "Evergreen Lane?" she scoffed. "To go along with Evergreen Manors, and Evergreen Mall, and Evergreen Bowling Alley. Is there anything in this neighborhood that isn't named after the school?"

I answered without turning away from the window. The street she was mocking was surrounded by thick, lush trees reaching so high they blocked the rays of the morning sun. Their fallen leaves dotted the single stretch of pavement that cut through nature and we sent them flying into the air as we drove—a riot of reds and golds swirling in our wake.

"The Evergreens are an old family, Mom. They moved in over a hundred years ago, bought up the entire town, and built this school."

She hummed and then flipped on the radio. That was the end of the history lesson.

Sinking back into my seat, I sighed. Two hours and now all that separated me from my new school was a two-minute drive up a tree-lined lane.

I rubbed my hands down my thighs, smoothing out my dress. I wasn't nervous exactly, I was excited to be here, but I did wonder how a poor girl from the projects would fit in at a school the whole town was named after.

Mom crested the hill and there it was. I shot forward in my seat.

Evergreen unfolded before me, even more amazing than I pictured and I had been pouring over the school catalog since I received my letter of acceptance.

Sitting on one hundred and fifty acres of land was a structure of gray sandstone, turrets, and arches. It was like something out of a movie, or maybe something from a country we have never been able to visit.

Mom whistled. "Nice digs."

"Yep," I breathed.

As our car rumbled closer to the wrought-iron gates, I noticed three figures standing just past the entrance. Mom pulled the car up to the curb and killed the engine.

I stepped out just as one of the people peeled herself out of the pack. A girl about my age slipped through the gap in the fence and raced up to me.

"Hello, I'm Val—*oompf!*"

Squealing, the stranger threw her arms around me and squeezed me hard enough to burst me like a jelly donut. "You must be Valentina! It's so cool you're here." She lurched back and grabbed my hands. "My name is Sofia Richards. I'll be your *student guide*." She punctuated that with an eye roll, but the smile didn't leave her face.

"Nice to—" The words lodged in my throat as I took her in. There was stunning and then there was Sofia Richards. Her auburn hair caught the wind and it flew around her in a silken halo. It was almost as gorgeous as the dancing brown eyes and the full, pink lips stretched into a grin. There wasn't a single blemish or pimple touching her fair skin.

I wasn't ugly by anyone's definition, but next to her, I might as well have been a toad. You wouldn't have thought we belonged to the same species if it wasn't for the identical blue uniform dress that she wore. Blue for freshman. We weren't only the same species; we were also in the same class.

"—meet you," I finally stuttered. "Sorry we're late. I didn't mean to keep you waiting."

She flapped a hand. "Don't worry about it. I love you so much right now. You got me out of a whole day of classes. I'm going to give you the official tour and then"—she put her hand to her mouth, lowering her voice—"the *unofficial* one. By the end of the day, you'll know everything you need to about this place."

"Great, I'll just get my stuff."

I moved away but a hand on my arm stopped me. "No, they got it." She turned around and called to the two men waiting behind the gate. A closer look showed they were wearing uniforms of a different kind marking them as school staff. The two men sprang into action and crossed to the car, pulling out my suitcases when Mom popped the trunk.

"They'll take it up to your dorm room," she explained, "while I show you around."

"Looks like you're all set, kid." I twisted around and looked at Mom over the roof of the car. "I'm going to head out, but call me later. Not too late though, I'll be out with the girls."

"Alright, bye, M—" She narrowed her eyes. "Bye, *Olivia*," I corrected. "I'll see you on Parents' Day."

She shrugged. "If I come. Who's got time to be doing this two-hour drive every other day?"

"Love you too," I deadpanned.

She cackled, threw me a kiss, and slid back into the driver's seat. I shook my head as I pulled open the back door and leaned over Adam. The five-month-old watched me with huge, solemn eyes while I planted a kiss on his forehead.

"Bye, Adam. I'll miss you. I love you. See you soon."

"Aww," Sofia cried when I stepped out. "Who is this little cutie?"

"My baby brother, Adam," I said while she hooked her arm through mine. "They don't make them any cuter than him."

She laughed and we waved goodbye when Mom honked and pulled away from the curb.

"Was that your mom or your sister?" Sofia asked, keeping up the questioning while she led me through the gates and I took my first steps onto Evergreen campus.

"My mom," I said absentmindedly as I took in everything around me. It was a good thing eyes couldn't truly fall out of your head or mine would be rolling down the cobblestone path.

An ocean of green surrounded us only broken by a magnificent bubbling fountain, gardens, and benches scattered throughout.

"Olivia is one of a kind," I continued.

Sofia chuckled. "I bet she's got nothing on my parents. On my move-in day, Mom was so into texting that she walked into a wall. The great Madeline Richards had to go around with a massive bruise on her forehead."

"Wait, not *the* Madeline Richards. Owner of—"

"Honey Hair Care," she finished. "Yep, that's her."

Her tone said this was no big deal, my gaping mouth said otherwise. "She's your mom?" I cried. "But I'm obsessed with her stuff. One of my suitcases—the big one—is filled to the brim with Honey products. Her shampoo has you smelling like a wood nymph with gardenias in your hair and sunshine coming out of your ass. No wonder you're sporting that auburn halo of loveliness."

Sofia threw her head back laughing. "Auburn halo of loveliness? Wood nymphs? Do you always say exactly what's on your mind?"

"Yep." I put a little pop on the "p."

Sofia squeezed my arm. "Good. Then you and I are going to get along just fine."

My lips twitched in the beginnings of a smile. I had a feeling I had made my first friend.

The two of us passed under a single stone arch and something caught my eye. I pointed at the top of the arch. "The inscription. What does it mean?"

Sofia followed my eyes. "Quae sequenda traditio. It means 'tradition is everything.'"

I nodded and turned my attention back to the academy looming before us. My head went all the way back as I took it in.

"This is the main building," Sofia spoke up. "The dorms, swimming pool, courts, track, and greenhouse are in the back, but since you'll be spending most of the next four years of your life here, this is where we'll start."

"Cool with me."

Twelve-foot heavy oak doors stood open before us. As we stepped inside, I saw an E and A emblazoned in the wood. "It's like a medieval fortress," I marveled. "Seems like we stepped back in time."

"Back in time is right," she said under her breath. "You'll soon figure out how stuck in the past Evergreen is. These uniforms for one. Girls have to wear dresses and skirts while the boys have pants and polos. They refuse to change it or the class colors. Just wait until next year when we have to wear yellow." She shuddered. "No one looks good in yellow."

I had a sneaking suspicion that there wasn't a single thing that Sofia didn't look good in, but I focused on the courtyard we stepped into instead of arguing with her.

The trees were shedding their leaves in here as well and they crunched under my feet. It was a satisfying sound to go along with the birds hopping along the ground, chirping as they plucked goodies only they could see from the cobblestones.

Gray columns lined the open space, supporting the second, third, and fourth floors of the academy and I could see the heads of my new classmates through the spotless window panes. A smaller version of the fountain rested in the middle of the courtyard and clear, cool water shot from beneath the feet of a stone man in long robes.

"That's the founder of the school, Francis Evergreen," Sofia supplied when she caught me looking. "Come on, let's sit."

Sofia took off, pulling me along, and led me to the lip of the fountain. She sat down and patted the spot next to her.

"Is this the part where I pump you for info?" I asked. "Teachers to suck up to. The best spot in the library. How to sneak out after curfew without getting caught."

Sofia bumped my shoulder. "No, this is the part where I pump *you* for info."

I blinked. "Me?"

"That's right." Turning to face me, she pulled her legs up and folded them under her. There was an eager glint to her eyes that surprised me. "I'll be honest, I was the first to volunteer to be your student guide and it wasn't only to get out of classes. Everyone is dying to know what your deal is, so spill it."

"My... deal?"

She bobbed her head. "Yes! You're the first student in over fifty years to transfer in during the middle of the semester. Evergreen is known for the fact that, when they close admissions, it's *closed*. They don't let anyone else in until the start of the new term. They even turned away the son of a European duke and he offered to fund a new wing. We've all been taking bets about how special the new girl must be if she got administration to bend the rules."

I gaped. "Bets? So people know about me already?"

She gave me a look. "Um, yeah. Did you think you were going to fly under the radar?"

"Well, no, but..."

Sofia grabbed my hands. "So, what is it? Child prodigy? Cured a disease? Performed with the philharmonic? Started a nonprofit that changed the lives of millions?"

I noted right away she didn't ask if my family offered to fund any wings. No mystery why. Wheezing up in Mom's ancient Chevy with the rusted doors and bumpers held to the car with straps and strings was a good indicator that we didn't have money.

I shook my head. "Sorry to disappoint but I'm not special. I graduated Joe Young Middle School with a B average and the closest I've gotten to the philharmonic is the recorder I played in fourth grade. They took it away from me five minutes after I put it to my mouth and gave me a triangle instead."

She leaned away, a faint hint of surprise in her face. "But then... what is it?"

"Nothing. I applied and they made an exception."

"But they never make exceptions," she protested. "There must be a reason. Do you not want to tell me?"

She sounded so hurt at the idea it pushed back my irritation at her not believing me. There was a reason I had gotten in and it wasn't for the ones she was thinking of. It was also not something I would tell her.

"The only thing special about me is that I dance," I offered to save our budding friendship. "I was the best in my school back home."

"Ohh." Sofia immediately brightened up. "That explains it. Evergreen is all about having the best, but you'll find that out soon enough."

"What does that—?"

"Come on." She grabbed my arm and shot to her feet. "We've got to get this tour started."

My shoulder is going to be real sore by the end of this.

We passed under the columns and walked up to another set of double doors. I gasped—yeah, gasped—when Sofia threw them open.

We set foot on polished marble gleaming in the light of the chandeliers. The outside of Evergreen Academy was old-world medieval charm, but the inside was what you'd expect of a high-priced prep school. Chaise lounges lined the walls, and above them were heavy drapes blocking the light from the morning sun and plunging the hallway in a darkness that only the chandeliers could pierce. I didn't mind it. It gave the place kind of a romantic vibe.

My eyes drifted down and landed on a vending machine halfway down the hall. "Oh, sweet. I'm starving. I was too worked up to eat this morning." I slipped out of Sofia's grasp and moved over to the machine. It took me all of five seconds to see it wasn't a vending machine. Actually, I had no clue what it was.

"Uh, Sofia...?"

"It's a customize-your-soda machine," she explained as she came to my side. "See." She tapped the screen and it came to life at her touch. "You choose your soda and then you get crazy with the flavors. I suggest strawberry root beer. It shouldn't work, but somehow it does."

"Strawberry root beer?" I whispered. Of all the things I had already seen, this was blowing my mind biggest of all. "I can't believe this is my life now."

She giggled. "You can thank Milton Meadows. His mom owns Meadows Theaters and she donated these to the school. I think she was hoping it would get him good college references, but all it got him was laid. I don't think he minded the trade-off."

My eyes were glued to the screen as I flipped through the flavors. "He got laid for a soda machine?"

She gave me a wry look. "Like I said, the strawberry root beer is out of control. Plus, the arrival of these broke the no-soda ban. I almost jumped his bones too."

"Soda used to be banned?"

She nodded. "Yep. Along with everything else that's good and wonderful. Get ready, Valentina, because you're about to eat healthier than you ever have in your life. They keep us on a strict diet here and this beautiful machine before you doles out our only treat. We're allowed no more than two a week and I"—she slipped her hand into the hidden pocket of her dress and pulled out her id card—"am giving my last one of the week to you."

Something stirred inside me as she swiped her card where a coin slot should have been and the machine hummed to life. When it was done, I took out my cup of strawberry root beer, sipped it, and let loose an embarrassing moan. "That. Is. Delicious."

"Right!"

"Where's the Milton guy? I'm about to jump his bones too."

We burst into giggles, huddled against the weird little machine, and in that moment, I knew for sure, Sofia and I were going to be tight.

This time, I threaded my hand through hers before handing over my drink. "Alright, student guide, what else do I need to know?"

She took a sip before answering. "First off, this is where you live." Her free hand swept out to encompass the hall. "Freshmen are on the first floor. Sophomores on the second. Juniors on the third. You get the idea. All of our classes are down here so you shouldn't get lost, but I'll show you around just in case."

I bobbed my head. Seemed pretty simple so far.

"The freshman class is split in two. There's the front class and the back class. You and I are in the back class. We don't share any lessons with the front, which sucks because half of my junior prep friends are in the front class. We still get to have lunch together though. Also…"

I tried to soak up every word that fell from Sofia's lips as she led me through the school. I was only a month behind the other freshmen, coming in during October while everyone else had been here since September first, but already I felt way behind. Sofia seemed to know everyone and everything. She showed me the broom closet where people sneaked cigarettes. She told me the best way to make nice with all the teachers, and she taught me the dos and don'ts that never made the handbook.

"What's this room?"

I pulled up in front of a solid oak door with no sign. It was the only one in the eerily quiet hallway we had stepped into.

"Oh, that. It's nothing." Sofia glanced at the door, then back toward the direction we had been heading in. "We can't go in there."

"Why not? What's in there?"

"Nothing. It's just a club room." I got a familiar tug on my arm. "This way, I want to show you the auditorium."

I stepped away and we continued away from the door. Sofia kept up a steady stream of rules and information as we went.

"Don't go up to the other floors unless invited. Everyone stays where they're put."

"Wear the uniform dress, not the skirt and blazer. All the girls are wearing the dress."

"Don't sit up front in Professor Rossman's class. The man's a genius but gets so deep in his equations that he forgets to shower. You don't want to inhale that stink."

I wrinkled my nose at that. "Good tip."

"But never sit in the back in Professor Markham's class. She loves calling on people in the back."

"Right. Got it."

She kept up a steady stream of advice as she took me out the back door of the school. I whistled, cutting her off midstream.

Sofia released me and walked out ahead. She swept out her hands. "So, this is the rest of Evergreen Academy. What do you think?"

I would have said it was magnificent if my tongue would have come unglued. Instead, all I managed was "Whoa."

There were more buildings back here. Four looked like miniatures of the main building, one was clearly a greenhouse, and another I guessed was the sports complex from the sign above the door with a racket and hockey stick logo. Taking up the expansive acres were the tennis courts, basketball courts, soccer field, football fields, and all the other things Sofia promised.

One look also told me there wasn't a single soul out here either. Everyone was still in class.

I glanced over at Sofia while we tromped across the lawn. "Thanks for missing class to show me around."

"Of course. I told you I volunteered. I wanted to snatch you up first before the other freshies got their claws in you."

I chuckled. "So what about you? What makes you special?"

She heaved a sigh. "Nothing sadly. I graduated with a 4.0 and won the science fair all three years of junior prep school, but inventing a new shampoo formula that makes it easier to penetrate the hair shaft was only enough to get me an interview. It was the Richards' bank account that got me the rest of the way."

I goggled at her. "You invented a new shampoo?"

"Yep." Her tone was totally casual as we crushed green blades of grass beneath our school-issued leather shoes. We closed the distance to the building Sofia pointed out as the freshman dorm. "The Honeysuckle Dream shampoo line was my creation, but that was back when I was trying to earn Mom's approval."

I picked up on the note of bitterness lacing her words, but I didn't comment on it. "I think that makes you plenty special."

Sofia stopped in front of the door and looked at me over her shoulder. "Thanks, you're sweet. You've already complimented my smarts and my hair. Keep 'em coming."

We laughed and stepped inside. Once again, I was struck by the ancient charm outside coupled with the modern feel on the inside. In here was the appearance of a hotel lobby with the warm beige décor and before us was the sleek silver doors of the elevator.

"Sorry about this, Val." Sofia slipped into my nickname without me having to tell her. "But because you're a transfer you ended up with the short stick. Your dorm is on the sixth floor."

"What's wrong with that?" I asked as she pressed the button for the elevator.

She jerked her head at it. "This piece of crap is always breaking down. You'd think the richest school in the country would be on top of something like that, but no, they're cool with us hoofing it down the stairs. But no one wants to take those."

"Why not?"

She gave me a look I couldn't read. "You'll see."

Goodness, will I ever learn the ropes of this place?

Of course you will, another voice countered. *You'll figure it all out and everything will be just as you imagined. This is going to be your fresh start.*

I repeated that to myself as the elevator climbed floors, taking me to the place I would be claiming for the next year.

Everything is going to change. It will all be okay now. Everything is going to—

"This is you." Sofia broke through my mantra as the elevator came to a stop. "One good thing about being up here is that you're by yourself."

"I am?" I stepped out of the elevator and looked up and down the hall. It was true. There wasn't a single sign or decoration on the plain brown doors—a lack of personality to go with the pressing silence. My face fell. "Why is that a good thing? I don't want to be away from everyone."

She threw her arm around my shoulder. "It's a good thing because you don't have to listen to the asshole above you tap dancing until three a.m. or listen to your neighbor practice the same concerto for the fiftieth time. And you won't be away from everyone, you'll meet my friends tomorrow and the four of us will hang out all the time."

She sounded so sure, my apprehension fled.

Friends. Study sessions. Gossiping over lunch. A normal life.

Memory of the info in my welcome pack led me down the hall to room 605. It was a door like any other door, except for the electronic keypad waiting to do my bidding.

"They should have sent you the code." I looked over at Sofia. "If you don't remember, we'll have to go to the office and get it from Mrs. Bruner."

"I remember it. It came with a bunch of warnings not to share it with anyone else and never forget it. The letter even said if I put the wrong number in more than three times, it will trigger a deadbolt and set off an alarm. Why so intense about it?"

Her eyes left my face and drifted over my shoulder. "For the same reason there are cameras on both ends of the hall recording twenty-four seven and monitored by Gus and the rest of his security team." Sofia suddenly met my eyes. "They want to prevent another murder."

I stumbled back, goose bumps erupting on my skin as the breath left my body. "What did you just say?" I gasped.

As quick as flipping a switch, the smile returned to Sofia's lips. "Don't let me freak you out. It's not a big deal. I mean, murder is a big deal, but it was thirty-five years ago. A kid was found dead in his dorm room. They never found out who did it, but since then they beefed up security and keep beefing it up so that it never happens again. Parents don't shell out fifty grand a semester to a place that can't protect their kids."

"How—" I swallowed thickly, trying to find my voice. "How did I not hear about this?"

"They pay lawyers good money to make sure no one hears about it." She leaned in. "And you're better off never talking about it to anyone outside of these walls... or even the people in them."

I nodded. Here I was thinking it would take me a long time to learn the ropes, but I had already learned my first lesson.

Lesson Number One: Evergreen values its reputation above all.

I turned away from Sofia and tapped my code into the keypad. A soft chime signaled the door was unlocked and I pushed through into my new room.

I might have said "Whoa" again, but it was too small a word to encompass what my eyes were seeing.

Sofia walked in and spun on me, grinning away. "Like it?"

"Do I like it?" My head whipped this way and that trying to see it all at once.

A huge queen-sized tapestry bed took up the middle of the room. Next to my bed was a vanity on one side and a large oak desk on the other. The dark-stained wood matched the bookshelves perfectly as it did the leather armchair sitting in the corner on top of a plush carpet.

I shot away and burst through the door to my right. A bathroom—my own bathroom—was a porcelain paradise. The only splash of color was the pink wash basin and the gold knobs in the shower/tub combo. We didn't have a tub in my apartment back home, and I had a feeling I would be thoroughly abusing my new ability to take bubble baths.

"Do I like it?" I cried. "I love it!"

"Awesome." I rushed back out to find Sofia reaching for something on my desk. "Here. This is your class schedule, map, etc." She beamed at me as she handed it over. "Now with that, the school tour is officially over, and you and I are off the hook for the rest of the day." She rubbed her hands together like we were going to get up to some shit. "I've got birthday cake Oreos that I smuggled in after my last trip home. Wanna binge while I tell you all the juicy stuff?"

"Birthday cake Oreos? Girl, what you still doing here? Get them and let's do this."

I collapsed on my bed after Sofia took off, sinking into the downy arms of my cream comforter. I clutched the folder with my class schedule to my chest as if to keep in the bubbles of excitement that were rising and popping inside of me.

I pushed aside all thoughts of military-grade locks and unsolved murders. I didn't need to worry about Evergreen's past. It was the best school in the country and now I was one of its students, and after an incredible four years, I would change my family's life for the better.

Everything I had gone through—the sacrifice, the sleepless nights... the pain... it won't have been for nothing.

I tried another smile. Peeling my lips from my teeth and curling them up to my cheekbones. It felt strange, foreign... but it held.

Chapter Three

I pushed aside the skirt and plucked out another uniform dress. Sofia said all the girls were wearing the dress, and I wasn't looking to fight the trend. I was already the new girl they were taking bets on. Back home, I stood out for all the wrong reasons.

Olivia's loser boyfriends tended to dip their hands into her wallet. We never had very much, but when a guy was around, we had even less, which meant there wasn't much left over for Mom to buy me clothes to replace the ones with holes in them. It meant that when she had a job, she was working long hours and couldn't get me ready for school, do something with my thick hair, or teach me to manage the pimples and acne erupting on my adolescent face.

It meant that except for when I danced, the looks my classmates gave me were ones I didn't want to see.

"But that's over now."

I took down my dress and glided over to the vanity. My favorite song belted from my speakers and I couldn't resist a twirl as I held the dress to my body. My musical taste spanned the world and right now I was obsessed with Spanish pop singer, Alvaro Soler.

I reached behind me and twisted my hair behind my head. *Hair up today to show off my diamond teardrop earrings. Light makeup. Blazer. Silver tennis bracelet. White leather backpack.*

I grinned at my reflection. Oh yeah, I was ready for my first day.

Sofia was waiting for me when I stepped out of the elevator. She whistled.

"Damn, girl! You look hot."

"Hell yeah, I do." I spun around and smacked my ass. "You could fry an egg on this thing."

She snorted a laugh as I linked our arms, but it soon stuttered to a halt. "Wait... those earrings..." She scrunched up her face. "Aren't those from the Exquis Summer Catalog?"

I faced forward, breaking our gaze. "Are they?"

"Yes. I begged Mom for them but she said they were too expensive outside of a birthday gift. How—"

Sofia cut off the question, but I could practically hear it go through her mind. *How could I afford them?*

I let it hang in the air between us as we stepped out into the quad. This was nothing like the serene quiet of the day before. Now there were students, lots of them, streaming all over the field. The air was filled with a riot of shouts, laughter, and too-loud conversations as Evergreen kids met up with their friends in the few minutes before the bell rang.

"Ready for your first day?" Sofia asked.

I nodded. "You made sure of it."

Sofia was a treasure trove of info. After the tour, we spent the rest of the day stuffing our faces on contraband while she gave me all the details. We had only homeroom, chem, and English together as she placed in higher math courses, but she promised we could sit together and meet up for lunch.

We crossed the quad, keeping up a steady stream of chatter, until it became clear that something was up. I broke off and met the eyes of one student... then another... then five more.

Everyone was staring at me.

"I've definitely been picked out as the new girl."

"Don't stress," said Sofia. "Last night, I hit the group chat and told them all about you. The freshies know you're someone to look out for."

I swung my head around. "You did what?"

She picked up the pace, tugging me along. "Come on. The bell's about to ring and I want us to get seats next to each other."

Told them to look out for me? I glanced at the faces as we ran past. To be fair, none of them were hostile. If anything, most were curious, and from a few of the guys, even appreciative.

The two of us burst into a familiar hallway and strode past the soda machine as we made for the door at the end of the hall.

Half of my homeroom class was inside, and when we walked in, a dozen pair of eyes turned to look at me except one. Professor Markham didn't lift her eyes from her computer. I wondered if I should go up and introduce myself, but Sofia dragged me away before I could complete the thought.

We marched up to a wooden cabinet. "Cell phones in here." She opened it and placed her phone in one of the numbered slots. "We can get them back at the end of the day."

I nodded and placed my new cell in the slot with my student ID. I closed it, then followed her to the row of desks closest to the window. Sofia sat and pointed to the seat in front of her.

I plopped down and spun around to chat her up while the clock ticked down to the first bell.

Ding. Ding. Ding.

"Class, your attention, please." The class immediately fell silent.

I faced forward as Markham rose from her seat and surveyed the room over the rim of her glasses. She was an older woman, early fifties I would guess, and everything about her screamed professor from the round-framed glasses, to the smart pantsuit, to the smudge of ink on her chin.

"The media room is having technical difficulties so I will relay the announcements before you begin *silent* reading." Her eyes shot to a group of boys sitting in the back and they quickly lost their grins. "The votes were tallied and this year the theme of the Halloween ball will be a masquerade."

"Yeah!" The class erupted into whoops and cheers. Sofia grabbed my shoulders and shook me like a rag doll.

"This is going to be epic!" she squealed.

"That is enough." Markham's soft reprimand quieted the class quicker than a shout. "As I was saying, students will be given special permission the weekend before Halloween to leave campus to purchase your outfits and masks for the ball. If you're not—"

Bang!

The class door flew open and all eyes snapped to the entrance.

It's hard to describe the first time I saw him. I think I was a bit dazzled because it's the only reason for the words floating through my head whenever I think of that morning.

"Gorgeous..."

His rumpled uniform shirt hung completely open, buttons undone to reveal a toned, pale chest. The guy's blazer was slung over his shoulder, hanging off the crook of his finger while his backpack was clutched in the other as it trailed the floor. My eyes left his belly button and skimmed the natural dips of his abs as they made their way past the strong chin, full lips, and finally stunning blue eyes—and saw they were staring right back at me. The sun streamed through the high windows, reflecting off perfect teeth as his lips curled into a grin.

I knew right away he had caught me checking him out and I tore my gaze away as heat rose to my cheeks.

"Mr. Van Zandt!" Markham cried. "How dare you walk in here looking like that? Button that shirt at once and get in proper attire!"

"My bad." The words flowed from his lips smooth as honey and I snuck a peek at him through my lashes. He didn't look the least bit cowed by Markham's fury. "I had to rush to get dressed. I was handling some... official business."

The professor lifted her chin. "Be that as it may, *official* business is no excuse for being late or out of uniform."

Clicking his tongue, he gave her a two-finger salute as he crossed the room. "Right you are. Won't happen again, mama."

My mouth dropped open.

Markham turned so red I thought she would pass out from the rush of blood to her face. "It's Professor Markham to you!"

"Oh, snap," the guy said lazily. He didn't bother to look at her as he turned down the row next to me and Sofia. "Isn't that what I said?"

I sat up a little straighter in my seat. I couldn't help it; Mr. Van Zandt was staring right at me. He loped up to my desk and stopped, towering over me as my breath caught.

Then he turned to the kid next to me and snapped his fingers. "Nah, playboy. You need to hop out of that seat. I'll be the one sitting next to the new girl. We need to get to know each other better."

"Right. Sorry, Jaxson." To my complete shock, the boy snatched up his things and scrambled to a free desk at the back of the room.

Jaxson Van Zandt.

The name slipped into my mind and spread like smoke, invading every corner as he plopped down next to me and gave me another grin. It was hard to believe a mere mortal could be as handsome as the boy sitting in front of me. The only thing that came close to an imperfection was the growing, blond peach fuzz sprouting from a recently shaved head.

"What's your name, new girl?"

"Umm…" I looked toward the front but Markham had gone back to her computer. From the way she was stabbing the keys, I could tell she wasn't happy, although she didn't say another word to Jaxson. I turned back to him. "It's Valentina Moon."

He inclined his head as he did up the buttons of his shirt. I fought to keep my eyes on his face. "Cool name. Where you from?"

"I'm from a town called Wakefield."

"No joke?" He pointed over his shoulder. "That's my girl Claire's town."

I followed his finger and got my second shock of the morning. Claire gave me a small smile as she waved. "Hey, Val. It's good to see you."

"Claire Montgomery? Oh my gosh. How did I not know you were here?" A better question might have been why was I surprised she was here. Claire Montgomery had gone to my middle school and it was obvious to everyone that she was going to be the first of us to get out of our neighborhood. I wasn't a child prodigy, but she was. She had been leaving school early to take classes at the local community college while the rest of us were still goofing off in English. "This is amazing. We should—"

"You can have your little reunion later." Jaxson brought my attention back to him. "You and I are talking now."

I bristled at his smirk. *What is with this guy? Where does he get off acting like he runs the place?*

"I heard you were hot," he continued. "I also heard you can dance like no one's business and you're going to challenge Isabella's spot as head of the Diamonds." He slumped back in his seat, shaking his head. "That's bold, baby."

My niggle of irritation grew into a full-blown wave. "I'm not your baby," I snapped. "And I don't know what the hell you're talking about."

Multiple intakes of breath made me look away from Jaxson. The rest of the class was staring at me with wide eyes, even Markham had stopped assaulting her computer long enough to watch our exchange.

The only one with a smile on their face was Jaxson. He tossed his head back and laughed. "This one's tough," he said between chuckles. "That's cool. I like my ladies feisty, but—" His mirth dried up in a flash and he gave me a look that pinned me to my seat. "I don't like 'em clueless. You need to learn how things work around here, *baby*."

"You need to—!"

Hands seized me. Sofia's nails dug into the folds of my blazer, bringing my tirade to a halt. "I'll tell her, Jaxson," my friend said quickly. "I'm her student guide. I'll take care of it."

He nodded curtly and turned back to the front. We were dismissed.

I pounced on Sofia the second we stepped out of class. "What was that?" I shot a glare at Jaxson's back as he strode down the hall. "Why did you stop me from telling that asshole off?"

Sofia grabbed my arm and pulled me away from the crowd. "Because you can't tell that asshole off," she hissed. "That's Jaxson Van Zandt." She sighed. "Look, this is my fault. There's a lot more I need to tell you about this school, but I can't now." She glanced at her watch. "I have to get to trig, but we'll talk at lunch. Until then, stay *away* from Jaxson."

This situation, and the deadly serious look on her face, had me confused, but I nodded all the same. "Fine. Lunch."

She gave me one last smile before walking off. For the time being, I pushed thoughts of rude jerks aside and consulted my schedule. I had Spanish and Algebra I next and then it was lunchtime. I had gotten pretty lucky in that I was placed in all the same classes I was taking at Joe Young High. Evergreen Academy was a competitive place and I couldn't afford to fall behind.

Three hours later, I stumbled out of Professor Rossman's class in a daze.

Polynomials? What in the flip, flipping hell are polynomials?! And that was just the word I could make out among all that nonsense.

It was like Rossman had slipped into another language. I couldn't understand him or the hieroglyphics he had written on the board.

I trudged to my locker and threw my books inside. What was I going to do? Were all my classes going to be this advanced? How would I ever keep up?

Those questions plagued me as I followed a crowd of students to the cafeteria. Sofia had showed it to me on the tour. I had seen the marble floors, glass dining tables, leather upholstered seats, and the dais at the front of the room which held one single table. I had seen it all, so I didn't pause my moping to goggle over it again.

I was standing in line for lunch when someone grabbed my arm.

"Hey, girl. How's it going so far?"

I shook my head. "I'm sunk, Sofia. I didn't have a clue what was going on in Spanish or algebra. My first day and I'm behind."

She put her arm around my shoulder and squeezed. "Don't look like that. Evergreen is tough, but you're just as good as anyone. If you really need help you can sign up for tutoring. Head to the library after classes and they'll hook you up with someone who'll help you."

I lifted my head, perking up. "Okay. Good idea."

I asked about her classes while we stepped up and accepted our trays of brown rice avocado rolls, miso soup, and crunchy green bean salad. Sofia was right, I have never seen so much green on my plate, but I had a feeling I would appreciate my meals a lot more than she did.

"Come on. My friends already grabbed our table."

Sofia led me across the polished floors to a table in the middle of the cafeteria. Three faces looked up as we got closer, one of them familiar.

"Hey, Claire."

She smiled over the top of her book. "Val, it's so awesome you're here," she said as I pulled out a chair. "We never got to hang out much at Joe Young, but I hope we can now."

"Definitely."

"Claire you know," said Sofia, "and this is Paisley Winters, and Eric Eden."

The two gave me a wave. Paisley was as pretty as her name. Her long brown hair was piled on top of her head with little wisps hanging around her face. When she smiled, her elfin nose wrinkled.

"I've heard so much about you and we've just met," remarked Paisley. "I hope you live up to the hype."

I grinned. "I do."

She laughed. "For sure, I like you already."

Eric stuck out his hand for me to shake. "Not sure if I like you yet," he said with a smile playing at his lips. He was equally as handsome and I was starting to think everyone here was a special brand of attractive. He kept his coarse brown hair cut short, but had the cutest dimples. "My bet was that you were like a chess grand master or something. I lost good money on you."

"Sorry to disappoint," I teased. "What else did people bet?"

"Some thought royalty," Sofia spoke up.

Paisley raised her hand. "That was my guess."

"A few put their money on Pulitzer prize winner."

"And then, of course," Sofia went on, "there were those who thought you sucked the headmaster off."

I choked on my brown rice roll. "W-what?"

Eric shrugged. "It was more a dig on him than you. The guy is a tight-ass. He desperately needs to get laid and anyone who can unravel that wound-up, stuffy old jerk would deserve a reward."

"Right. Cool," I replied easily. Underneath the table, I placed a hand on my squirming stomach. Time to change the subject. "All I can do is dance, but I think my skills at that have been greatly exaggerated."

"What do you mean?" Claire lifted her eyes from her book. "I remember you in middle school. You were seriously good."

I shrugged. I knew I was a good dancer. We didn't need much money for me to flip on the radio or dance along to music videos. I loved to dance and I taught myself to be good at it, but still...

"I don't know if I measure up to people here who could afford dance lessons and coaches and formal training."

A look passed between me and Claire. "I get that," she said softly.

"I don't know about that." Something in Eric's voice made me look up. His eyes were narrowed into slits. "Even the mediocre can rise to the top at this school."

I blinked at the venom in his voice. Sofia twisted around to see what he was looking at and then spun on him. "Careful, Eric. Don't let anyone hear you talking like that."

"About what?" I looked over my shoulder and my eyes fell on Jaxson Van Zandt immediately. His blazer was nowhere in sight and his shirt was buttoned but not all the way. I was certain the peep show he was giving the cafeteria was against the rules, but he didn't seem to care any more than he did this morning.

Jaxson didn't head for the lunch line. He strolled across the room, collecting stares as he went, and climbed the dais. I scoffed as he sat down in one of the four empty seats.

"So you don't like that jerk either?" I kept my voice low. "Why not?"

Eric made a face at Sofia. "You mean you haven't told her?"

"I was getting to that," she said through gritted teeth. She shifted away from him to face me. "Look, Val, I should have told you all of this yesterday, but you looked so freaked after I told you about the murder that I didn't want to scare you off this place."

"Okay, so what did you leave out?"

She took a breath. "Jaxson Van Zandt... is a Knight."

I looked from her to the grave faces staring back at me. "Am I supposed to know what that means?"

"It means," Paisley cut in, "that he's in charge. There may be a whole administration office with little worker bees banging away at their computers, but Jaxson and the other Knights are the ones who really run this school—at least in the ways that matter."

I made a face. "Excuse me? You guys are messing with me, right? There's no way a fifteen-year-old boy is running anything."

"*That* fifteen-year-old boy is," Eric spat, "and it's not right. My dad and my grandmother were Knights. I should have been chosen."

My head was spinning. What were they talking about? No one was making any sense.

Sofia grasped my shoulder. "Val, do you remember that arch in front of the school? 'Tradition is everything.' Well, about a hundred years ago, Francis Evergreen founded this school and the Knights. This was back before guidance counselors and suggestion boxes when students were expected to settle problems among themselves.

"The old man's idea was that the Knights would be an extension of him. They'd keep the students in line, uphold the traditions of the school, punish those who needed to get in check, and leave him free to juggle his many mistresses. Through the years, new headmasters and headmistresses took over the school but they kept the Knights on. They were too good at their job and Evergreen was amassing a reputation as the best school in the world. Why mess with what was working?"

I put up a hand. "Alright, hold on. You're serious? You're seriously serious about this?"

Sofia, Paisley, Eric, even Claire nodded.

"I didn't believe it at first either," Claire admitted, "but you saw Jaxson with Professor Markham this morning. Does she seem like the kind of woman who would put up with that if she didn't have to? Not even professors can go against the Knights."

I looked up at the dais as her words sunk in. This guy held a title so important?

"But he talks like he stepped out of a music video and can't seem to remember anyone's name," I protested. "Who in the world thought it was a good idea to make him a whatever."

"I don't know but I'd love to talk to them," said Eric. "No one knows who chooses or how they make their choice, but either way, I'm a legacy. The last four Knights graduated and I should have been picked to take a spot."

"But why would you want that?" I asked.

His brows drew together. "Why would I want that? Why would I want to freely roam the school? Why would I want to be above the rules? Why would I want to have so much power that even seniors have to listen to me? Why would I want to follow in my dad's footsteps?"

I threw up my hands. "Okay, I get it. Stupid question."

"As for your other question," said Sofia. "Jaxson did grow up in a studio surrounded by the best names in music. That probably has something to do with him talking like a music video."

"He did?"

Paisley bobbed her head. "Val, haven't you heard of Levi Van Zandt? The—"

My hand shot out and gripped Sofia's forearm. "The most famous music producer since Jerry Wexler?!"

"Ouch!" Sofia cried.

I ignored her. "But he's produced almost every single one of my favorite artists and he—"

"—is Jaxson's father," Paisley finished.

I sunk into my seat. I had spoken to music royalty today... and he was an ass.

"So that's it," I croaked. "That's why they're picked. The Knights are people with money, influence, and a music collection I would kill for."

Claire shook her head. "Not all of the Knights have had money. The current ones do, but I've been researching them ever since I've got here and women and even students on scholarship have been chosen. There's no pattern. Four freshmen just open their lockers one day and find the card."

"The card?"

She nodded. "It's about the size of a playing card and just like one, it has the picture of a knight. One day it just appears and no one's ever seen who puts them there."

"So they get this magic card and... that's it? Everyone just has to do what they say? Even upperclassmen? What if they tell you to streak across campus? Or smuggle drugs in your crack?" Somehow I was buying into this nonsense and I had a lot of questions.

Sofia cracked a smile. "The point of them is to uphold the standards of the school. They wouldn't tell you to do something illegal and no one would expect you to go along with it if they did. But they do get a lot of perks. You remember that clubroom we passed on the tour that I told you not to go into? That room is theirs. It's what they get for being all important."

Eric nodded. "The Knights *are* important. Evergreen is probably the most competitive place in the world and it's loaded with geniuses, rich kids, and future masters of the world. Having a beef with someone here has bigger repercussions than in a regular high school. The Knights make sure it never gets out of hand."

"I get that, but still," I said. "This isn't the 1800s and they're a bunch of freshmen. If people didn't listen to them, what could they do about it?"

The table fell silent. I looked between their faces. "What? Why does anyone listen to them?"

Paisley lifted her head, looking me in the eyes. "Because if they don't... they get marked."

"They get what?"

"Paisley!" She snapped her mouth shut at Sofia's shout. "Stop it. That hasn't happened in years and it's not going to happen again because"—Sofia took my chin and made me look at her—"no one is going to go against the Knights or get on their radar. Right?"

I nodded in her hold. "Don't have to worry about me. I'm here to make the most of this opportunity, study my ass off, and get into a great college. Messing with people like Jaxson isn't on my list."

"Cool, then we're good." Sofia took up her chopsticks and went back to her lunch. But I had one more question.

"Who are the other Knights?"

Eric pointed over my shoulder. "You can see for yourself. The rest of the chosen just walked in." I twisted around to look. "Their names are Ezra Lennox, Maverick Beaumont, and—"

My chair crashed to the ground with a deafening sound. Every eye in the room latched on to me as I lurched to my feet.

It can't be. It can't be!

Our gaze connected and Sofia's worried cries faded under the roaring in my ears. His silver eyes swept over my face, lighting with recognition. It made sense that those orbs were silver because they were as cold as metal and as unfeeling as him. I prayed that I would never have to see those eyes again outside of the nightmares they haunted. I hoped that I would never again meet—

"Ryder Shea."

Chapter Four

M y tormentor. My bully. My worst enemy.

He stared back at me... then his eyes slid away and he kept walking without breaking his stride.

Sofia righted my chair and yanked me back down. "What was that about? Do you know him?"

I tried to speak, but the lump in my throat near strangled me. "H-he—"

Paisley leaned in and winked. "Let me guess. You are swooning over their collective hotness. I don't blame you."

Shaking, I peeked at the dais. Ryder was handsome but it had never been his looks that were the problem. I watched him take a seat and then looked away. My stomach was heaving; I couldn't stand the sight of him.

Instead, I moved over to the other Knights.

"The giant is Maverick."

I didn't have to guess who the giant was. He towered over the other boys, and while they all appeared in shape, he was ripped. Maverick bent over to drop his backpack at the feet of his chair and his polo rode up high enough to reveal his abs. I think a few people truly did swoon.

"Maverick is the son of Marcus Beaumont and namesake of Maverick Technologies. You can thank his daddy for the security system. He's also captain of the Kings. The boy dominates in football and soccer."

I didn't reply. There wasn't a hint of emotion on Maverick's angular face, or a hint of hair on his head, but it made him look mysterious instead of frightening.

"That's Ezra Lennox." Paisley moved on. "His mother is media maven, Amelia Lennox. She started as a reporter, cracked some of the biggest stories in the industry, and now owns three news stations and a restaurant."

Ezra.

Such a unique name for the most conventional-looking person I had ever seen. Unlike the other boys, Ezra was in full uniform and not so much as a thread was out of place. His leather shoes gleamed in the artificial lights, and even from this far, I could see he had a manicure. Strait-laced as he appeared, it didn't dampen those dark, tempting eyes or the confidence in his gait as he moved. Like the rest of the boys, he had a buzz cut.

"And last, but not least, is Ryder—who you seem to know."

"Yeah," I croaked. The words were ripped from my throat. "I know all about Ryder Shea."

I tried to fight it, but the memory sucked me back in.

"What?" he jeered. "What kind of idiot doesn't know how to swim?"

Water ran down his face and followed the cruel lines of his mouth. His smile was nasty as we stood at the rim of the pool. The water lapped at the sides, beckoning me in, but I couldn't take the plunge.

I balled my fists. "Why are you such a jerk now, Ryder? I don't have to get in if I don't want to."

"You think so?"

That was all the warning I got before he grabbed me and threw me in. I screamed as I plummeted into the pool and water filled my open mouth.

I choked. Coughing, sputtering, panicking as I sank.

"Help! Help!"

Laughter met my cries, filling my ears until my head sank below the water again.

I kicked out desperately. My arms windmilled as I fought my way to the surface.

He stood at the edge of the pool, stiff and immovable.

"Ryder, please," I screamed. "I c-can't swim!"

My eyes sought his, the pure unadulterated fear shining through... and complete coldness reflecting back.

I stopped screaming, stopped pleading... and the water claimed me again.

My world grew hazy—bending and twisting in the refracted sunlight. Those cold eyes would be the last thing I ever—

A hand broke through the surface and tangled in my hair. I cried out as Ryder hauled me back up and deposited me on the sandstone.

Pool water surged from my throat. I vomited and hacked onto the ground, tears running down my face, while Ryder walked off without a backward glance.

The memory shook me loose and I came to with a stinging pain in my palms. I had dug my nails in deep enough to draw blood.

I couldn't believe he was here... but then, I should have known he would be. Of course, he would be.

"Valentina?"

I snapped back to reality. "Hmm, what?"

Sofia was giving me a funny look. "I said, how do you know Ryder?"

My gaze went back toward the dais but Ryder wasn't looking my way. He was sitting in the middle of the table and, as if waiting for a cue, four girls appeared out of nowhere and placed lunch trays in front of the boys.

"My mom... used to work for his dad," I said simply.

"Your mom worked for Shea Industries?" Paisley responded, sounding way more impressed than she should.

"She was his secretary. Sometimes she brought me along when they worked out of his house or she couldn't find a sitter."

She hummed. "It's a shame what happened to him though. Ryder's dad. They say Benjamin Shea just disappeared without a trace. The news was going crazy last year, saying he might have been kidnapped and held for ransom."

"Only problem with that was there was no ransom," Claire put in. "And after fourteen months, it doesn't look like there will be."

"I keep saying the guy ran off," Eric added. "My dad's one of the shareholders of Shea Industries and there were whisperings that Benjamin might be replaced as C.E.O. With all the scandals, he was losing the company projects and respect."

"So, what?" Sofia said. "He doesn't want the embarrassment of being kicked out of his own company so he disappears and leaves his wife and child behind?"

I let their words fade in the background as I kept my sight fixed on Ryder. He was in the middle of listening to Jaxson. Something interesting by the way Jaxson's hands were waving. Suddenly, the table erupted into guffaws, Ryder included, and my lips curled.

"Oh, look. It laughs."

"Whoa, okay," Sofia said, picking up on my comment. "You obviously don't like him."

"What's to like?" I looked at his head. "Although, when I knew him, he had hair."

"At the start of the year, they all had hair," said Eric. "They shaved it when they accepted their position as a Knight. It lets the whole school, and whoever chose them, know that they're in charge now."

Anger blossomed in the pit of my stomach, mixing with all the other negative emotions. "Who in their right mind would make him a Knight?"

"Don't know, but with whatever bad history you two have, it's more reason for you to stay clear of Ryder and his boys."

"That won't be a problem for me. I don't know if I can say the same for him."

In a blink, Ryder's head snapped up and he finally met my gaze. As if he was listening. As if he knew every word that had passed through my mind and out of my lips...

He smirked.

I SAID GOODBYE TO MY new friends and bolted from the cafeteria. I needed to put as much distance between me and Ryder Shea as possible.

It shouldn't have surprised me that he was here. Honestly, I should have thought of this. The Sheas were richer than sin. Shea Industries built half of the skyscrapers that made up the New York skyline. His money, coupled with the fact that beneath that evil mind was a brilliant one, meant that Ryder was a shoo-in for Evergreen.

My eyes stung with unshed tears as I dove for my locker. I threw it open and shoved my head inside. I was so stupid to think I could have a second chance. A fresh start.

No, stop it. Don't give up. Don't let him take this from you too.

That thought stopped me cold. I took a breath, holding it until my lungs screamed for air, then I slowly let it out.

Too much had happened. Too much had been taken from me. I *would not* let this chance go.

Ryder and his gang could do whatever they wanted; it has nothing to do with me. There's no reason I would need to have a thing to do with Ryder, Jaxson, Maverick, or Ezra.

My heartbeat returned to normal. Everything would be okay.

I pulled my head out of the locker and slammed it shut.

Then my eyes locked with Ryder's.

"Ahh!" I screamed. I lurched back, clutching my chest. "What the hell?!"

"Valentina Moon." Ryder leaned back onto my locker, folding his arms. "What the fuck are you doing here?"

"Getting my backpack for art class," I snapped. "What are *you* doing here?"

"I can't believe it's really you." His eyes raked my body and I couldn't help pulling my blazer tighter. Ryder's smile widened at the gesture.

It was wrong. It was so wrong how beautiful he was. Neither the cruel curve of his lips or the stubby black hairs where thick raven locks used to be could change that. He was beautiful. Exquisitely perfect like that of a Greek statue—gorgeous, cold, unfeeling... lifeless.

Ryder cocked his head, resting it against my locker. "So how did you do it? You're too stupid to have won a scholarship, so that's out."

I bristled.

"But you're also too poor to afford the tuition. So how did you get in?"

"I applied. I got accepted." I gave him a shit-eating grin. "That easy enough for you to follow?"

He clicked his tongue. "Come on. This is me you're talking to. We both know it was more than that. There was a bet going around that you sucked the headmaster's dick for a spot, but that's not your style." He shook his head. "No, I put my money on your whore of a mother doing it for you."

My hands balled into fists. "Watch it!"

"You know." He went on like I hadn't spoken. Outside of our little world, we were drawing an audience. "I heard that Olivia Dearest had gone and got herself knocked up again. Does she know who the father of this kid is?"

A red mist descended on my vision and I launched forward. There was no time to think or I may have stopped myself. I placed my hands on his chest and shoved. "Don't you *ever* talk about Adam! Ever!"

Ryder stumbled back laughing as gasps went up in the crowd forming around us.

I folded my arms to stop myself from hitting him again. "Besides, aren't *you* the one who doesn't know where their daddy is?"

A flicker of emotion flashed across his face. It was gone as quickly as it came, but there was no denying that I had struck a nerve. I smirked. "How long has it been now? Fourteen months since the great Benjamin Shea disappeared without a word? But that's not before the months he spent in the news cycle, caught with woman after woman, many of them whose services he *paid* for." I could hear the harsh words dripping from my lips but I couldn't seem to stop them. They were being fed by another part of me—one I thought I had locked away. "And you call my mom a whore."

Ryder's face didn't change as I spoke. "Good one. Going for the most likely dead, cheating dad." The matter-of-fact way he said that made me shiver. He was so blank. Empty. "Looks like you caught a backbone in the projects. It was bound to happen sometime. But you're going to want to be careful, Val. Haven't you heard? I run things in this school."

"The only thing you run is that trash mouth."

"It's true. This mouth is trashy." Ryder closed the distance between us. He leaned in close, putting his lips to my ear. "It has been ever since I put it on yours."

My body shook with rage and embarrassment. Tears prickled behind my eyes but I wouldn't let them fall in front of him. "Just stay away from me," I forced out. "You and your little Knights."

"Maybe I'll do that"—he pulled back and smiled into my face—"or maybe I won't."

He walked backward, tossing me a wink as the crowd parted for him. "See you around, Val."

I stood rooted to the spot. It took the final bell sounding for me to snap out of it. Picking up the pace, I grabbed my bag out of my locker and hurried to the second wing. Evergreen hated tardiness almost as much as cheating, and I wouldn't be late because of *him*.

I clung to my positivity as my shoes squeaked across the floors. *That show was just to rattle me. Ryder hates me. He doesn't want to breathe the same air as me and he's made no secret of it. He'll keep his distance and I'll focus on my life.*

I felt slightly better by the time I pushed through into Art Studio I and came to a stop just past the doorway. It was incredible in here.

Students were scattered about the room donning smocks, mixing paint, and setting up easels. Above their heads, artwork of many styles and colors covered the walls. Every part of Evergreen had charm, but this was the first room I had stepped into with personality.

"Made it by the skin of your teeth." Her amused voice brought my attention to the front of the room. A woman in paint-splattered overalls stepped away from the desk and stuck out a hand. "You must be my new student, Valentina."

The woman smiled and it lit up her whole face. The dusting of freckles on her cheeks stood out clearer. Her green eyes sparkled brighter. I don't think I had ever met anyone whose smile packed such a punch except for Ryder—but it was for a different reason in his case.

"Welcome," she continued. "My name is Scarlett LeBlanc. Please, none of that Professor LeBlanc stuff. Just call me Scarlett. They brought me in to lighten up your stuffy little prep school lives and, Hera help me, that's what I'm going to do."

I giggled. I liked Scarlett instantly.

She cocked her head. "Goodness, you are a pretty little thing, aren't you?"

I didn't know how to answer, but this didn't seem like a question that required one. Scarlett released my hand and clapped. "So, I know it's your first day, but I'm afraid I'm going to have to drop you right in it. Today the students start their art projects.

It's due at the end of the month and counts for a quarter of your grade."

Wow. Dropping me in it was right.

"Everyone is pairing up and creating a painting that reflects who their partner truly is. This is more than a portrait. Any old bastard can draw what they see; I want you to capture what others don't."

"Um, okay. I can do that."

I couldn't do that. I wasn't even among the old bastards that could draw what they see. I couldn't draw at all.

"It's actually perfect that you're here," she went on, "because we have an odd number. I thought Maverick would have to partner with me, but since you're here, you can do the project together."

The floor went out from under me. "Did you just say Maverick?"

"Yes, Maverick Beaumont," she said cheerily, unaware of my growing horror. "He's in the back so go over and introduce yourself."

I slowly turned around. Just moments after swearing I would stay away from the Knights... this happens.

Maverick didn't look up from his easel when I greeted him. I stepped around him and dropped my backpack next to a free stool. This was a great spot. We were right next to the window and it granted us a perfect view of the grounds.

I turned away from the window and looked at him again. He was intent on his task, eyes fixed on his palette while he mixed paint, transforming them into his desired colors.

"Hey, did you hear me? I said I'm your new partner."

He didn't lift his head. "I heard."

"Cool. My name is Valentina Moon."

"I know who you are."

His voice was surprisingly soft for such a big guy. It wasn't soft as in high-pitched, but more like the bass of your favorite song. Not loud enough to crowd out the other instruments, but without it, the music was lacking.

I waited for him to say more. "Aren't you going to introduce yourself?"

"You know who I am too."

The dude's full of himself, isn't he? Accurate, but that's not the point.

"I don't know who anyone is," I countered. "This is my first day. But out of everyone, I need to know you if we're going to do this project."

Maverick finally turned his attention to me and amber locked with green. I had never met anyone with amber eyes before, but it turns out they were just as captivating as the books described. Maverick was even cuter up close.

Stop it! It doesn't matter how cute he is. If he hangs around Ryder then he is just as bad.

"...trying to find out?"

I blinked. "What?"

"I said, what do you want to know?"

"Oh, um... okay, let's do this." I reached behind me and grabbed my chair. I placed it right next to him and climbed up. Maverick's brows lifted at my sudden invasion of his space. "What do you like to do?"

He lifted his shoulders. "I don't know. Stuff."

"I can't scrawl 'stuff' across the canvas. Come on, dude. Dig deep. How about this: you're sitting in your dorm room, your

Wi-Fi is out, and your phone is dead. How would you pass the time?"

"I'd pass it by fixing my Wi-Fi."

I threw up my hands. "You're not going to make this easy for me, are you?"

Maverick set down his palette and I saw a ghost of a smile on his lips. "I am making it easy. That's what I like to do. Fix things. Build things. Code things."

"Oh." I sat up a little straighter. This was progress. "What kind of things do you build?"

Another shrug. "Electronics. Computers. Robots."

"Wow. I made a clock out of a potato once."

He was grinning now. "Should I file that away under things to know about Valentina Moon?"

I flushed. I liked the way he said my name. It went well with his throaty, bass voice.

"It is one of my biggest accomplishments, so yes."

"Cool, and what else do I need to know?"

I rolled my eyes toward the ceiling as I thought. "Let's see. I love dancing, music in languages I don't know, and holding chocolate on my tongue until it melts into sweet goodness. Your turn."

Maverick rose from his seat. My gaze traveled up and up until it passed over his smooth chin and landed on his face. "We should start. Scarlett will be over in a minute to find out why we're not painting."

With that, he strode off to get a smock, and after a minute, I got up to do as he said. The project wasn't due for weeks; I would have time to pick up the questioning. Here's hoping he would get more descriptive.

Ten minutes later, I was staring at a blank canvas. What was I supposed to do now?

I glanced over to Maverick to find him looking back at me. His amber orbs swept my face, staring with an intensity that brought heat to my cheeks. Then he broke contact and leaned over his canvas.

He's painting me, I realized with a start. *Maybe I should be painting him too.*

I couldn't think of another idea so I swirled my brush in the brown paint and got to work.

The two of us worked in complete silence for the next hour. At one point, Scarlett came over and opened our window, but I didn't break from looking at Maverick to the painting. Maverick. Painting. Maverick. Painting.

Every now and then our eyes connected as we studied each other and I felt the bubbles make a comeback, growing and bursting in my stomach.

I put the final touch on Maverick's head and then I sat back. "Done." Maverick pulled back and got to his feet. "No, wait. Don't—"

It was too late. Maverick moved to my side and saw my portrait in all of its glory.

"Wow," he began. "People tell me I'm handsome... apparently they're wrong."

A snort ripped from my lips. I giggled as I took in the lopsided head, overly large eyes, and jagged slash for a mouth. "File that away under info about Maverick Beaumont: he's funny."

"Keep that one a secret." I could hear amusement in his tone. "Like this painting."

"Haha. I get it. I suck."

A breeze came through the window and played with my hair, sending the wisps dancing in my face. I reached up to brush it away, and smeared paint all over my cheek.

Maverick walked away as I grumbled under my breath. "Great. That's just great, Moon."

I let out a soft squeak when firm fingers grasped my chin. I stared at Maverick, body still, as he tilted my head up and pressed a cool cloth to my cheek. For a big guy, his hands were gentle, and despite the coolness of the cloth, my skin was burning under his touch.

I was supposed to be wary of him... but at that exact moment, I couldn't remember why.

See him for who he really is.

Is this who Maverick Beaumont was? A secretly funny, gentle guy who was slow to open up?

Did I have to stay away from him? Being a Knight doesn't mean he's Ryder's friend.

The thought no sooner passed my mind that a vision of the four of them laughing at lunch followed it.

They were friends. And the only way I would have the life I wanted here was to let Ryder nowhere near it.

Maverick dropped his hand. "Class is over."

I looked up. Students were packing their bags and putting away their smocks so I rose to do the same. "So." I pointed at the back of his canvas. "Do I get to see mine?"

"Maybe some other time." Maverick took the painting down and I was granted only the barest flash of red before it and he were gone.

"TODAY HAS BEEN A DAY."

The soda machine had no reply for me, but that was cool. Soon it would be giving me something to make this day better. After crazy hard classes, bizarre hundred-year-old traditions, and running into Ryder Shea again, I could safely say this wasn't how I pictured my first day.

But now it's time to turn it around. Focus on what I can do.

I accepted my strawberry root beer and took a long sip, letting the sweet, sharp goodness chase away any lingering dark feelings. That's right; I was going to focus on what I can do, and top of the list was tackling crazy-hard classes.

I followed a familiar path to the library and found myself standing before oak double doors. I hid my drink behind the fold of my skirt and slipped inside.

"Excuse me?"

A man sitting behind a desk weighted down with books lifted his head. He squinted at me like he was wondering what I could possibly be doing here. "Yes?"

"Where do I go for tutoring?"

"G stack. Next to the computers."

"Thanks."

The book stacks were marked by letters and I was starting next to Z. I kept going, marveling at the serene, quiet atmosphere. There wasn't much light in here for a library, but I didn't mind the shadowed corners or the floating whispers of turned pages.

I had always loved libraries. Not for the books, but for the squishy beanbag chairs in the children's section. For the kind librarians who let you stay as long as you wanted to avoid the bullies outside or the sleazy boyfriend waiting at home.

I turned the corner at H stack and my eyes lit on the computers. A head appeared over the top of a computer in the back and I made my way to them.

"Hey, are you the tutor? I was hoping you could help me with—"

They turned to face me.

My mouth dropped open. "You've got to be kidding me."

Ezra Lennox lifted a brow. "Excuse me?"

"You're the tutor?"

A wide, pleasant smile settled on his lips. "That's me."

I glanced around like I was expecting the camera crew to pop out and yell "Gotcha." I wanted to stay *away* from these guys. Why was that so impossible?

"Are you looking for a tutor?"

I bit my lip as those eyes looked me up and down. The desk lamp shone on part of his body, but his face was caught in the dimness of the library. It made his already dark eyes appear inky black. I don't know why it unsettled me. He seemed perfectly harmless sitting straight-backed in his chair—his suit neat and pressed, his manicured hands drumming on the table, that smile on his lips. There was just something about—

"I said, are you looking for a tutor?"

I shook myself. "Um, yeah, but—"

Ezra patted the chair next to him. "Please, sit down."

I thought about ignoring the command, just turning and walking out, but the weight of my backpack and the assignments within them made me pull out a chair and sit.

Ezra latched on to the drink in my hand. He grinned. "What are you doing with that? This is a library, you know."

"I was thirsty," I defended. "Plus, I was craving something fierce. The strawberry root beer is insanely good."

His brows drew together. "Strawberry root beer?"

"It shouldn't work, but it does."

"Hmm. Let's see."

Ezra leaned in, and before I could comprehend what was happening, he wrapped his slender fingers around my wrist and brought my drink to his mouth. He didn't look away from me as his lips closed on my straw.

My heart picked up speed and went racing away. We were close. So impossibly close with only inches separating us while he sipped. I should have pulled away. I should have *looked away* but those jet-black orbs kept me pinned.

Ezra hummed. "You're right," he whispered when he was done. "It does work."

"That's... mine," I croaked much too late.

He chuckled. "So what do you need help with, new girl?"

I was abruptly reminded of why I was here. "It's math," I said quickly. "Evergreen is moving faster than my old school and I don't want to fall behind."

He inclined his head. "Lucky for you I'm a math tutor."

We were still sitting much too close. I moved back and Ezra automatically moved with me, maintaining the same distance.

"But unlucky for you," he continued, "if I decide not to take you on."

I screwed up my face. "What? Why wouldn't you tutor me? Isn't that your job and— Can you give me some space?" I hissed when another attempt to put distance between us failed.

"No." Ezra's lips stretched into a grin. "This is a library. We have to whisper. How else will you hear me if we don't sit next to each other?"

"Write me a damn note." I put my hand on his shoulder and pushed him back. "I like my space."

I pulled away but his hand flashed out and held me fast. "Hey!"

"Jaxson said you were feisty." If it was possible, his eyes had darkened even more. "Tough. Someone we would need to look out for."

I swallowed. "Yeah? And... what did Ryder say?" I whispered.

Ezra cocked his head. "Ryder? Nothing. Why? Should he have said something?"

I didn't reply.

"Nope, it was Jaxson who told me all about you," he continued. The charming, sweet smile melted away. His expression became harder—sharper. "But while my boy is a good judge of character, I prefer to decide these things for myself."

Without warning, he dropped my hand. "As you would have heard, I'm a busy guy and I don't have time for bullshit. Tutoring looks good on a college app, but not even that's worth it for stupid little girls who aren't serious."

I reared up. "What did you just—"

His soft words cut right through my rant. "If I'm going to tutor you, then you're going to work harder than you ever have. You're not going to complain I'm going too fast, because I'm not. You're not going to say I didn't explain it well, because I did. And you're not going to come back to me with anything less than an A. Do we understand each other?"

Tight as a bowstring, I met his gaze without flinching. "Perfectly."

"Good. Then you'll meet me here tomorrow at three o'clock. If you're late, I'm gone."

"I won't be late."

"Until then." Ezra smiled as he got to his feet. "One more thing—" He reached down and plucked my soda from my hands. "You don't mind if I have this, do you? I ran out my limit for the week."

I sputtered. "I do mind actually!"

He grinned at me with my straw between his teeth. "Then call it punishment for bringing food in here. I'm a Knight; I can't let you get away with breaking the rules." He winked. "No matter how cute you are."

Ezra loped off before my mouth remembered how to form words.

What is with these guys? It's probably a good thing no one knows who chooses the Knights or that fool would be hearing from me.

Shaking my head, I took my homework out of my bag and got to work—pushing aside all thoughts of flirty, funny, handsome guys who just happened to share the same title.

Chapter Five

The pain tore a cry from my throat. No matter how many times, it still hurt and the tears still came.

They wracked my body, choking me until I couldn't breathe... until I wished I wasn't breathing. Then the pain would stop. If I was dead, this would all go away.

My fingers wrapped around the handle of the knife.

I would make the pain stop.

I woke with a shout. Sweat covered my body, soaking into my sheets, and I threw them off me in a blind panic. This was the first time in weeks I had the dream. I thought this was finally over—that my new determination to change my life was taking root.

Though, I had a good feeling why it had come back.

My breaths came in rapid pants as the remnants of the nightmare slipped back into my subconscious. I clutched my chest.

I always felt strange after the dreams. Not just the racing heart or the churning stomach, but a feeling deep inside. It was a raw, achy sense like someone was scraping sandpaper against my soul.

Scratch, scratch, scratch.

Slowly but surely, it was being eroded away.

"It's alright. It's over. It's just a nightmare." Encircling my knees, I rocked back and forth as I repeated my mantra. "It's just a nightmare. It's over. It's all over."

When I felt like I could breathe again, I reached for my cell phone. It took a few tries for me to pull up the number, my hands were shaking so badly, but soon the phone was ringing.

"Val?" Mom's concerned voice came through the speakers. "You alright? It's after midnight."

"Sorry," I rasped. My throat was sore. I must have been yelling in my sleep again. "But I figured you were up."

"We're both up actually. Adam's been doing this thing where he doesn't sleep. Can't wait for him to grow out of that phase."

Despite myself, I cracked a smile. "Read to him next to the open window. He likes the sound of traffic. Puts him right back to sleep."

"Ooh, good tip. So what's up with you, kid? You liking your new school?"

Cold gray eyes flashed across my mind. "It's good, but did you know that R—"

I cut myself off. Olivia would have told me if she knew about Ryder being here. She wasn't the one I needed to ask.

"Did I know what?"

"Did you know that... I have my own bedroom and bathroom? It's great, Mom. Bigger than our whole apartment."

"Sweet, baby. I'm going to have to come up and bunk with you."

"I thought the drive was too long," I teased. I felt the tension slowly leak from my body as my sweat cooled. I was fine. I was safe now.

"It is, but it turns out I miss you, so what can you do?"

I chuckled. "I miss you guys too. Hey, can you put Adam on?"

"Sure. Give me a sec."

I sank back into my pillow.

I came to Evergreen for a new life and it was what I would have. The girl who experienced that pain would only exist in my nightmares.

No one, not even Ryder Shea, would bring her back.

I WOKE EARLY THE NEXT morning and went through my routine. Curling my hair, putting on my makeup, finding the perfect accessories. I finished up, gathered my things, and headed outside. I was crossing the quad when I heard a shout.

"I told you to keep your fucking hands off!"

I slowed down. A small crowd was forming in front of me, surrounding two boys. One was red faced and panting, while the other was grinning away. Both were wearing yellow uniforms for sophomores.

"Hey, dude," the smirky one said. "It's your girl who can't keep her hands off of me."

Red Face became Purple Face. He launched himself at the other boy and they fell to the ground in a tangle of limbs.

I was rooted to the spot, not knowing what to do other than watch. A shadow fell over me and I turned just in time to see Ryder bearing down on me. All of the Knights were. I tensed until I noticed they weren't looking at me.

The four of them walked around and I twisted to follow them. The circle around the fight broke apart the moment they strolled up.

"Boys, boys," Ezra said, a smile on his face. "That's enough of that."

To drive his point home, Maverick bent down and grabbed one of the boys by the collar. He hauled him to his feet like he didn't weigh a thing. Red/Purple Face struggled in Maverick's hold while the other kid scrambled to his feet and came after him again. Jaxson stepped into his path.

"Slow up, playboy. Ezra said you're done, so you're done."

"This doesn't have anything to do with you!" shouted Smirky.

"Actually, it does, Shawn," said Ezra. "Your father owns the largest medical supply company in the country, while Tobias's mom owns a quarter of the private hospitals. You two aren't going to ruin that business relationship with a girl both of you won't remember five years from now."

I was in serious danger of being late to class, but I couldn't look away. Was I seeing the Knights in action? Well, some of them anyway. Ryder was just standing there.

"Fucking hell, I won't remember," Tobias spat. "I won't have anything to do with this piece of shit!"

Ezra shook his head. "That won't do. This is how it's going to work. Shawn is going to stop being an asshole, and you're going to handle your issues with your girlfriend with her. Both of you are going to shake hands right now and make up."

Shawn bared his teeth. "How about this instead? You four fuck off and—"

Ryder moved so fast I would have missed it if I blinked. He grabbed Shawn around the neck and kicked the back of his knees. One second he was upright, the next he knelt in the dirt, crying out as Ryder forced his head down.

"Ezra, I don't think he heard you." Ryder's words were calm and unhurried. "What was it they were going to do?"

Ezra chuckled. "Stop being an asshole, handle their own shit, kiss and make up."

Ryder yanked the kid's head up. "And what do you say?"

The smirk was nowhere to be seen now. Honestly, I kind of felt bad for him. I knew what it was like to be on the other side of Ryder's *charming* personality.

"Y-yes, Ezra," Shawn stuttered out. "Sorry."

Ezra stepped aside and pointed to the now still boy in Maverick's hand. He had calmed down quick when Ryder sprang into action.

"Sorry, Tobias." Ryder released him and Shawn wasted no time in scurrying away. Maverick dropped Tobias and he did the same.

The four of them fell back in line and sauntered off like nothing happened.

So that's Knight business.

I don't know how effective it was at solving the problem, but they had ended the fight. Another thing they did was show me how much power the Knights really had.

"LUNCH LOOKS GOOD TODAY."

Sofia accepted her tray of steamed chicken lettuce wraps and sweet potato soup. She grimaced. "I'd give anything for something deep-fried and dripping with oil. I mean it. I'm not above sexual favors."

I bumped her shoulder, before accepting mine. "Out of your stash already?"

She nodded, lips turned up in a pout. "I'd do something about it if we were allowed off campus. But no, they keep us trapped in here like prisoners."

I looked around at the high ceilings, expensive tables, and five-star meals. *Some prison.*

"At least we're going to have some fun tonight."

"We are?" I asked on the way to our table. It was Friday which meant I had survived my first school week at Evergreen Academy—albeit barely.

"Oh, I forgot you're not in the group chat. Tonight, the Diamonds are having a sleepover, and since I'm going, you're going."

The Diamonds. Why did that sound familiar?

"Hey, guys," I said to Eric, Paisley, and Claire. "Are you going to this sleepover too?"

"I am," Paisley replied, "but Claire isn't." She shot her an exasperated look. "She has to study."

"We have a history test on Monday," she explained.

"I should be studying too," I admitted. "Ezra's a beast. I got one question wrong on his practice test and he assigned me homework. *He* gave *me* homework! Can you believe that?"

Eric laughed. "The guy's intense, but he's all about being the best and taking over his mom's empire. Every single part of his life has to be perfect, right down to his poor mentees."

"Yep," Paisley agreed. "That's why no one works with him."

I threw up my hands. "Thanks for the warning, guys."

They erupted into laughter. "It's not our fault," Sofia said. "I thought you were staying away from the Knights."

I grumbled under my breath. "Not easy to do when one insists on sitting next to you in homeroom, is your art partner, or the only way for you not to fail math." I snuck a peek at the dais. "At least I don't have to deal with Ryder."

Apparently, I wasn't so unlucky in life. Ryder was in the front class so we didn't share any lessons. Even better than that, he hadn't approached me—or even looked in my direction—since we got into it on Tuesday. I was right about him wanting nothing to do with me, and the feeling was mutual.

Ryder was leaning back in his seat, his head tilted toward the ceiling as his friends chattered around him. He looked lost in thought, so lost he didn't move when a long-haired girl set his lunch down in front of him. She popped a kiss on his cheek before moving away and sitting down at the table just before the dais, but Ryder's silver grays stayed fixed on the ceiling.

I wonder what thoughts go through the mind of the devil.

"Staring at Ryder again?"

I jerked. "What? No!"

Sofia gave me a knowing look. "Don't worry about him. He's not going tonight, but *you* are. You can do math tomorrow."

I could fight her but she would only use the password I had given her the day before to burst into my room and drag me out. "A party does sound fun."

She squealed and threw her arms around me.

We got back to our lunch and the topic changed to classes and homework. The day passed quickly and soon the final bell was ringing my freedom. I hurried out of Tamaran's social studies class and beat it for my locker. I wanted to get back to my dorm and figure out my outfit for the sleepover/party.

I wasn't invited to many—any—parties back home in Wakefield. I didn't want to mess up on my first one.

"Valentina?"

I skidded to a stop. Spinning around, I saw Scarlett waving at me from the doorway of the art studio. "Can you come in here for a second?"

"Sure."

I walked over to her and she stood aside to let me pass. The room was empty but it looked like a horde of people had stepped out only seconds ago. Smocks were on the floor and open jars of paint on the easels.

"Do you need help cleaning up?"

Scarlett shook her head. "That's sweet, but I have little helpers for that." She pointed across the room at my spot. "I wanted to see you because I looked over the painting you did of Maverick and... yikes."

I choked. "Scarlett, you're a teacher! You're not allowed to say that."

She clapped her hand over her mouth. Her eyes danced as she smothered a laugh. "I haven't been much of one or I would have helped you out sooner. I can see you didn't take art in your old school."

"No. It was optional at Joe Young and with dance as an elective; I signed up for that in a second."

She put her arm around my shoulder and drew me to her side. Together we moved over to my easel. "Well, you have to take it here and at the Evergreen Junior Prep school. A lot of these students had me already, and I don't want you to be at a disadvantage. I can work with you after school if you'd like."

"Really? That would be great. Thank you." Evergreen truly was a great school. No teacher at Joe Young would have given up their afternoons for me.

Scarlett waved away my thanks. "I have to make sure you do Maverick justice. He made an incredible painting of you."

"He did?"

"Yep." Scarlett dropped her arm and went over to Maverick's station. The painting Maverick had refused to let me see was hiding behind the white cloth.

I froze when she ripped it off.

"Wow..." was all I got out before words deserted me.

Incredible seemed too small a word for the job Maverick had done. In the painting I was hunched over the canvas, my face screwed up in concentration. Maverick had gotten every detail down to the wrinkle between my eyes and the way I chewed my lip when I was thinking. The eyes of the girl staring back at me sparkled with a light mix of gold paint, and I wondered if I really looked this beautiful or if it was just how he saw me.

"He's good, isn't he?" There was a note of pride in her voice. "So how about Tuesdays and Thursdays after school?"

I already had tutoring with Ezra on Mondays and Wednesdays, but one look at Maverick's painting told me I wasn't on his level. I needed to up my game if I was going to ace our art project. "Tuesdays and Thursdays it is."

I said bye to Scarlett and headed out. Maverick's painting took over my thoughts as I got my things out of my locker and made for the freshman dorm. Maverick wasn't full of himself like Jaxson, a taskmaster like Ezra, or a sadist like Ryder. Of the four Knights, he seemed the most chill—content to paint and dodge questions about who he was.

It's like I thought when I first saw him. He's mysterious. He'll make me work for it, but if I dig deeper, maybe I'll meet the guy who creates such beauty.

I clutched my backpack tighter. Hold on. What was I thinking? I didn't sound like an art partner, I sounded like a girl with a crush. But did I have a crush on Maverick? I couldn't remember the last time I had one of those.

I crossed the quad and let myself in through the dorm's entrance. *You don't have time for crushes even if this was one. And you definitely don't have time to crush on Ryder's friends. Maverick seems okay but I can only imagine the things Ryder has said about me to him.*

My eyes lit upon the elevator and the sign taped to the metal doors.

Out of order.

Veering off, I made for the staircase instead.

It was just a painting, I thought as I climbed the steps. *There's no reason to read into—*

"Ahh, yes!"

A moan promptly ripped me out of my thoughts. *What the fuck?*

I slowed down as the moaning got louder. Rounding the corner, my eyes popped when they landed on the people in the stairwell. I recognized the girl instantly. She was the one who brought Ryder his lunch. Even with her face screwed up like that, I could see she was pretty. Her legs were wrapped around his waist while he pressed her up against the wall.

There was no mistaking that bald back of the head. That was Ryder, and that was the girl's panties hanging off her ankle.

I didn't give a thought to them seeing me. I darted up the stairs and ran past, not stopping until I was safely in my dorm with the electronic lock clicking into place.

I JUMPED WHEN THE DOOR flew open. "Sofia, I almost burned myself!"

She laughed as she plopped down on my bed. "Sorry. You ready to go?"

"My hair's done." I set down the hot iron and gave my curls one last fluff. "I haven't picked out my outfit."

"I'll handle that."

I caught a glimpse of her in the mirror. Sofia had gone for matching silk lavender shorts and a tank top.

"Sof, tell me if I'm right. Is the reason no one takes the stairs because students like to take advantage of the fact that there are no cameras in there?"

She shot me a look over her shoulder. "Got it in one. They monitor the cameras all day and night, and will report us if a boy comes into our rooms, or we go into theirs. So people end up screwing in the stairs." She sighed. "It's shameless, but I've had a few late-night hookups in there too. You do what you gotta do."

Necessity or not, I did not want to see Ryder handling his business ever again. I think I would be putting in the next complaint about the broken-down elevators.

"Ooh. This one for sure." Sofia pulled out a pink cotton tank and pink plaid shorts. She giggled. "You have to wear the matching bunny slippers too."

I accepted my outfit and tossed her a grin. "Don't think I won't. I'm shameless too."

She lost her smile. "Wait, no. I was kidding."

Laughing, I darted away and snatched them from the closet. I was halfway to my bathroom when she tackled me. We collapsed on my bed in a shrieking heap.

"Put them back!"

"Never!"

I was laughing so hard I thought my sides would split open. It was hard to imagine I could be happier than I was right now.

"I CAN'T BELIEVE YOU wore the shoes," Sofia mumbled under her breath.

I was right behind her as we stepped onto the ground floor. "I can't believe you thought I wouldn't." I poked her in the back. "Anyway, I spent so much time fighting you off; I never got to hear more about this sleepover. Who is throwing it again?"

"The Diamonds." The words floated over her shoulder as she led me down the hall. "They are the last thing you need to know about this place and then my duties as student guide will be complete."

"Goodness. You've been holding out more from me?"

She chuckled as we pulled up in front of the last door at the end of the hall. Music poured from the cracks, loud enough to vibrate the walls.

"It's not as big as the Knights," she assured me. "And despite what people have been saying, I don't think you need to be worried about Isabella."

My eyes popped. "Worried? About what? And what are people saying?"

She shook her head. "You really need to get in the group chat."

Sofia popped open the door and the noise drowned out my reply. About a dozen girls turned on us when we stepped inside. A few of them I knew from my classes. One was Paisley and I waved at her. A couple I had only passed in the hallway, and one—

The girl from the stairwell. She looked up and stared me right in the face. I stiffened, waiting for the hint of recognition, but her eyes just slid off me and she went back to talking to the girl next to her.

She looked good. Everyone here looked good. It was all slinky lingerie, spaghetti strap tops, and shorts short enough to show off their cheeks.

Sofia grabbed my hand and dragged me over to the desk/food table. I sucked in a breath at the spread. Cookies, candy, soda, chips, you name it. Every single thing banned from our diet was laid out before me.

"How did they score this?" I asked before I snagged a handful of Cheetos and shoved them in my mouth. The moan that escaped me was pornographic.

"Isabella gets special permission to leave campus on the weekends to train with her instructor. She brings back the best stuff. Why did you think I wanted to come tonight?"

Sofia disappeared about a quarter bowl of chips before pulling me away. We huddled into the corner between the wall and wardrobe. "Okay, listen up. Final lesson." Sofia gestured with her chin. "You see those girls by the bathroom?"

I followed her eyes. Staircase girl was standing there with two other girls. The three of them were stunningly gorgeous, more proof this was some kind of admission requirement.

"The girl with the long black hair is Airi Tanaka. She moved here from Japan when we were in junior school. Her dad is a diplomat and her mom is the founder of Tantalizing Perfumes."

"I know that brand," I replied. "It's like a hundred dollars an ounce."

She nodded. "That would be cool enough if Airi didn't have more going for her. She's a world-class violinist, and I mean world-class. She turned down an offer to travel with the London Orchestra. She would have been the youngest in history to get the position."

Wow. The girl I just saw being screwed against the wall was a talented musician. "Huh. Shame about her taste in men."

"What?"

"Nothing. Go on."

"The girl with the blonde pixie cut is Natalie Bard. Chess player. She has traveled the world, and she's beaten almost everyone she's come up against."

"Impressive."

Natalie swatted Airi's shoulder, laughing about something she said. She wasn't just rocking a pixie cut. Natalie also sported a row of piercings in her ear, one in her lip, and another through her nose. She didn't look anything like the chess geeks from my old school.

"And last but not least." My eyes drifted to the final girl. "Isabella Bruno."

"Isabella," I repeated. "She's the one whose name I keep hearing."

"She's the leader of the Diamonds and set to become the youngest principal dancer in the world. People thought you were going to challenge her title when you showed up."

"Her title?" I looked away from the group to make a face at Sofia. "Why would I do that? *How* would I do that?"

"Remember I told you this school was obsessed with the best?" She jerked her thumb in their direction. "Well, that's them. The Diamonds are made up of the best in the school. Best grades, best athlete, best musician, and best dancer." Sofia rolled her eyes. "They take it very seriously. But then, why wouldn't they? They get loads of special treatment. I mean the fact that we're standing here at Isabella's party snacking on Cheetos and chips. All of this is against the rules, but she's not worried about getting caught."

"So, people thought that because I said I dance, I was going after Isabella?" I scoffed. "I don't even know ballet."

She shook her head. "It's not the best ballet dancer. It's the best dancer period. And Isabella's not sharing the spotlight with anyone."

"I don't want her spotlight. This isn't anything new. Evergreen's got their version of the popular kids and they banded together to soak up all the attention and glory. They can have it."

Sofia nudged my arm. "Does that mean you're not trying out for the dance team?"

I looked away. Sofia had said "dance team" the day before at lunch and I lit up like a Christmas tree. I was itching to dance. My little spins around my room weren't cutting it, but sadly tryouts were closed and wouldn't be opening up until next year.

"If I can get in next year, I'll go for it," I admitted. "But if I do, it will only be because I love it, not because I want to be a Diamond." I glanced over at Airi, Natalie, and Isabella. "And can I ask what's with the names? Knights, Kings, and Diamonds? Is that on purpose?"

She rolled her eyes again. "The Knights and Kings are, but Isabella started the Diamond thing in junior prep when she announced she was planning to take over. The best of the best always banded together; they were just never arrogant enough to give themselves a name until her."

We glanced at the girls, looked back at each other, and burst out laughing. I may not be the best of the best, but I liked my little no-name group of friends just fine.

"Why are you guys giggling in a corner? You planning something?"

I turned around, and then looked down. A short, stocky girl with shockingly red hair grinned up at me.

"Nothing good," Sofia answered. She gestured between us. "Val, this is Ciara O'Brien. She's super cool."

Ciara tossed her hair. "It's true, I am."

"Cool enough to help us devour ninety percent of what's on that desk?" I asked.

Ciara laughed. "Hell, yeah. Love this school. Hate the food."

We bolted across the room, junk food on our minds, when three girls stepped into our path.

"Look who it is. I don't think we've been introduced."

Sofia didn't have to tell me that Isabella Bruno was a ballerina. It was obvious in her lithe, slender form, almost impossible height, and the way she moved like everyone else was earthbound but she had been graced with the gift to float. She cocked her head and soft, brown waves fell around her face, and a lovely face it was.

Isabella held out her hand. "You must be Valentina. I've heard a lot about you."

"That's me." I shook. "Cool party."

"Thanks." She pointed on either side of her. "This is Airi and Natalie. We're the Diamonds."

Whoa. She even put it in her introduction. "Nice to meet you guys. I love your hair," I said to Airi.

Airi brushed the jet-black waterfall behind her shoulders and smiled. "Ooh, she's sweet." She suddenly shot forward and stuck her face in my neck. Airi pulled back before I could get out a shout.

"She smells sweet too," Airi went on. "Let me guess: Passion from the Charmante collection."

I clapped my hand to my neck. "You can tell my perfume from one sniff?"

She grinned. "It's a gift."

"It's weird is what it is." Isabella sighed. "I told you to stop doing that. You're freaking the new girl out, and we can't have that if she's going to be one of us."

Isabella's expression didn't change but that seemed like the perfect opening. We might as well get this out of the way right now. "Look, I know the group chat has been hot with talk about me, but despite what people have been saying, I'm not looking to show anyone up. I'm a dancer, but I only do it for fun, and I'm not formally trained. I'm no challenge."

I let out a small "eep" when I was suddenly tugged forward. Isabella grabbed my shoulders in a surprisingly strong grip. "Don't do that. Don't sell yourself short. You are the first transfer in fifty years, and the headmaster wouldn't have done it if you weren't special." She leaned in close, putting her face in mine.

"But the thing is—"

"I'm sure you've heard about me too and that I want to protect my position as head of the Diamonds. I do, and I will."

I blinked. Wow, this girl was intense.

"But they are wrong to think I don't welcome competition. Want to know how you become the best?"

"Actually, I—"

"It's by going up against people stronger than you and coming out on top." Her eyes probed mine—seeking, searching, creeping me out. "I embrace every challenge because I don't lose. I *never* lose."

We stood there, staring much too deeply in each other's eyes. She seemed to be waiting for me to say something.

"Not a loser," I finally said. "Got it."

Isabella smiled and released me. "Great. So we understand each other."

I nodded rather than reply.

"Bella! They're here!"

The six of us shifted our attention to a girl from my history class. For some reason, she was pointing at the window.

"Finally," Isabella breathed. "We can get this party started."

Isabella, Airi, and Natalie walked off without another word. My audience with the Diamonds was over.

"You guys were no help," I said to them while we continued our mission to the snacks.

"Sorry," said Sofia. "I was just surprised to hear so many words come out of Isabella's mouth. She barely talks to anyone outside of her clique."

I reached for a can of Sprite and popped the top. "So should I be honored that—"

"Hey, Maverick," said a flirty voice. I choked. "I like your PJs."

I couldn't have heard that right.

I spun around. Not only did I hear Maverick, I was seeing him climb over the windowsill. He practically had to bend in half to fit his bulk through the window, but in he came... followed by Ezra... then Jaxson... then—

Every part of me went rigid at the sight of Ryder.

The Knights strode into the room as more boys streamed in. Keeping with the party dress code, they looked more ready for a photo shoot than they did to go to sleep. Ezra and Ryder had gone with drawstring pants that hung low on their waist and tight white shirts. Maverick opted for a tank that left no bit of his muscles to the imagination, while Jaxson stood before the party completely shirtless.

"Sofia," I said through gritted teeth. "You said he wasn't coming."

"He said in the group chat that he wasn't."

"What is he doing here anyway? I thought boys get in trouble for being in a girl's room."

"They do," Ciara piped up. "That's why they came in through the window. No cameras outside."

"Come on, Val, don't worry about him. It's a party, everyone is here to have fun."

As if on cue, Isabella turned the music up even louder. Girls peeled themselves off the walls and found boys to drag on the makeshift dance floor. The party had started.

Sofia snagged my hand. "Let's dance!"

"In a minute," I shouted over the music. I held up my drink. "I'm going to finish this first."

She shrugged and she and Ciara ran off instead. Paisley joined them and my friends let loose.

I moved into the space between the desk and the bed and my gaze fell unseeingly to the floor. The truth was I was trying to talk myself out of leaving right then. I did not want to be here if Ryder was. I knew he would find some way to ruin the night for me. Why give him the chance?

"I must not be working you hard enough."

My head shot up. Ezra grinned, flashing perfect teeth, as he closed the distance between us.

"If you've got time to be out partying," he finished.

"You're working me plenty hard." The words were out of my mouth before I could stop them. I cringed as Ezra's brows shot up his forehead. "You know what I mean."

Ezra glanced down and stifled a laugh. "What the fuck is on your feet?"

My eyes snapped to my bunny slippers. If I thought I was cringing before.

"I... uh... wore them because..."

He rested his hand on the wall above my head and leaned in until not even a whisper could fit between us. His grin was level with my gaze, and I tilted my head back until all I could see were those darkening eyes.

"Because what?"

"Because I'm... shameless," I whispered.

He laughed—a soft, rich sound that filled my ears and brought a flush to my cheeks. Why was this guy always practically on top of me?

"What does that mean?" he asked.

"It's a long story."

He hummed, nodding his head. "A story I plan on getting out of you... in between working you as hard as I can."

That line would have reduced any other girl to goo. I just clicked my tongue. "Wow, Ezra. And they say you're the prim and proper one."

"They say a lot of things." Ezra wrapped his fingers around my soda and tugged it free. "You'll have to figure out what's true."

With that, he rose up and turned away. I looked down at my empty hand. "Why do you keep stealing my sodas?!"

His laughter floated over his shoulder as he strode off.

As I watched his retreating back, I pressed my hand to my cheek. It was still warm.

Is this what it's like?

Attraction, crushes, desire... sex. Is this how it all normally works?

I glanced around at the scantily clad prep school kids grinding in the middle of a dorm twice the size of my apartment.

Or at least what passes for normal in Evergreen.

I looked past the dancers and spotted the only other person against the wall. I went over to Maverick.

"Hey."

"Hey," he replied without looking up. Maverick was sitting in the desk chair fiddling with something. In his lap was a pile of parts.

"What are you doing?" Maverick stopped and held out his hand. I bent over, squinting at the tiny square resting on his finger. "What am I looking at?"

"It's a button cam."

"That's a camera?" I looked down at his lap. "And is that your phone?"

He inclined his head. "Had to take it apart for the camera."

"Right... but now you have no phone."

"I'll get another one."

"Why are you making a button cam in the middle of a party?"

"I'm not."

I made a face. "Excuse me?"

Maverick lifted his head high enough for me to see his faint smile. "I was building the cam in my room when Jaxson dragged me out and brought me here."

"Hmm. Things to file under Maverick: handy but helpless against boys half his size."

He barked a laugh before he caught himself. It seemed to surprise him as much as it did me. Maverick was the king of the half grin, but this was the first time I had heard him laugh. "You're snarky, Valentina Moon." He gave me a smile—a real one—and the bubbles came back full force. "I kinda like it."

I ducked my head. Maybe I should tell him I saw the painting. Let him know how much I loved it.

Or maybe you should walk away now before Ryder makes an appearance or whatever is going on in your body gets out of hand. If this is a crush, you're not having it on one of the Knights.

"Val, that's it!" Hands seized me. "You're dancing with us now!"

I didn't fight being dragged away. Sofia, Paisley, and Ciara had saved me from deciding whether to stay or go.

We pushed through into the mess of bodies just as the song changed. "No way," I cried over the music. "Alvaro Soler."

I had only been obsessively listening to this guy's songs for the past week. Isabella needed to take it down about fifty notches, but I had nothing to say against her taste in music. His perfect voice filled the room and I was lost.

I didn't think about who was watching. I let the music take over and moved my body as it demanded. Dipping, swaying, and working my hips to a song about freedom that I didn't know the words to. That didn't matter. The only thing you needed to understand about music was how it made you feel. How it could drown out the sound of fighting and replace it with beautiful noise. How it could take you to another place. A place where all you needed to do was dance.

The song was over much too soon and I opened my eyes. I stopped dead at the opened-mouth stares from the room. The crowd around me had moved away, leaving me my own little spot to dance while they watched.

"Damn, girl," Sofia whistled. "You really *can* dance."

I wasn't embarrassed. I loved dancing and didn't mind doing it in front of people, but those people usually weren't Isabella Bruno or Ryder Shea.

I stiffened as I caught the looks on their faces. Neither one was scowling, but they also weren't smiling. If Isabella didn't see me as competition before, I had a feeling she did now. And as for Ryder, he dropped his blank stare and turned to Airi, going back to chatting her up in the darkened corner.

Another Spanish song came on and I reached for Sofia's hands. "Do you know how to dance to this? 'Cause I could use a partner."

"Is this the part where I admit to dancing around the living room with my nanny... this summer?"

We giggled and got to it, switching out every now and then to dance with Ciara and Paisley. They didn't know the moves at first, but picked them up quickly. We were having so much fun—not caring about who was watching while we twirled and sashayed—until others decided to join in.

Michael sidled up to us. "Hey, Paisley."

That was it. Two words and Paisley promptly dropped my hands and plastered herself against Michael.

Ciara, Sofia, and I formed a threesome but the boys weren't done picking apart my group. In no less than five minutes, I went from dancing with them to dancing alone. Sofia was grinding on a dude from homeroom and Ciara wandered off hand in hand with some guy to a private corner.

I didn't mind. Isabella's playlist was bumping and I was into every song. I threw myself into a spin and stumbled into a hard chest.

"Oops, sor—"

A hand snaked around my waist. "No problem, baby, but it looks like you could use a partner."

I jerked back, but Jaxson's tight hold didn't let me go far. "Thanks," I said, pushing against his bare chest. "But I'm cool dancing alone."

"You're even cooler"—a yelp escaped my lips as I was suddenly dipped—"dancing with me."

Jaxson picked me up and spun me out. My hair went soaring, blocking out the whirling room, until I was brought back. I barely had time to catch myself before he slid his hand up my thigh, wrapping it around his waist as he lifted me and twirled us both around.

I laughed breathlessly, gazing down at him while my curtain of hair made Jaxson all I could see. "You're pretty good at this."

His lips pulled back into a grin that revealed one sharp canine. "You sound surprised."

I slid down his body as he gently put me back on my feet. Taking my hands, he draped them over his shoulders, and instead of pulling away, I linked them together. Nothing separated my body from his. We moved so perfectly in sync. Jaxson seemed to know the moves I would make before I made them—before I thought them.

I had never felt so in tune with a dance partner. My heart was racing, pounding, leaping out of control... or maybe it was his. I could feel his heart beating against my body, and without thinking, I moved my hand down and rested it on his chest.

His heart was just as out of control as mine was. I didn't know what to think, and then his hand was on mine—curling around my fingers and holding them still. Our eyes locked and I was trapped.

Crystal blue pools sucked me in, beckoning me like a siren to my death. It would have been a mistake, but such a beautiful one.

His hot breath ghosted over my mouth and my pulse quickened. Every good, sensible reason for why I couldn't do this flew out of my head.

Our lips closed the distance.

"Okay!"

The music went off so quickly, it jarred me. I lurched out of Jaxson's hands and the fog I had fallen under.

What. Just. Happened?

Isabella stepped away from the speakers and clapped her hands. "Circle up, people. It's time to get interesting."

Interesting? What did that mean?

Apparently, I was the only one who didn't know because everyone else was heading for the floor and forming a circle. Sofia sat down and waved me over. I took my spot next to her, and across from me, Ryder settled in with Jaxson on one side and Ezra on the other. Maverick didn't move from his chair or button cam.

"Truth or dare," Isabella announced. Airi stepped up to her side with a smirk I didn't like. "The usual rules apply. If you refuse to answer your truth or do your dare, then you"—Airi's hands whipped out and revealed what was behind her back—"drink."

My nails dragged through the carpet as I clenched my fists.

"Ready?" Cheers and whoops rang out. "Great, then first...." Her eyes scanned the circle until they landed on me. "Valentina."

I expected this. The bottle was passed around until Sofia handed it to me. I set it down in front of me without looking at it.

"Truth or dare?"

"Tru—"

"Don't think about lying." The sound of that sickly honeyed voice made me swing my head to Ryder. "The penalty for that is even worse."

I looked him right in the eye as I said, "Truth."

"How did you convince the headmaster to let you transfer in late?"

I blinked. That I wasn't expecting, but I guess it's the question hanging over everyone's mind. What made the new girl so special?

"I wasn't late," I said honestly, finally revealing the info I hadn't shared with even Sofia. "I applied on time and was accepted."

A wrinkle appeared between her brow. "Then why did you start late?"

I kept my tone even. "It's only one question per truth, right?"

Isabella nudged Natalie who shot me a smile. "Truth or dare, Val?" Natalie asked.

"Truth."

"Why did you start school late?"

My nails dug deeper into my palm. The room was completely silent as they waited for my answer. "Family stuff."

"Uh-uh." She waved a finger at me. I could see she was enjoying this. "Specifics or drink up."

My stomach heaved at the thought. I pushed the bottle further away. "I... have a baby brother," I forced out. "My mom needed help looking after him while she searched for a better job. The headmaster was understanding."

She cocked her head. "Hmm, how unlike him."

I didn't reply.

The game kept going, and when the next question, and the next, and the next was directed at me, I got the real point of the game loud and clear.

A girl sitting next to Airi was up next. "New girl, truth or dare?"

"Truth." There was no way I was saying dare.

"How many?"

"How many what?"

She rolled her eyes. "You know. How many people have you slept with?"

I clenched my teeth. "Zero."

"What?" She frowned at me. "Hey, you can't lie."

"I'm not lying. I've never had sex."

I heard a few murmurs of disbelief. People shared looks with each other as though the idea of me being a virgin was so out there.

Airi grinned at me. "Valentina, truth or dare?"

"Truth."

"What other sexual flavors have you indulged in?" She licked her lips. "Blow jobs? Hand jobs? Anal? Sexting? Name 'em, my sweet-smelling friend."

This girl's flavor was nutty. I'd like that if she wasn't joining in on this interrogation.

I smiled back. "None. None. None. And... oh yeah, none. Sorry, guys, but my sex life is nonexistent. Might want to pick a new line of questioning."

Maybe I shouldn't have said that because they happily took up the challenge. Except for Paisley, Ciara, and Sofia, everyone chose me and threw me the craziest and most personal questions they could think of. I got everything from when I got my first period, to my taste in porn, and one guy even asked me if I've ever killed a man. By the time they got to Jaxson, I was sick of having that bottle sitting in front of me.

Jaxson took one look at me and snorted. "Don't look so scared, baby. I ain't here for this truth shit and it's getting real boring. Yo, listen up. Lay off my girl Val and play the game for real. If I don't start seeing some skin, the Knights are out."

He expressed it in typical Jaxson fashion, but at that moment, I could have kissed him. Maybe he wasn't such an ass after all.

"Speaking of which." Jaxson turned on Natalie. "Truth or dare?"

"Dare," Natalie answered without hesitation.

"Strip. I'm talking full nude."

I was wrong about the ass thing.

"Gladly."

Shouts and cheers went up as Natalie got to her feet. It wasn't until she ripped her bra off that I averted my eyes. When the cheers got deafening, I figured the panties were gone too.

A sudden chorus of groans made me pick my eyes off the floor. Natalie winked as she buttoned up her pants. "Sorry, but you didn't say I had to stay naked for the whole game. I told you it's all about the specificity."

"I'll remember that for next time," Jaxson replied.

I'd have shaken my head at him, but I wasn't worried about Jaxson Van Zandt anymore. Now, it was Ryder's turn. I knew it was coming no matter what Jaxson said.

"Moon."

"Truth." The word was out of my mouth before Ryder finished saying my name. I waited tensely. Ryder wasn't like the rest. He knew me. He knew my family. He knew all the awful things he had done to make me cry and beg him to stop. He knew the questions to ask.

"Val, is it true..."

My body was tighter than a bowstring.

"...that you like to sneak around and watch people fuck?"

I jerked like he'd slapped me. "What?! No!"

His smile was wicked. "Liar."

"I'm not lying!" I cried, cheeks flaming. "What is wrong with you?!"

"With me? I wasn't the one peeping on you in the stairwell." He pointed at the bottle. "Now, drink."

"I'm not drinking, Ryder. I wasn't peeping on anyone!"

The circle was watching our exchange in rapt fascination, their eyes ping-ponging between us.

"No? Then how long did you stand there looking, listening, wishing it was you?" He scoffed. "It's kind of sad really. You're not getting it from anyone else so you get off watching other people." He spat the final word like he believed it with every fiber of his being. "Pathetic."

I lurched to my feet.

"Alright! This has been fun!" Sofia grabbed me around the waist, holding me back. "But we've got homework. See you around."

She practically dragged me to the door.

Ryder followed our retreat. His eyes were dark, fathomless pools. "Don't think this gets you out of your penalty. I'll be coming to collect."

I freed an arm and flipped him off. "Why don't you collect this, you piece of—!"

Sofia yanked open the door and tossed me out, slamming it shut on my rant. "Are you insane?!" she shrieked. "You can't talk to him like that! Do you have any idea what he can do to you?!"

I barely heard her.

Scratch, scratch, scratch.

Collapsing against the wall, I clutched my chest as that familiar ache flared inside of me. Scraping, tearing, ripping apart my soul in an anger that was all-consuming. It was going to swallow me again. It was—

"Val, it's okay." A gentle voice broke through my mist. "I'm sorry I yelled at you." Arms encircled me and brought me to my feet. "Come on. I know what will make you feel better."

I let her take me. I wasn't in a position to put up a fight.

We stepped out of the hallway, but Sofia didn't turn us toward the staircase. Instead, we slipped out into the night. A rush of fresh, chilling air to my face cooled the tears that threatened to fall.

"There's a spot I like to go," Sofia began. "Coach Panzer set it up and used it for when she was hooking up with Professor Rossman. But she's been telling the girls that men are dogs lately so I think that's on the rocks. The lock is busted so we should be able to get in."

Our feet were soundless as we crossed the quad, but the night wasn't. Cicadas chirped and sang to the moon. Hundreds of small voices coming together to make themselves heard.

We approached the sports complex, but veered off just before the doors of the gym. Skirting the building, Sofia brought me around to a door I had never paid attention to before. It opened without a problem.

"It's up there."

She kept an arm around me as we climbed the staircase and topped the landing. In front of us was a rusty door with the letters E and A painted on the face.

Sofia released me to open it. Slowly, I approached.

"Oh, wait. One sec." Sofia darted through the door and disappeared. I trailed after her and stepped onto the roof just as the lights flicked on.

"Wow," I breathed.

"It's cool, isn't it. Panzer did a good job."

I couldn't disagree. The roof of the gym had been transformed from an oversized bucket for rainwater and dead leaves, to a cozy hideaway. Fairy lights had been strung along the small ledge of the roof. It perfectly lit up the couches and potted plants that had been set around a tiny coffee table in the middle of the space.

Sofia ran over to the sofa. "As long as you ignore the fact that Rossman and Panzer got naked on this, it's a nice spot to chill out."

A chuckle escaped my lips. I sat next to her and pulled my legs onto the cushion. "Won't we get in trouble for being here?"

"Yes, but that's why we won't get caught."

"But the dorm cameras..."

"Gus only cares about keeping people out of our rooms, not keeping us in them. He won't report us, but Panzer would flip her lid if she found us up here so be careful."

I rested my chin on my knees. "Okay."

We fell silent. It stretched between us, begging to be broken, but I made no move to.

"I'm sorry about in there," she finally spoke up. "I didn't know they were going to grill you like that."

"It's not your fault."

"It is. We should have left sooner." I felt a hand slip into mine. "They asked you all that stuff about your town and your family..."

I shook my head. "I'm not ashamed of Mom, Adam, or where I come from."

"But your dad..."

I balled my fists. Having to share that I didn't know who my dad was to half of my class sucked. The guy ran out on Olivia before I was born and she wouldn't even speak his name.

I hated having to tell them that, but Ryder was right there and he knew the whole story. If I hadn't spilled, he would have.

"I don't care about my dad," I rasped. "Things have been tough, but when it mattered, Mom is always there for me."

"I wish I could say the same thing." I turned to look at her. "I never see my dad. They've been trying to take Honey Hair global so he spends all his time overseas. I haven't seen him in eight months, and you want to know how many times he's called me since?"

I didn't need to ask. Her tone told me it wasn't nearly enough. "What about your mom?" I whispered.

"Madam Madeline is even worse," she spat through curled lips. "She lives only twenty minutes away and before that she was right down the hall. The reason she didn't spend time with me was just because she didn't want to."

I squeezed her hand tighter.

"It's okay though. I have Carmen. She's been my nanny since I was two weeks old, and although she stopped working for us when I came to Evergreen, she still calls me every week."

"I'm glad you have her."

We fell silent again.

The next time Sofia broke it, it was to say what I had been expecting. "So that was intense in there with you and Ryder. Was it always like that between you?"

"No," I said honestly. "I mean, we were never exactly friends, but he wasn't always such a beast. He was the rich son of Benjamin Shea and I was the daughter of the secretary. I only ran into him when Mom brought me to his house, but when she did, he was nice enough."

"What happened?"

"I don't know for sure," I said into the night air. I stared unseeingly over the edge of the roof, not turning to face Sofia. "But I guess it was his dad."

"His dad going missing?"

I shook my head. "His dad showing up in every tabloid and blog with a different woman on his arm. The guy was a bastard plain and simple. He cheated on Ryder's mom and didn't care who knew."

"Yeah, I... saw some of that."

"In the worst of it, Ryder's mom, Caroline, took to locking herself in her room and never coming out. I'd be there, and butlers and maids would go in and out of her room, but she never did. I think it got to him. Messed him up."

"So he took it out on you?"

I didn't reply.

"What did he do?" she pressed.

"What didn't he do? He picked on me. Spread lies about me to his friends. Threw me in a pool and almost drowned me. Once he threatened to put his mom's jewelry in Olivia's purse and have her arrested. He said I'd be put in foster care and he'd never have to see me again."

"Holy shit," she gasped. "What the hell is wrong with him?"

"I was so scared he'd really do it that I pawed through her things when she came home. I did that every day for a month."

"I'm so sorry, Val." She let out a sigh as she fell back onto the cushions. "No wonder you can't stand to be around him. I should have let you beat his face in."

"No, you were right to get me out of there." I mimicked her and leaned back. The sky was bathed in stars and the beauty of the sight was filling me up. It was easy to feel calm and at peace when you looked at the glittering skies. Space was a harsh, cold, unforgiving vacuum, but those brilliant balls of light survived. If they could pierce the unending gloom surrounding their life, maybe I could too.

"Squaring off with Ryder wouldn't have changed anything," I said. "He'll be just as horrible tomorrow. And the day after that. And the day after that. I'm the one who has to change and put it all behind me. That's the only way he won't have power over me anymore."

"We'll get better at avoiding him. I'm talking bird calls and hand signals if we see him coming."

A smile tugged at my lips. "And code names."

"And escape routes. If he comes in a room we're in, we'll be hopping out the nearest window."

I snorted a laugh. "What are we going to do about stairwell hookups?"

"Easy. We hang a rope ladder outside of your window and you'll never take the stairs again."

I was howling now. I tipped over into her lap as we devolved into giggles.

"You've got it all figured out," I said as I looked up at her. "I can't think of a better plan."

She hummed. "I don't think it's going to help you with Maverick, Ezra, or *Jaxson*."

"Oh no," I groaned.

"Oh no is right! You and Jaxson were burning up the rug, girl. It. Was. Hot."

I clapped my hand over my mouth. I couldn't let her peep my grin. "Sof, please. We were just dancing."

"Liar." Her fingers went skittering over my stomach and I squealed. "He was going to kiss you, and you were going to let him. Admit it."

"Not under pain of death. Jaxson is just so... Jaxson." I grabbed my stomach to keep the emerging bubbles at bay. They were little traitors. "He's funny, and cute, and can dance—"

"I'm not hearing a downside."

"—but he also likes to get girls to strip and is feeling his title as a Knight way too much. Not to mention Ryder."

"All very true, but still... you were going to kiss him!" Her shout was followed by another tickle attack that almost sent me to the floor. "And don't think I didn't see you getting snuggly in a corner with Ezra, or laughing with Maverick."

"It w-wasn't what it l-looked like," I cried breathlessly.

"If only Isabella hadn't stopped the music and started the inquisition. I have a feeling Jaxson would have changed a few of your sex answers tonight."

I gaped at her wiggling brows. "Sofia! I hate you so much right now."

"More lies," she teased. "You're lucky we're not still playing or I'd make you drink."

"Why are we picking on me? Don't you think I noticed you grinding up on Jeremiah? What's going on with that?"

"Oh my gosh, I haven't told you yet. So, last summer he and I..."

I let Sofia's words wash over me. The night had started badly, but couldn't have ended better than this. I could take whatever Ryder had to throw at me. I had great friends and went to the top school in the country. Nothing would stop me from having the best four years of my life.

Chapter Six

"Class, your attention."

I lifted my head from my math homework in time to see the students from the AV club wheel in the television. Joe Young High delivered their announcements over a staticky intercom that made every person speaking sound like they had the flu. But of course, Evergreen had to do it better.

I grinned to myself. *Four weeks here and I'm still comparing everything to my old school.*

Professor Markham clicked the television on and the screen lit up with the morning announcers: Catrina Bell and Ezra Lennox.

Ezra smiled broadly at the camera. "Good morning, fellow classmates, and welcome to another day at Evergreen Academy." I bit back a laugh. I would never get used to seeing Ezra all sweet, smiling, and polite. People who were all of those things didn't assign you twenty practice problems for getting an A minus.

I grimaced at the worksheets on my desk. *I really should drop this guy as a tutor, but knowing him... he'd come after me.*

My mind drifted back to the day before. Sitting among the tomes—Ezra's arm draped on the back of my chair and his breath in my ear, whispering so we wouldn't disturb the people sharing our table.

My cheeks heated up like a Florida summer. Okay, maybe there was more than one reason I hadn't gotten a new tutor.

"...this weekend. I know we're all looking forward to it," Ezra said sunnily, "but first, our headmaster with a message."

Ezra and his co-host disappeared from the screen and were replaced by a man I had only met in person once: Headmaster Evergreen.

I scrunched down in my seat—as though the weight of his gaze was reaching through the screen and pressing on me.

"Good morning, freshman class."

Headmaster Evergreen was a thin man. No matter what suit I saw him in morning after morning; it always looked like he was swimming in it. But despite that, every other part of him fell into the stereotype. His beard was neatly trimmed, thick glasses perched on the edge of his nose, and there was a slight thinning on the top.

"As you all know, the Halloween masquerade ball is tomorrow night. As such, afternoon classes will be canceled so you can purchase what you need for the dance."

A squeal behind me made me turn to Sofia. "We're going shopping together," said my best friend. "It's happening. Don't try to get out of it."

I laughed. "I won't. I need an outfit anyway."

"...expect you to remember you represent this school at all times." The headmaster's voice broke through our conversation. "Conduct yourself in a proper manner while you off campus and return on time. No excuses."

I had the strongest urge to say "yes, sir" even though he wasn't in the room.

"Thank you." The screen went dark and then Ezra and Catarina were back.

I dropped my head and picked up my pencil to return to my math. A shadow fell over my paper.

"So who you going with to this dance, Val?"

Maybe it was him using my actual name for once that made me answer. "The girl behind me." I shot Jaxson a smile as he scraped his chair over to my desk. He paid no mind to the daggers Markham was shooting our way. I did care, but ignoring a guy like Jaxson was impossible. He demanded attention like a burning building. "Why?"

He grinned. "Don't get excited; I wasn't asking. I'll be deejaying the dance."

"You will? They didn't want a professional?"

His grin widened. "They did, and that's what they got."

I rolled my eyes.

"And it's good you don't have a date. I don't want to be up there watching you grind that ass on anyone else."

Propping my head on my palm, I smiled at him. "Who I grind my ass on is my business," I returned. "So just don't watch."

Chuckling, Jaxson leaned in until I was enveloped in his spicy, sweet scent. His blue eyes danced as we fell into a routine that was becoming familiar. "I do like 'em feisty, but you take it to a whole other level, girl." His gaze swept my face in a way that was blatantly appreciative. It pulled a blush to my cheeks. "You'll save me a dance tomorrow night."

"Are you asking me or telling me?" I replied, brows raised.

"You pick." Jaxson reached out and brushed a curl behind my ear, leaving a trail of goose bumps in his wake. "The result will be the same."

He was pulling back and returning to his desk before I thought of something to say.

Sofia tapped my shoulder. I caught her look and winced. "Don't say it."

"Don't say what?" she replied, careful to make sure her voice didn't carry. "Don't say you both need to pop into the stairwell and bang it out already. Okay, I won't say it."

If I thought my face was on fire before. "No one is banging anything," I hissed. "Where do you get this stuff from?"

Her smile told me how much she was enjoying this. "You two flirt literally every morning."

I snuck a peek at Jaxson, but he was absorbed with talking to Claire. "Yeah, and then he spends the rest of the day flirting with everyone else. It doesn't mean anything, and even if it did"—my throat grew tight—"I'm not ready for a relationship with anyone."

"Whatever you say," she sang.

I pointedly turned my back on her and went back to my work. Things were going well for me. My grades were up. I wouldn't be taking a Diamond spot as highest GPA in the class, but I was maintaining an A/B average. Sofia, Claire, Eric, Paisley, and I were tight. We ate together every day and goofed around campus on the weekends. And most importantly, I haven't dealt with Ryder since the party.

Like the rest of us, he was too busy with school and whatever he did as a Knight to make my life miserable, and I was more than happy with that. Life in Evergreen was good; I wouldn't mess with that by getting into a relationship I wasn't ready for.

And I repeated that to Sofia as we headed for the school gates that afternoon. "I've already got a gorgeous date," I said. "There's no way I could trade up."

Sofia swept her hair over her shoulders. "That's true. You can't do better than me."

I laughed. "So where are we going first?"

First years streamed around us, all heading for the shuttles waiting beyond the gates. There was a buzz of excitement in the air. After all this hard work, we were more than ready to blow off some steam.

"Dress first," Sofia announced. "Then we'll find masks to match. If they had given us more time to shop, we could have gotten them custom-made. I tried to get Madam Madeline to order me a mask, but... she was busy."

I drifted closer and bumped her shoulder. I wished there was something I could say to make her feel better, but the only thing that could do that was her parents giving a crap.

"Anyway, a costume shop will have to do."

Together we strode down the paved path and escaped through the gates. Five darkly tinted shuttles with the school's name on the side waited for us.

We walked up to the nearest shuttle and fell in line. We were all going to the same place: Evergreen Promenade.

I climbed up and waved to Eric and Claire in the back. We took the free seats next to them.

The second my butt hit the seat, I caught sight of Isabella Bruno. She glided down the aisle and, one by one, her posse followed after her. In the last few weeks, I'd gotten to know all the Diamonds, even if some were only by sight—like advertised: they were all top in the school in some way or other, and they all milked it. Claiming the lunch table nearest the Knights, throwing parties in their dorms, getting special treatment from the professors. They weren't on the same level as Jaxson, Ezra, Maverick, and Ryder, but they were close.

Lesson Number Two: There is a hierarchy in Evergreen, and it matters.

"You missed the homecoming dance, Val." My eyes slid from Isabella to Eric. "The parties here are the best."

"I'm excited. I missed the homecoming dance at my old school too."

Claire frowned. "Oh no, did you get sick again?"

"Again?" Sofia asked.

"I got sick my last year in middle school," I explained. "Mono. It was awful."

"Val was out of school for months," Claire added.

"Yeah, but that wasn't why I missed homecoming. I couldn't afford a dress and decided it was better not to give the kids another reason to make fun of me."

"Oh." Claire dropped her eyes and the conversation. I read all over her face that she was remembering what I went through in middle school. By the time the bus pulled away from the curb, we had moved on to another topic.

The ride into town was short, but that didn't mean there wasn't a lot to see. The difference in this neighborhood and my own was staggering. The streets I used to walk were littered with trash and cigarette butts while these were pristine. The view from the windows I looked out of boasted grimy buildings and smoggy air, while there were rolling hills and trees as far as the eye could see. Topping a few of those hills were the mansions many of the students called home—Sofia being one of them.

She pressed her finger against the glass. "See that brown one? That's my place." I bobbed my head in awe. Even from here I could see it was gorgeous. "Ooh! You should stay with us over winter break. It'll be so much fun!"

"I'll ask my mom," I replied as the mansion faded in the distance. "But I couldn't stay the whole break. She'll need help with Adam."

"Whatever, as long as you come."

Ten minutes later, we were turning into the promenade. There was practically a stampede when the doors opened up. Students found their friends and ran off in a dozen directions, hunting down their favorite stores.

Sofia seized my hand the moment we stepped down. "Okay, first Maxfield, then Dynasty, then Saks, and if we haven't found dresses by then... we panic."

I laughed. "Alright, let's do it."

I looked over at Eric and Claire. "You guys coming with us?"

Eric shook his head. "Got my suit already. I only came out to get off campus." He gave us a salute as he walked off. "See you guys later. I'll be the one with the chocolate ring around his mouth."

"You better be packing some chocolate for me," Sofia called after him. She turned on us, beaming. "Let's go."

"Wait." Claire backed away. "I'm going to Green Mart for my dress." She cut eyes to me. "Val, shouldn't you— I mean, do you want to come with me?"

"Oh, right," said Sofia. She dropped my hand.

"Why don't we *all* go together? We do Green Mart and then hit Sofia's stores."

The girls agreed, dropping their uncomfortable looks, and we took off.

Green Mart had the bargain finds you'd expect of a supermarket, but they didn't have a great selection of party dresses. Claire looked through the clearance racks until she found a black and emerald one-shoulder dress that we gushed over.

On the way back to the promenade, Claire broke off from the group. "I'm going to drop my bag on the bus then catch up with you guys."

I nodded. Claire was far from the only kid on scholarship, but that didn't mean she wanted to flaunt it. Not all the rich kids were as nice as Sofia.

"Okay, Maxfield is on the end of this street. I saw a dress on their website last night that was killer."

She dragged me off to the boutique. Sofia burst through the doors and left me standing on the welcome mat.

My eyes swept the cream carpets, lounges, and color displays. I had never been in a store like this. I had never *walked* down a street that had stores like this.

These clothes are so—

"Hello, can I help you?"

I jumped.

A store attendant had materialized at my side. She was impeccably dressed—not a hair out of place and makeup done with an expert hand. The clothes she wore no doubt equaled six months of Mom's paycheck, and from the way she scanned me up and down, she was seeing if mine did too.

I tugged my blazer closed and her eyes immediately fell on the Evergreen patch. Her whole face changed.

"Good afternoon, ma'am," she said cheerily. "My name is Christine. You must be here for the Evergreen Halloween ball. We've gotten multiple orders to be picked up tonight. Are we holding something in the back for you?"

"No, I haven't found my dress yet."

"Not a problem, ma'am. I would be more than happy to assist you. Can you tell me more about what you're looking for?"

Biting my lip, I glanced around at the parade of obscenely expensive clothes. "I was thinking blue. Like a dark or midnight blue."

"I know just the thing. Why don't you sit down and enjoy a cup of tea while I pull a few dresses for you?" She looked me up and down again, but this time her look was shrewd over snobbish. "Size zero. C-cup."

I clapped my hands over my chest. "Um, yes."

"Perfect. I'll be back in a moment."

She took off before I could get a word out. Not seeing why not, I padded across the carpet to the middle of the room where couches and a small coffee table took up the space. Resting on the table was a fine tea set. I touched my hand to the teapot. It was still warm.

I never felt so bizarre as when I filled my dainty cup with Earl Grey tea and relaxed onto the lounge. I was definitely not in Wakefield anymore.

"Val? Valentina?" Sofia emerged from the back of the store. "There you are. I found it. What do you think?"

It was a strapless bloodred mermaid dress. My mouth dropped. "Dude, if you don't get that, I will."

She squealed, clutching it to her chest. "No way, it's mine. I'm going to try it on. Don't move."

"I'll be here." I waved her off and went back to my tea.

"Ma'am?" Christine returned with her choice in tow. "What do you think of this?"

I sucked in a breath—and my tea—and choked. I fell into a coughing fit as Christine held up the dress.

"—love the Brodeur." A voice cut through my hacking, sounding from the dressing rooms Sofia had disappeared into. "But there will be diamonds on my mask so I need something to…" Isabella, Airi, and Natalie stepped out onto the floor. Isabella trailed off and frowned at Christine. "Chris, what are you doing? I told you Mother won't approve a dress over two thousand and this isn't even in the right color or size. Put it back."

"This is not for you, Bella." How often do you have to shop here to get on nickname terms with the attendant? Christine turned to me. "It's for her. What do you think?" she asked, holding the dress up proudly.

Three pairs of eyes landed on me, but I only had eyes for the dress. I had never seen anything so beautiful in my life. It beckoned me forward and I climbed out of my seat to get a closer look. A midnight blue masterpiece of tulle, lace, and jewels stared back at me. The top was sheer, showing off the shoulders, sides, and back, but intricate beadwork covered the front. The rest of the dress cascaded to the floor in a waterfall that shifted from blue to black as it caught the light.

"Valentina?" Isabella looked at me like she had no idea what I was doing here. "But she can't afford that either." She didn't sound like she was trying to be mean; on the contrary, she spoke like she was stating a simple fact.

Christina lost her smile. "Excuse me?"

"She doesn't—"

"Actually, I think it's perfect." I met Isabella's eyes steadily. "If it fits, I'll take it."

Christina perked back up. "Excellent. I'll put this in your dressing room."

"What is this?" Isabella folded her arms. "Am I missing something? You said your mother works in a daycare and your dad took off before you were born."

"She does. And he did."

Her brows drew together. "Then why are you pretending you can afford a four thousand dollar dress?"

I lifted my shoulders. "Who's pretending?"

I stepped around her and went into the dressing room. I knew the moment I slid the dress over my thighs that this would be the one. A look in the mirror only confirmed it.

I left the dressing room, the gown slung over my arm, and slapped my credit card on the counter while Isabella, Airi, and Natalie watched.

Chapter Seven

My fingers glided over the stones, following the curves and dips of the mask. I hadn't put it on yet. I was having too much fun staring at it.

My bedroom door flew open. "Val? You ready?"

"You've got to learn to knock," I replied without turning around. "What if I had been naked?"

"You never get naked—hence the trouble getting rid of your V-card."

"Shut up," I laughed. "I'm not having trouble."

"Mm hmm. Especially in that dress," she purred. The figure in the mirror looked even more amazing in the red mermaid dress than when I saw her the day before. Sofia had piled her silken hair on top of her head and let the curls fall on one side of her face. She completed the look with the red and white Venetian-style mask perched on her nose.

"Let me see you."

Sofia grasped my shoulder and spun me around. She whistled. "You look amazing. Jaxson won't be able to keep his hands off you."

The bubbles made a reappearance. "Yes, he will," I said firmly. "Everyone is keeping their hands to themselves."

"Everyone except me." Sofia took my mask and turned me back around. "I may wander off with Jeremiah at some point," she said while she carefully placed it on my face and tied the ribbon beneath my bun. "Will you be okay on your own?"

"I'll be fine. You two have fun."

"Thanks, Val." She stepped away to let me have the full effect. I could barely believe that reflection was me. The dress molded to my body like I was poured into it, and the mask... Somehow we had managed to find the exact shade of blue as my dress. A *Phantom of the Opera*–style filigree mask that covered more of my face on one side, but was studded with glittering stones that drew attention to my light dusting of eye shadow.

I was ready.

THE DANCE WAS BEING held in the sports complex, but if I hadn't known that beforehand, I wouldn't have recognized it. The gym had been decorated to disguise everything from the bleachers to the hardwood floors. I placed my heels on the dark carpet that was now surrounding a black, makeshift dance floor. Heavy curtains hung from the ceiling covering up the paneled walls and scoreboards. And that was not the only thing hanging from the ceiling.

I marveled at the hanging lights and spinning spotlights as much as I did all the people around me. It was hard to make anyone out between the darkened room, pounding music, and jeweled masks, but it was clear everyone had dressed to impress.

Sofia waved to someone across the room. "Okay, Val. I'll catch up with you later."

"Wait. What? I didn't know you were ditching me the second we stepped inside."

She giggled and pressed a kiss to my cheek. "You don't need me. I see someone else is ready to take my spot."

I froze. *Jaxson?*

Sofia disappeared into the crowd as a hand settled on the small of my back. A single word drifted over my shoulder.

"Valentina."

"Ezra."

That was the only person it could have been. I knew that voice for all the times it whispered in my ear, and I knew that touch from the ripples it enticed from my skin with every accidental brush. I turned and met his obsidian eyes—the exact shade as the mask that obscured his features.

The part of his face I could see curled into a smile. "Val, I was hoping to find you." He didn't move his hand from my back.

"Why? To give me more homework?" I teased.

His grip tightened ever so slightly. "To ask you to dance."

I blinked. "Dance?"

"That's right." He tilted his head toward the middle of the room. "This song is my favorite. Dance with me."

He was leading me off before I could give an answer, but it didn't occur to me to say no. I didn't recognize the song, but it was a slow one playing for a thin crowd. Students were still filing in and only a few had made their way to the dance floor.

We stepped past them until we reached the middle of the dance floor. Ezra spun me around, keeping one hand on the small of my back, and with the other, he grasped my fingers and linked them together. I expected him to pull us closer but instead he maintained a polite distance: the perfect gentleman.

I didn't do much waltzing in my old life, but he was a good leader. We swayed smoothly without stepping on each other's toes, and the hand on my back stayed firm. It didn't slide up or down, and yet, I was highly aware of it. It felt like his touch was burning through the fabric of my dress and radiating inside of me. I was warm, jittery, and I couldn't think about anything but that hand, or his penetrating gaze.

I should say something. I knew I should say something but I didn't know what.

"So...you can dance?"

Stupid.

Ezra inclined his head. "I had to learn to go to my mom's banquets and award dinners. You get quite an education to prepare for the spotlight."

"I've read a few of your mom's articles, seen her segments, and that was before I knew who you were. She's amazing."

"That she is," he said simply.

I studied him. There was nothing on his face to say if he really agreed or if he was saying what you're supposed to. It wasn't the first time I had that thought. Sometimes I thought I was getting flashes of the real Ezra... and other times I wondered if that was just what I wanted to believe.

That thought pushed my next comment from my lips. "They say that's why you're such a perfectionist. Because you're trying to make sure your image is as perfect as the one you need to take her place. Smiling, put together, rigid." A picture was forming in my mind. "A mannequin."

Yes, that was it. If Ryder was the Greek statue with a face of chiseled beauty and a heart of stone, Ezra Lennox was the mannequin—living out a plastic life that exists only to be on display for others.

He laughed. "A mannequin? Ouch. And here I thought you were going to be nice to me for once."

"For once? What are you talking about? Since when have I ever not been nice to you? I think you have this relationship turned around."

A smile played at his lips. "Are you kidding? You're always pushing me away, telling me off for getting in your space, and refusing to share. And now you're calling me a mannequin. I'm starting to think you don't like me very much, Valentina."

"I do like you," I blurted. I winced internally as his brows climbed his forehead. It came out before I could stop it, but now it was hanging in the air between us. I had to keep going. "I didn't mean what I said as an insult. I understand showing a different face to the world," I whispered. "Not everyone can... or should... see what's beneath."

Ezra stopped dancing, just for a moment, but the pause let me know my words had struck him.

I was getting too heavy—saying too much, but instead of heeding the warning in my mind, I pushed forward. "I see the guy that works really hard to help me. I see the guy who likes weird-flavored sodas, and secretly has a raunchy sense of humor. You're not as perfect as you appear."

"Is that a good thing or a bad thing?"

"A good thing," I replied. "Everyone else can see the plastic person, Ezra, but I can see more. I *want* to see more. I've always known perfect doesn't exist."

Ezra's eyes glided over my face—a slow, lazy sweep that didn't hide what he was doing. "I wouldn't say that."

He smiled at me, and one tugged at my lips until I was doing the same.

It wasn't a conscious thought. One moment my hand was in his, and then I was sliding it up his arm and draping it around his neck.

The melody swirled around us, blocking everything out and plunging me into a world where there was only me and him, dancing much too far apart.

I don't know who closed the distance first. But in the next breath, my body was pressed against his and, in the other, were my lips.

It was a chaste kiss—a butterfly kiss is what Olivia would have called it. So light you don't notice it at first, but when you do, their presence delights. I knew about butterfly kisses, but what I didn't know was the zinging electricity that would surge through my body. It lit my every nerve on fire—a heat that was the complete opposite of the tender kiss—and I broke apart with a gasp.

We were both panting. My heart was pounding so hard I was sure the entire room could hear it. *What was that?* I had never felt anything like that. I didn't know it was possible to feel like that. I wanted to do it again, and run as far as possible at the same time.

I chanced a look around and saw no one looking in our direction. A hand on my cheek brought me back.

"Is something wrong?"

"I..." *I shouldn't have done that. You're not the only one wearing a mask. But unlike yours, there is nothing good hiding beneath mine.*

I took a breath. "Ezra, I—"

"Alright, alright, alright!" I half jumped out of my skin. Jaxson had taken his place on stage and, as if that was the cue, kids began surging onto the dance floor—bumping into us as they descended on the stage. "Enough of this shit, time for some real music!"

Ezra shook his head. "This guy. I bet that was on purpose."

"On purpose?" I pressed a finger to my lips. "Because you..."

He met my gaze head-on. "Kissed you? Likely. The guy hasn't shut up about you since you got here. I think he was hoping to steal your first kiss."

"Who said it was my first?" I shot back, cheeks warming. I looked up at Jaxson, but if he was watching me, I couldn't tell through his green mask. "I hope this doesn't start some stupid war between you guys."

"Us?" He appeared thrown by the very idea. "Jaxson wouldn't turn on me for that. It'll take a lot more to get rid of that guy. We can handle liking the same girl."

Goodness, Ezra was so unnaturally blunt. "You guys do seem pretty close," I replied, not ready to touch the idea of him and Jaxson liking me. "All four of you." The question had been pressing on my mind and I couldn't resist the chance to ask. "How did you become friends? I can't think of people more different than the four of you."

Ezra's face changed. It was so subtle; I don't think anyone else would have noticed. Suddenly, the wide genuine smile was replaced with the one I was realizing was fake. "Never thought much about it," he replied. "We're friends. That's it."

His hand shot out and snagged mine. "But do you really want to talk about them when there is something much more interesting we could be doing?" Ezra placed his hand on the back of my neck and leaned in.

"Wait." I turned my head away. "Not like this."

Ezra slowly dropped his hands, backing away. He didn't ask me what I meant.

I looked in his eyes and a million things sprang to my lips—all my mixed-up thoughts on how I felt, or thought I felt, and what I wanted, or thought I wanted. It all begged to come out.

I looked at him... then I picked up my dress and walked away. Ezra didn't come after me.

I freed myself from the grip of the crowd and stumbled off the dance floor. The effects of the kiss lingered. My body was overly warm and my lips tingled like I had put on too much peppermint lip gloss.

I ran straight to the food table and the bowl of cool fruit punch. I was downing my third cup when someone tapped me on the shoulder.

"Val, you okay?"

I didn't speak or turn to face Sofia. I just shook my head.

She grabbed my hand when I reached for the ladle a fourth time. "You might want to slow down. It's probably spiked."

"What?" I lurched away, slapping a hand to my throat.

Sofia caught me and spun me to face her. "Relax. I don't know for sure," she yelled over the music. Jaxson was ramping it up. "It's still early so they might not have gotten to it yet. But what's this look on your face? Did something happen with Ezra?"

"Yes, we kissed, but I shouldn't have done it." The words poured from my lips. "I told you I wasn't ready for anything and he basically admitted to liking me, but then I ran off and—"

Sofia tapped her ear, giving me a clueless look. "I can't hear you!" she shouted. "What did you say?"

I looked around quick and spotted a slight part in the curtains. "Come on!" I grabbed her hand and tugged. We weaved through the bodies as I made for a quieter spot. I passed by someone and reached for the curtains.

"Hey," they cried after me. "There's a line!"

Ignoring him, we were plunged into darkness as we slipped inside. "Okay," I began. "We were dancing and then—"

"Someone is eager."

I clapped my mouth shut, spinning around to find the source of the voice. "Who's there?"

"Who else but Madame Shari? You may come in."

Come in? I crept forward, my eyes adjusting to pierce the gloom, and slowly I put my hand out...

...and it passed through another break in the curtains. The act allowed a shimmer of light to come through and I pushed on, stepping inside.

It felt as though I stepped into another world. Gone were the hidden faces and sweeping strobe's spotlight, in here a soft glow emanated from the fairy lights woven through the dark red drapes. Squashy gold and black cushions surrounded a small table placed in the middle of the space, and sitting at that table was a thin woman with kohl-rimmed eyes and heavy makeup.

Her lips curled into a smile. "Ah. It's you. I was hoping you'd come." She swept out her hand. "You may sit down."

Sofia laughed. "We're not here for this. We just needed a place to talk."

"Well, while you're here..."

"It's cool," I interrupted. Postponing a talk about my mixed-up feelings wasn't the worst thing. "We're here so I'll give it a try. What do you want me to do?"

"Sit down, Valentina."

Sofia heaved a sigh. "I'm going to catch up with Jeremiah. Find me when you're done." She left and I took my seat.

Madame Shari smiled at me from across the table.

"How do you know my name?" I asked.

"Don't be too impressed. I was given names and pictures beforehand to add to the effect." I was surprised to receive such an honest answer. "But the rest, I will learn from you. I will see through to your soul and know the struggles that lie ahead, and in the past." Madame Shari lifted her hands and resting on her palm was a stack of cards. "After tonight... you will too."

"Right, so you want me to pick a card. Bring 'em on."

She leaned forward and fanned the cards out on the damask cloth. They were beautiful, hand-painted works of art in a swirly red and gold design that shimmer in the lights.

Her voice came to me in a whisper. "Choose three."

I placed my finger on the cards and one by one slid them toward her. She flipped over the card in the middle.

"The Magician," she announced. "Strong, powerful, resourceful and... deceitful."

"What does that—"

She flipped over the card to my right. "The High Priestess. Secrets. Tells of things that are not yet known, but vital for the path ahead."

I frowned at her. The air was becoming thick—cloying. I suddenly felt penned in by all these drapes.

"And last," she spoke in hushed tones. She picked the final card up with red-painted fingernails and flipped it on its back. A man wearing brightly colored clothes and a foolish grin stared back at me. "The Fool."

"And?" I met her eyes, but she didn't reply. "What does it mean?"

The silence spread between us like spilled tea, and with every second, I grew more weirded out. "Are you going to say—?"

"Valentina, have you ever heard of Walter McMillian?"

I blinked at this change in topic. "Walter McMillian? No, I have no clue who that is."

"He was a student here. He won the first ever scholarship to Evergreen Academy. Smart. Tough. Well-liked."

"I'm sorry." I held up a hand. "What does this have to do with anything?"

"But Walter," she plowed on, "he didn't know the rules— No, he knew the rules, but he thought he didn't have to follow them. He didn't understand the world he stepped into was nothing like the one he left."

Pinpricks of sweat dotted my forehead. I fanned myself as I fidgeted on the cushion.

"Walter wanted change but quae sequenda traditio. Trad—"

"Tradition is everything."

She smiled at me. "That's right. And as tradition demanded, when Walter wouldn't fall back in line, *they* had to act."

I leaned forward, bumping my chest against the table. "Who's they?"

"It doesn't matter so much as what happened next. You see, brave little Walter was killed."

My nails dug into the cloth. "Killed? You mean—"

"Murdered," she stated blankly. "And the mark he left on the legacy of Evergreen was wiped out."

Irritation bubbled in the pit of my stomach. "Why are you telling me this? What does this have to do with my fortune?"

"Everything." Madame Shari looked down at the overturned cards. "The Magician. The High Priestess. The Fool. You need to be strong, Valentina. Quick, intelligent, and not afraid to fight because"—she slid the Fool card toward me—"you're destined to share Walter's fate."

I lurched to my feet. "That's not funny! What's wrong with you? You're taking this game a little too far."

She shrugged. I wasn't finding her smile so pleasant now. "You don't believe me. Why? It's not so strange that you would share the same fate as Walter... you already share his room."

I turned and walked out. The heat, the swallowing drapes, that creepy dead-eyed stare were all too much. I needed to get out.

I swept out into the gym. My dress wrinkled in my fists as I sped for the doors, picking up the pace as I got nearer. The band around my chest tightened as my breaths came in shorter pants.

"You see... brave little Walter was killed."

Bursting through the doors, I sucked in deep lungfuls as the night air smacked my feverish face. I didn't stop. My feet took me around the building toward the door to the roof.

I just need a few minutes, and then I'll—

I rounded the corner and slammed into a warm body.

"Ow!" I cried.

Large hands encircled my forearms, steadying me. "Valentina? What are you doing out here?"

My head snapped up. "Maverick?"

It was him—standing before me in an incredible tux that screamed money as loud as it screamed what a great body he had, molding to the curves of his muscles like it was painted on. Maverick wasn't wearing a mask which allowed me the perfect look at the surprise breaking through his normally blank features.

"What are you doing out here?" he repeated.

"I just..." How did I begin to explain my night or my reasons for needing to get away? "I needed some air. Why are you out here?"

He dropped his hands and I found myself missing the loss. "Same," he said simply.

Maverick backed up and propped himself on the door I was looking to get through. I considered asking him to move, but going up there would reveal our secret spot. Instead, I moved over to him and adopted his position.

"It's spooky out here." I rubbed my arms where his hands had been. The skin was prickling. "But the peace and quiet is nice."

I fixed my eyes on the side of his face, but he didn't turn to look at me. Before us loomed the thick copse of trees that made up the woods surrounding the academy.

I lightly hip-checked him. "You don't like parties, do you?"

He was quiet for so long I thought he wouldn't answer. "No," he said after the silence had grown almost unbearable. "Too much noise. Too many people."

"There's a lot of noise and people at soccer and football games, but yet, you're captain of both teams—dominating the field."

"That's different," he protested. "When I'm playing it's like—it's like—" I sensed his frustration as he tried to explain. "It's like when building a hard drive or writing code or... never mind."

I picked up where he gave up. "It's like you're in control."

His head twisted around, facing me. I went on. "I get that. It's like... when I'm dancing I don't care who's watching me or what they're thinking. It's the only time I feel I know exactly what I'm doing." I laughed. "But put me in front of a class full of people to present my crappy art project, I near wet myself."

Maverick chuckled, a lopsided smile breaking through. "Your painting wasn't that bad."

I sighed. "I don't think people got it." The end of October had come which meant we had to reveal the paintings we had done of each other. My bright idea had been to paint Maverick with his chest cracked open to reveal gears and wires inside. Even with lessons from Scarlett twice a week, half the class screwed up their faces squinting at the canvas. "I didn't mean it like you were cold or robotic. It's just one of the things I like about you is how you can see the potential in things."

He blinked. "Like about me?"

"You don't see a cell phone; you see a button cam or a re-mote. All the things it could be." My mouth was running full speed with no sign of slowing down. "And that's what I think when I see you. That if I open you up, I'll discover what makes you tick and all the parts that make you who you are and..."

I trailed off as I finally caught the look he was giving me. I groaned. "And I should have stopped talking five minutes ago."

Maverick laughed, tossing his head back. I liked his laugh. It started low and rolled out of his chest, deep and honest for how rare it was. I knew when I heard his laugh, it was because I earned it.

I leaned against the cold metal of the door. "I liked the paint-ing you did of me." Maverick hadn't gone with the one he drew of me the first day we met. When he ripped off the blanket, my eyes widened at the strokes and colors that came together to show me the night of the sleepover—my hips out and hair flying as I danced in my bunny slippers. There was no one else in the paint-ing, as though I had been the only person he had seen.

"I don't know how you do it," I breathe. "You make me look beautiful; I wonder if you're actually painting some other girl."

"I did not make you look that way." He spoke so softly the wind almost took his words away before it reached my ears. "You are beautiful."

I bit my lip as the bubble machine in my stomach turned up to maximum. I felt them growing, bursting, popping, and spreading out into my body and making me float. Or at least, that's what it felt like.

I hip-checked him again, but this time I didn't pull back, let-ting my hip, and then the rest of my body fold into his side. I feared Maverick might pull away. It was obvious to everyone that he didn't like people in his space, and he liked them touching him even less, so a soft gasp escaped my lips when an arm wound around my shoulder.

I held completely still as though even a twitch could break the spell. Maybe it would have. Maybe it *should* have. I should pull away, go inside, and dance the night away in my four-thou-sand-dollar dress. I had no business being out here in Maverick's arms.

Taking a deep breath, the smell of him filled me up instead of a blast of courage. A sharp, woodsy scent that mixed in with something that was purely Maverick. It blew away all my thoughts of leaving. I rested my head on his chest as the arm around me moved up until his fingers found my chin. I didn't fight him as he tilted my head back and pressed his lips to mine. Kissing him in that moment was the only thing I could have done.

This kiss was nothing like the one I shared with Ezra—chaste and sweet under the watchful eyes of a crowd. Maverick had no reason to hold back and he didn't.

He crushed me to his body, tangling his fingers in my hair as our mouths moved feverishly. He nipped my bottom lip and I gasped, giving him all the invitation he needed to deepen the kiss—his tongue teasing mine to play.

I wasn't on fire. I wasn't burning. No, with Maverick I flew. I was cresting, soaring, spinning as sunbursts exploded in my mind.

Something was poking me in the side, disturbing one of the best kisses of my life. I shifted to get away from the doorknob...

...and went down.

"Ahh!"

My ankle folded like tissue paper, ripping our lips apart as I crumpled to the ground.

"Shit!" Maverick dropped to my side. "Val, are you okay?"

"I'm fine." I laughed. "I don't wear a lot of heels at home. I guess this was destined to happen. Hmm, why didn't Madame Shari predict that?"

"What?"

I shook my head. "Nothing. Just help me up."

"No, stay here. I'll get ice."

Maverick was up and running before I could stop him, leaving me alone in the darkness.

I climbed to my feet. My ankle was okay, but I wasn't feeling the eerie silence of the woods. At least there was light, stars, and cozy chairs on the roof.

I turned to go. *I can catch up with Maverick inside and—*

"...no..."

I froze. *What was that? Did I just hear?*

"...no..."

That was a voice. I twisted around looking for who spoke. Nothing but woods and rolling grass met my eyes. The wind brought another word to my ear.

"...stop..."

My eyes flicked to the woods. *Someone is in there? But why would they be there in the middle of the night?*

I took a step, then stopped. It was probably nothing. A couple of kids hooking up or—

But they said stop.

I was off and across the lawn before the thought was complete. What if someone needed help?

The trees whispered to me as I ran, calling me into their depths. I passed through the tree line and skidded to a halt, listening closely.

"...you did..."

My head whipped to the left. *There.*

I didn't run. This time I stepped lightly over the earthen path.

"...everyone will know," came the hushed voice, "what you really are."

The darkness was thicker under the entwined branches of the pines. I could barely see the hand in front of my face as I felt my way.

"Keep your mouth shut!" That snarled reply stopped me dead. I sensed the venom, the anger... the familiarity... in that voice as though it was my own.

I took one more step, and I saw them.

In the distance, I made out two figures in the scant moonlight. They were upset—arguing from the way their hands were waving. I squinted trying to see through the shadows to their faces.

"...isn't a game."

"...won't stop me."

I edged closer. *That voice. I think I know... that voice.*

Suddenly the bodies collided, as if one had thrown themselves on the other. I saw them grappling—struggling with each other as I desperately tried to make out a face.

"Argh!" A shout and then something went flying through the air. I couldn't see what it was.

"I promised you would regret this!"

"Oh no," I breathed. Of course, I knew that voice. "Ryder."

No sooner had the name passed my lips than the bodies sprang apart. I tried to find Ryder, and my eyes fixed on one of them in time to see metal glint in the gloom as they raised their arm high.

A scream ripped from my throat. "Ryder!" I surged forward, racing toward him, and screamed for the third time that night as an unseen root snagged my foot. I fell hard, crying out as pain exploded in my knee.

I heard a muttered curse, the thud of retreating footsteps, and then "Valentina!"

Wincing, I dragged myself through the dirt and grabbed on to a tree. Rough bark scraped my palms as I heaved myself up.

"Ryder?"

I looked around frantically. I couldn't make anything out now, not even shadows. "Ryder!"

Nothing.

Carefully, I stepped further in, my eyes scanning the trees for a flicker of movement. What if Ryder was still in here with the person who had the knife?

What if Ryder was the person who had the knife?

I shivered at the chill that thought sent up my spine. Who was I in here with?

I took another step.

Crack.

Something broke under my heel that was not a twig. I reached down and my fingers brushed against a smooth surface. I held it up.

A red and white mask stared back at me.

Chapter Eight

I dreamed of blood that night.

Hoarse screams ripped me out of sleep. I rose with a groan, giving up any chance of going back to bed that night. A glance at the clock told me it was five a.m.

I kicked the tangled covers away from me and scrabbled for my phone. Moments later, the dial tone was ringing in my ear.

"What the hell, kid?" Olivia griped by way of hello. "Do you have any idea what time it—"

"M-Mom," I sobbed.

"Val?" Mom's voice changed in an instant. "Baby, what's wrong? What happened?"

"I had the d-dream again."

"Okay, well, what do you do when you have the dream?"

"Mom—"

"What do you do, Val?" she repeated, tone soothing.

My jaw worked and I tried to reply. "I... turn on all the lights."

"That's right. Are the lights on?"

"No," I admitted. I hated how small my voice sounded.

"Okay, get up, turn on the lights, and I'll be right here."

It took a few times of her repeating that for me to finally slide one leg off the bed, then another. I crossed the room with quick

126

steps and flicked on the lights. The tightness in my chest eased the moment it chased away the darkness.

"Okay, they're on."

"Good, baby, then what's next?"

"I call you."

"Check. Best mom in the world is right here. So only one more thing to do. What is it?"

I climbed back into bed and huddled between my pillows. "I remember that... it's just a dream," I replied as I pulled my knees to my chin. "But that's it, Mom." A tear rolled down my face and soaked into the sheet. "It's not a dream."

"It is," she said firmly. "It's only a dream."

I shook my head. "Tonight was so awful."

"Why? Tell me what happened."

The words poured out of me with no more prompting. "There was this Halloween dance, and a fortune teller. She told me the story of a student who went to Evergreen, and she said that he used to live in my dorm. Mom, he was murdered here." My skin crawled as I thought of his presence in this room—of his body on my floor.

"I'm sure that's not true."

"But she said—"

"She is a know-nothing fake who gets a kick out of telling scary fortunes. She was messing with you, love."

"Maybe." I swallowed. "Maybe you're right."

"Of course I'm right."

"But after when I went outside..."

"What, Val?" Mom prompted when I trailed off.

What do I say? I ran into the woods and saw Ryder fighting with someone I couldn't see. Yelling about them paying for what they did, and then the glint of what I'm sure was a knife. But who was holding it?

I ran back into the party after I found the mask, searching for a teacher that would raise the alarm and start a search of the woods. But when I skidded inside the gym, my eyes landed on him right away.

Ryder was there. It was impossible to mistake him. Those silver eyes pierced me as he stood harmless in front of the punch bowl, sipping his drink with one hand while a blue mask hung from his fingertips. No expression graced his face. Nothing to give away what I had just witnessed.

I took a step toward him and Ryder turned and disappeared into the crowd. Filled with confusion, I stared after him until I realized everyone was staring at me.

My dress was ruined—covered in leaves, dirt, and broken twigs. I didn't look for Sofia, or attempt to chase after Ryder. At that point, I left the gym, racing back to my dorm.

"It's nothing," I finally said. "I didn't have as much fun at the party as I thought I would."

"There will be more parties. I remember they were endless when I was in high school."

"They are here too despite them being banned." The tension leaked from my body and I curled into my pillows. I reached for my blanket and pulled it to my chin. "Even with cameras and security guards, they find a way."

"I'm not surprised. You find a way too. Get your head out of those books, my little egghead, and have some fun."

I smiled. "Aren't you supposed to tell me the opposite?"

"Nah. I want you to live like a teenager. It's past time you did."

I nodded even though she couldn't see me. "Then you'll be proud to know I was very irresponsible and shelled out four thousand dollars for a dress. A dress that I ruined in one night."

She whistled. "Wow, kid. You're not talking about the way I used to ruin dresses, right?"

"Mom!"

Her laughter echoed through the phone. "Just checking."

"I shouldn't have spent so much," I continued, "but it was so pretty and I was practically dared to buy it." I chewed my lip, wondering how mad Mom would get at what I was going to say next. "Mom, if you need—"

"No."

"Just to help with the bills—"

"No!" I snapped my mouth shut. "We talked about this, Val. I got my job at the daycare. Good pay. Free childcare. Adam and I are doing fine. You just focus on getting that diploma, going to college, and getting a good job." Her tone softened. "Then you can set me up in a nice house and pamper me in the way that I deserve."

I chuckled. "Alright, Mom. So how is Adam?"

"The boy's got teeth."

"Seriously?" A thread of warmth went through me. "Already?"

"Yep, and he knows how to use them. Yesterday, he..."

I pushed away thoughts of Walter McMillian and the lingering fear from my dream. It had been a long, confusing, terrifying night, but I was safe here. Everything would be okay.

"I SWEAR THAT'S WHAT I saw," I whispered to Sofia as we crossed the quad Monday morning. I had spent the whole weekend locked in my room, worrying about what to do, and fighting sleep. I had texted Sofia everything that happened that night, but with the nightmares and Madame Shari's warning throwing me off-balance, I asked her to give me space to process. My time was up.

"He was arguing with someone and it got heated. Then one of them pulled a knife."

"Are you sure it was a knife?" she asked. "Are you absolutely sure? You were in pitch-black woods."

"It... looked like a knife. I mean it was dark, but..." Uncertainty crept into my mind. "They ran when I called out for Ryder. Whatever was going on, wasn't good."

"And you didn't see who it was?"

I shook my head. "I barely made out Ryder. I only knew it was him because I'll never mistake that voice."

"But you found that mask."

"Yes, and it must have belonged to who he was fighting with because Ryder still had his when I saw him afterward."

"One of the freshmen then if they were at the masquerade."

We stepped into the hall. I kept my voice low as we dodged students. "I felt sick thinking that I should have tried to find out who they were—*where* they were. Ryder is a monster. It must have been him who started the fight."

"If a student had been knifed or went missing, security would be swarming the place." We stopped in front of my locker, leaning in close. "You said Ryder got back before you so he must have rabbited out of there when you showed up. No time to chase that person down and finish what he started."

I bobbed my head. "Right, of course." I needed to hear this. Her logic was talking me down. "So you don't think I should tell someone? A professor? The headmaster?"

She shook her head firmly. "You don't have anything to tell them and it would be your word against Ryder's. He could tell them it was just Knight business, and they would swallow it. The point is we don't know what was going on, and the only one who could tell you is Ryder." She squeezed my hand. "So don't freak, Val."

"Okay." I squeezed back. "Thank you." With my free hand, I spun my locker dial.

"Good. So if you're really okay now...?"

I nodded.

She grinned. "Then you can tell me all about making out with Ezra *and* Maverick in the same night?"

"Wow." I removed my lock and palmed it. "That almost feels like a different night and another girl." I threw open my locker, then shrugged off my bag to riffle inside for my books.

"But it was Friday night and *you*. I want every... single... detail..."

"I don't know if you want *every* detail. The truth is I messed it up both times and I still haven't changed my mind about not dating. What do you think I should do?"

There was no answer.

"Sofia?" I lifted my head. "Hey, are you okay?"

Sofia had gone sickly pale. Her jaw trembled, and I saw her eyes were wide as she stared at something over my shoulder. She took a step back.

"What's up with you?"

I turned to look. Hanging from the top of my locker was a single card. Frowning, I reached for it.

"Val, don't—!"

I snagged it and pulled it out. "What is this? How did it get in here?"

There was a red "A" stamped onto solid black. I flipped it over. The man adorning the card wore brightly colored clothes, a two-bell hat, and a grin that looked almost sinister.

"A joker card."

"Look..."

I glanced up as the first whisper reached my ear. A crowd was forming around me, students pausing in their rush to homeroom to gather—all eyes were on the card.

I raised a brow. "There's nothing to see here, guys. You can keep moving."

No one did.

"Anyway," I said to my best friend, ignoring the growing crowd. "We should talk about all of this tonight, but— Sofia, are you okay?" She was starting to worry me. Her chin trembled and beads of sweat were collecting on her forehead. I rested my hand on her arm. "You look sick. Let me walk you to the nurse."

In a blink, her face twisted.

"Sofi—"

Smack!

I let out a small scream as the slap snapped my head around. My bookbag slipped through my fingers, crashing to the floor and scattering its contents everywhere.

I gaped at her, clutching my stinging cheek. "Sofia! What the fuck?!"

Gone was the ever-present bright smile. Her lips were curled into a snarl so fierce I took a step back, banging into my locker.

"I'm not your friend, bitch!" she spat.

The words struck me as hard as her slap. I jerked as they pierced through me and rebounded through my skin.

Sofia spun on her heels and elbowed through the crowd. She stomped off without another word—without looking back.

After she left, my silent audience broke apart too, leaving me standing alone.

I STUMBLED INTO HOMEROOM late. My head was spinning with what just happened. *Sofia hit me. Why would she do that? Why would she say that?*

I couldn't make sense of it, nor could I understand the silence the room was plunged in when the door swung shut behind me.

My eyes swept the room to the sight of upturned noses and hostile glares, and those were from the people who would look at me. Many turned their head away when I glanced at them—Sofia included.

My chest tightened at the sight of her. *Why is she being like this?*

"Miss Moon." I tore my eyes away and turned toward Markham. Her face carried the usual no-nonsense expression, and I waited for my telling off for being late. "Have a seat, please," she said simply.

Slowly, I picked up my feet and walked up to the phone box. Giving the class my back, I placed my cell inside as whispers broke out behind me.

I locked up the box and headed for my seat. More whispers followed me, and this time they were accompanied by hushed snickers. I didn't have to ask if they were talking about me, I felt the weight of their side-eyes pressing on me, making my hair stand on end.

What was going on?

I fixed on Sofia as I took my seat. She was looking out the window, pretending she couldn't see me coming.

"Sof?" I whispered. "What the hell was that back there? Is everything okay?"

No answer.

"Sofia?"

Her only movement was a slight tightening of her jaw.

My hands curled into fists. "Sofia?" I hissed. "You just smacked the crap out of me, at least you can tell me why!"

Screeech!

Metal scraped across the floor as Sofia pushed her chair back. She snatched her backpack up and stamped off to a desk in the back. I watched her go open-mouthed.

I swallowed hard. Pressure was building behind my eyes—a familiar prickling that warned of tears pushing against the flood-gates. *How could she just walk away from me like that?*

I shifted around in my seat and caught Claire's look before she quickly dropped her gaze. "Claire? What's going on with Sofia?"

My friend hunched over her desk, fixing her attention on her textbook.

"Claire?" Her cheeks pinked under my eyes, but she did not look up. She steadfastly ignored me. "Cla—"

The door banged open and all eyes snapped to the front as Jaxson strolled in. It was a familiar scene. He tossed a careless "Sorry I'm late. Knight business," at Markham as he crossed the room to his seat. An easy smile graced his lips as he ran his fingers through his growing blond hair, and the sight of him actually put me at ease.

Maybe he can tell me why everyone's lost it.

He passed by my desk, hitting me with a wave of his spicy sweet scent, and I reached for his arm. "Jaxson, I need to talk to y—"

My fingers brushed his skin.

"Yo!" Jaxson recoiled, shooting away from me like my touch burned. "What do you think you're doing?!"

My cheeks warmed as every eye turned on us. "Me? What is wrong with you? Why are you freaking out?"

His handsome face twisted into a scowl. "If you have to ask then it's clear you still don't know how it works around here, but you're going to find out real soon." He leveled a finger at me. "You were the Knight business."

"Me? What are you talking about?"

He scoffed. "Here's a tip for free: Get out of here."

"Get out of where? Class?" I reared up. "You can't kick me out of—"

"Get out of Evergreen." His words chilled me as effectively as the look in his eyes. This was a Jaxson I hadn't seen before. No playful smile. No flirting. No heart-pounding laugh. "Now, Valentina."

I stiffened. Jaxson never called me by my full name.

"Before we make you."

The words hung in the air as Jaxson streamed past me, ignoring the seat by my side that he had claimed all those weeks ago.

I sat there for a while as the snickers got louder. They were invading my brain, niggling inside and planting seeds of doubt. Had I done something? What was going on?

My mind turned up no answers to these questions.

Focus on something else, I thought. *Ignore them.*

I didn't know what else to do so I bent and took out my homework. Numbers and equations demanded my attention as I tried to complete my math, but whispers and laughter pressed in on me. The invisible band around my chest squeezed, tightening and tightening until I stopped breathing.

IF I THOUGHT MY MORNING would get better after homeroom, I was wrong. The strange silent treatment kept up through English and PE It wasn't just the students either. Professor Strange pretended she didn't see me every time I raised my hand.

By the time I pulled on my dress and made for the cafeteria, I didn't need to ask if something was off, I knew it was, and I knew it was entirely about me. I saw it in the filthy looks people I never even spoke to were throwing me. I felt it in the slap of my best friend.

But what did I do that would make the entire freshman class turn on me? Why was this happening?

I stepped through the doors of the lunchroom, and for the fourth time that day, the room fell silent. Clenching my fists, I lifted my chin and walked stiffly to the lunch line. I fell in behind two girls from my biology class.

Emma and Lola were deep in conversation until Emma noticed me over her friend's shoulder. She cut off mid-sentence.

"Oh, hi, Val," said Emma. She smiled at me. "Why don't you go ahead of us?"

"What?" I stepped back. "Why?"

She shrugged. "It's good today. Quinoa salad and tomato spinach grilled cheese." Her smile slipped. "Besides, I heard what you've been... going through." Emma and Lola both stepped to the side. "Please, go ahead."

After a few seconds, I returned their supportive smiles with one of relief. "Thanks, guys."

"No problem," Emma replied as I moved to take her place. I was taking down my tray when her next comment landed. "Lunch is so important, and we want to make sure you eat."

"Make sure I eat?" I glanced over my shoulder and went rigid at the change in her expression. The smile was morphing into one that was sharper, nastier.

"Yeah," Lola piped up. "We know about your little problems with food. Tell us: how many times did you have to stick your finger down your throat to get into that size zero?"

Sniggering rang out all around me as red stained my cheeks. My tray shook in my hands. "I don't know," I snapped. "I think it's the same as the number of nose jobs you got to get that beak."

Lola's hand flew to her nose. "I don't have a— Hey, don't walk away from me, bitch!"

I ignored her and stomped off. My feet carried me down my usual path to my table. I was a few feet away when I slowed down.

Where's my chair?

The chair next to Sofia was gone. An obvious gap that I knew meant something. Maybe I should have turned around, but I couldn't. I needed someone to tell me what was going on.

I stopped in front of my friends' table. They were in the middle of a conversation.

"—such a good time. You've got to send me the pictures you took at the dance."

"Guys, where is my seat?"

Neither Sofia, Paisley, Eric, nor Claire looked up.

"I'll send them to you tonight," said Sofia, sounding like her old self. "Text me to remind me."

"Sofia, can I talk to you?" I asked. "I don't know what happened to you today, but you can't go around hitting me."

"Also," began Claire, "we should start talking study groups now that finals are coming up."

"They aren't until the end of the month," Eric said. "I'll worry about them the week before."

Laughing, Paisley shoved his shoulder. "Then you'll be a sleep-wrecked mess and crying into your textbooks every night in the library."

"I'll accept my fate."

Fate. The word struck me as the four of them devolved into chuckles. It settled uncomfortably like a pit in my stomach.

That's it.

I slammed my tray on the table. The four of them jumped. "Guys, stop pretending you don't see me! What is wrong with everyone today?! Talk to me!"

Paisley shot me a look that didn't sit well on her pretty face. "We're *not* talking to you. So will you take the fucking hint, Moon, and *go away*!"

I flinched, my anger taking a hit. "But why? Guys, if I did something to piss you off, just tell me."

Paisley's response was to spin around in her seat, giving me her back.

I glanced at Eric for help. "Eric, what's up?"

His face was grave. "There's nothing we can do, Val. Just go."

I didn't know what was worse. Paisley's venom or Eric's resignation. "But, guys—"

"Damn, do you listen?!" I jerked my head up at the shout. "They said to go away!"

This had come from Kevin Jones—a boy from my art class who blushed when our hands touched reaching for the same brush.

"No one wants you here! Get out!" Kevin closed his hand over his bottled water and lobbed it at me. I ducked with a scream as it went whizzing through the spot my head was just in.

"Yeah! Get out!"

I was crouched on the floor when the first sandwich smacked my forehead and slid down my face. Then all hell broke loose.

Food rained down on me as furious as the shouts, screams, and insults they were hurling my way. I picked myself off the floor and ran. I stumbled when I slipped on a piece of lettuce, but didn't stop fleeing.

I cried out as another water bottle struck me in the back. Picking up the pace, I burst through the doors and slammed into a hard body. I bounced off them like a pinball and landed on my ass.

"Whoa there. Where do you think you're going?"

Dread filled my bones at the sound of his voice. I lifted my head and all four of them gazed down at me: Ezra, Jaxson, Maverick, and Ryder.

Ryder smirked. "Hold her."

"Wha—"

Maverick sprung forward and scooped me up. He crushed my back to his chest, facing me toward the other three boys, as he secured an arm like iron around my stomach.

"Hey! Get off! Let me go!"

"Shh, shh, shh," Ryder said. "There's no need for that." His voice was soft—almost gentle. He reached out and brushed the hair that had escaped my ponytail out of my eyes. He didn't pull back. "We're not going to hurt you"—his grin grew wicked—"physically."

"What's going on, Ryder?" I rasped. "What did you do?"

"Me?" He cocked his head. "I didn't do a thing. This was all you." He traced a path to my cheekbones. "I left you alone just like you wanted, Val, but I knew all I had to do was wait. Soon, you'd screw up and we'd be here. It was fate."

"Screw up? But I didn't do anything." My eyes found Ezra's. "Ezra, what is this? What's going on?"

His polite smile was firmly in place as he lifted his shoulder. "I'd say you were a smart girl and you'd figure this out," he said with mock pleasantness, "but I am your tutor, so I know you're not."

The boys laughed—even Maverick. I felt the rumble of his chest as he mocked me and it churned my stomach. It writhed and twisted like it did before I threw up. "Maverick," I whispered. "How can you be like this? The other night—"

"You talking about when you hooked up with my boy behind the gym?" Jaxson spoke up. He grinned as he rested his elbow on Ezra's shoulder. "That was like five— four seconds after you stuck your tongue down Ezra's throat?" He shook his head. "And everyone said the Virgin would be a challenge. Seems to me like she gives it up pretty easily."

I flushed.

"I never said that," Ryder joined in. His fingers were still on my face, stroking my cheek in a way that could have been mistaken for affectionate. "I told you she was a whore like her mother. I'd bet half my fortune she's lying about being a virgin too."

Jaxson hummed. "The whore thing would explain how she affords all these jewels and expensive dresses. Damn, why didn't we see it before? The girl's got customers."

"Stop it!" I shrieked when they laughed again. "What is wrong with you people?!"

They kept going like I hadn't spoken. "Well, I don't care who she gives her services to," Ezra said. "I won the bet. I was the first to hook up with her. Pay up."

I choked. "Wha—"

"Hold up." Ryder cut in. "It was which of you three slept with her first. You haven't won yet."

Jaxson shrugged. "I can settle that right now." He pinned me with his stare. "How much for a fuck, Val? I'll pay your rates."

"You piece of shit!" The words exploded out of me. "I'm not a prostitute!"

"Isn't that cheating anyway?" Ezra asked. "Let's just call it a kiss and give me my winnings." He smirked. "How much did we bet? Oh, yeah... one dollar."

The pressure was building behind my eyes. Every hateful word flayed me alive, peeling back my skin and exposing the raw, soft part of me that had allowed herself to hope, to trust three of the beasts surrounding me, to think that things could truly be different for me.

I should have known the final beast would never let that happen.

"Why, Ryder?" His hand had moved to my hair now, lazily wrapping a curl around his finger. "I've never done anything to you. Why do you hate me so much?"

His face changed. The taunting smirk disappeared behind his cold, stony mask. "This isn't about you and me. I didn't start this, Val, you did." He closed the distance between us until our noses brushed. His silver eyes filled my vision. "It was you," he whispered, "who went where she didn't belong, and saw what she wasn't supposed to see."

His hand left my hair and moved down my chin. He pressed his fingers gently to my lips. "And now they'll make sure you keep your pretty mouth quiet."

"W-what happened in those woods?" My mouth moved against him. "What did you do, Ryder?"

"It's all about what you did now. You saw it for yourself. Opened your locker and discovered your life had changed just like I did."

Opened my locker...

"You're marked, Val," he went on. "Your time in Evergreen is up. But it's okay because you never belonged here anyway. One way or another, I was going to get rid of you."

My body trembled. I was practically vibrating in Maverick's hold, but despite my tumultuous feelings, I looked Ryder right in the eyes. "I'm not going anywhere."

He chuckled. "You won't last the week. Save yourself the trouble and pack your bags now."

My eyes narrowed. "No."

Ryder heaved a sigh like I was being difficult. "Suit yourself, but don't say I didn't warn you. Just remember one thing." He tapped my lips. "Keep that whore mouth shut—"

I lunged forward and snapped, viciously biting down on his finger.

"Argh! Fuck!"

Ryder shot away from me, roughly yanking his finger from my teeth, and the surprise got Maverick to loosen his grip.

I reared back and buried my elbow in his gut. Maverick grunted in pain and his arm loosened some more. I took my chance.

I darted out of his hold and raced down the hallway faster than I had ever run in my life. Their shouts followed me down the hallway although their feet didn't. They weren't chasing me, but I didn't stop running.

My leather shoes squeaked as they scuffed the polished floors. My reflection ran with me, pacing me in the glass of the hall of windows, looking not nearly as awful as I felt. I lit upon the girls' bathroom at the end of the hall and dove inside. Breaths coming in rapid pants, my chest heaved as I sucked in air that did nothing to help. I fell against the door.

Scratch, scratch, scratch.

Nails dug into my chest as I slid onto the floor. The pressure was beneath my skin. It was boiling with rage and pain and feelings I couldn't name, but knew well. They scoured me, trying to rub me away—trying to undo all the work I had done to change.

It was too much. I couldn't stop it. I couldn't fight it.

When the first tear rolled down my cheek, I gave myself to the pain, and sobbed.

I LOCKED MYSELF IN the bathroom for the rest of lunch, ignoring the bangs on the door from other people trying to get in. I had earned my space. After all, I had just found out three boys I thought liked me had been betting to see which one could hook up with me first.

I didn't know who to be angrier at. Them or me. I should have stayed away from them like I resolved from the beginning, but all the time I spent with them made me believe I shouldn't judge them based on Ryder.

What a fucking idiot.

Sighing, I let my head fall back against the door. No one who could be friends with Ryder was a good guy. I should have seen that.

This isn't only about their bet, I reminded myself. My hand moved to the pocket of my dress and the single card that had been burning a hole in it all day.

Once I stopped crying, I turned my thoughts to what else Ryder said.

"I didn't start this, Val, you did. It was you who went where she didn't belong, and saw what she wasn't supposed to see."

"You've been marked."

I slipped the card from my pocket and met the hideous smile of the joker.

"But why do people have to listen to them?" I said into the empty space. "Because if they don't... they're marked."

I remembered what Paisley said that day. What I don't remember is why I didn't press for more information? Something had been done to me and I still didn't know exactly what or why.

This card had lost me my friends in the space of an hour. It lost me the good feelings of my classmates, and if what happened in homeroom and the cafeteria was anything to go by, it had cost me the protection of the staff. No one had spoken up to help me. How far would this go before someone did? What would I do if no one did?

I was no stranger to bullying. Joe Young Middle had been a brutal place for a girl with holes in her clothes and no money for lunch. Things had gotten slightly better in the month I was at Joe Young High, but still it was a relief to leave and start over in a better place. If I left Evergreen, there would be no going back there.

But that's what they want.

I knew that much for sure after my little chat with the Knights. They want me out of the academy and all for what I saw—or didn't see—in the woods.

But why?!

The corner of the card crumpled in my fist. I didn't tell anyone what I saw besides Sofia, I didn't *know* what I saw. Ryder fought with someone I couldn't see. I didn't even make out what the argument was about. Why did he think I could tell people? I couldn't identify who held the knife or say for sure it was a knife.

Around and around I went in my head, but by the time the final bell rang, I still had no answers.

I picked myself off the floor and went over to the sink. The cool water soothed my heated skin. I took my time washing the tear tracks from my face until every strip of makeup was gone. Water dripped down my pink cheeks as I met my gaze in the mirror. There was a blank look in my eyes that chilled me.

It reminded me of Ryder.

I WALKED INTO CHEMISTRY class feeling like the emotional equivalent of a wrung-out dishrag. I didn't react to the snickers that went up the moment I stepped inside.

I shared this class with Sofia, and normally we sat together, giggling over Chem notes. I scanned the room and found her in the back next to Natalie. We clearly wouldn't be doing that today.

I dropped my gaze and shuffled over to my desk.

A taunting laugh behind me made my hair stand on end. "Did you hear she locked herself in the bathroom?" Penelope Madlow said loud enough for her voice to carry. "Throwing up even though she didn't touch her food. That's one seriously bad case of bulimia when just the sight of it makes you stick your finger down your throat."

I dug my nails so hard in my palm it sang with pain, but I didn't respond. I wouldn't give them the satisfaction of replying to such a cheap shot. The Joe Young kids had gone after my body too, but they took shots at my mom saying she was too poor to feed me. That hurt worse than some made-up nonsense about eating disorders.

Professor Grass rose from his desk. "Alright, class, settle down." I don't think it was a reprimand. He said it so monotone it didn't sound like one either. "Open your textbooks to page one hundred. Read silently to yourselves."

"I bet you don't last the semester," Penelope hissed at my back. "You'll be running back to your slum with your tail between your legs."

Slowly, I twisted around in my seat. Penelope's smirk slipped when she saw the look in my eyes. "You'll be talking through your gums if you don't stop running that mouth. I went through things you would never believe in that 'slum'—way worse than your weak-ass digs and a handful of thrown salad. I'm not going anywhere and you can pass it around. There's nothing any of you can throw at me that will break me."

Penelope dropped her dumbfounded expression quick as a snarl formed on her lips. "We'll see about that."

I looked over her head at Sofia. She dropped her eyes the minute I caught her looking. She was the only one who would not look at me. The rest of the class had no problem leveling me with their hateful glares.

I didn't fully understand why this was happening, but I did know one thing. I was in this alone.

IT WAS A SLOG TO THE end of the day. In and out of class, students stuck their fingers in their mouths and pretended to heave as I walked by.

I waded through a sea of gags and hot breath as a crowd surrounded me in front of Professor Markham's class.

"Move," I said through gritted teeth.

"Or you'll what?" One of the boys lashed out and shoved me. Quick as a whip, I took my textbook and whacked his hand.

He yelped. "Bitch!"

The boy shot forward, hands out, but someone materialized in front of me.

"You out of your mind, fool?" Jaxson growled. He snagged my attacker's collar and twisted it until he choked. "You keep your fucking hands to yourself. It doesn't get physical." He said that but from the way the kid was turning blue, it was getting plenty physical. "You're standing outside Markham's class trying to start a fight. If she goes to a professor with bruises, they'll have to do something or get their stupid asses sued. No one touches her, and that's an order from the Knights."

He threw the boy back and he collapsed onto his friends, gasping for air, but he nodded so furiously I thought his head would fly off. "Yes, Jaxson. Sorry." Apologies went around the entire group.

I didn't know what to say. Jaxson defended me. He protected me from what those hateful eyes truly wanted to do. *Maybe he—*

"Everything else though... is fair game."

Dread filled my bones like lead, pinning me to the spot. I wasn't able to move as Jaxson finally turned on me. He grinned into my wide eyes. "Although, I may do something about that too if you take me up on my offer." He brushed the hair behind my ear in the way I secretly used to love—in a way I still loved. A shiver went through my body and I hated myself for it. "How much for a fuck?"

I stepped closer, getting right in his face. "I wouldn't fuck you for all the money in your bank account. Get out of my way."

"Still so feisty." Backing away, he tossed me a wink. "We'll see how long that lasts."

The crowd didn't stick around long after Jaxson left. Finally alone, I stepped through into Markham's class. She looked up from her computer when I entered. "Ah, Miss Moon."

I didn't respond and crossed the room for the phone box. I had nothing to say for the woman who sat there while her class mocked and taunted me. She most likely also heard everything that went on outside the door, but still she sat there typing away. There was no excuse for being such a coward.

I yanked out my phone and slammed it shut none-too-gently. I stomped back to the door.

"Miss Moon, please. Can I speak to you for a moment?"

I paused with my hand on the knob. I didn't turn around.

"Miss Moon, you are a very promising student. You've worked hard to catch up to your peers and I can see you're serious about doing well here."

That made me turn around. I looked at her in disbelief. "You want to talk about my grades right now? Seriously?"

"But," she went on like I hadn't spoken, "surviving in Evergreen Academy is about so much more than excelling at academics. I should know, I went to school here myself. This place is unlike any other and there are things— people—who will do what it takes to keep everyone in line."

For the first time since I started here, Professor Markham stepped out from her desk and stood in front of me. She gazed at me with an expression I couldn't read. "They say the nail that sticks out gets beaten down, and that is what they will try to do to you. You have to be strong if you're going to face what's ahead."

I tensed. What was this? She was talking like this was war instead of high school. "If you have such a good idea of what I'm going to face, why don't you do something about it?"

Markham lifted her chin. "If there is something I can do for you, I will."

"That is the vaguest offer of help I've ever heard."

Her face didn't change. "That should tell you, Miss Moon, that there isn't much I can do to help. Honestly... no one can help you now."

My throat bobbed as I swallowed. I tried to form a response—something along the lines of me not being scared—but the clammy, too-tight grip on my phone said otherwise. Nothing would come out, so I spun on my heels and left.

The hallways were clear when I stepped out—a welcome relief. I couldn't stand having people chase me around gagging when my own stomach was close to hurling. To think everything had been perfect only a few days ago.

I was halfway to my locker when I noticed the buzzing in my hand. I held up my phone and tapped the home screen.

138 messages.

I blinked. The group chat had been blowing up today. Sofia had added me in weeks ago, but it was usually only filled with notices about parties and pleas for homework help. It never went off like this.

Any guesses why today is so special?

My jaw clenched. I could only imagine what was being said about me, but if I didn't read these messages then imagination is all it would be. I don't need to know what they're saying.

I repeated that to myself as I rounded the corner to my locker.

I stopped dead.

Plastered all over the metal were dozens of joker cards in every style, color, and size. Those tiny little men laughed and smirked at me as I approached, much like the people I thought were my friends did the moment they saw that stupid card.

I've been marked.

They want the whole school to know it, and they want me to never forget it.

Steeling myself, I brushed away the card covering my lock, opened the locker, and gritted my teeth when even more cards spilled at my feet. I snatched out my things and left, leaving the cards untouched.

This wouldn't get to me.

They would never break me.

I MADE IT ALL THE WAY to my dorm before I broke down and opened the group chat. Letters blurred as I scrolled to the beginning of the thread.

I sank onto my bed when I saw the photo beneath the older messages cut-off line. It was a pic of me standing in front of my locker holding the card. Underneath it read:

"The new girl's been Marked. Spread it around."

Within minutes of Casey Stanton posting that picture, a flood of messages poured in. I bit my lip hard enough to bleed as I read them.

"It's about time. They should have Marked her the first day she mouthed off to Jaxson."

"At least we don't have to pretend we like the Virgin anymore."

That sentence smacked me in the face. Was that true? Was the last month of my life fake? Like Jaxson, Ryder, Maverick, and

Ezra, was everyone putting on a show until I made the wrong move and they could take me out?

"**Seriously, what's so special about her? How did she get into this school anyway? It's fresh hell sitting next to her in class. The Virgin is a fucking idiot.**"

"**Didn't you hear? 'The Virgin' is anything but. Turns out she was selling it in the slums to scrape up money to go here.**"

"**The only thing special about her is she didn't gag when she sucked Evergreen's wrinkled dick for admission.**"

"**Probably the only time she hasn't gagged.**"

That set off a round of LOLs that Jaxson, Maverick, Paisley, and *Sofia* joined in. The others pounced on Sofia the moment her name popped up.

"**Spill, Richards. What did she tell you about her customers?**"

Sofia: "**She's still saying she's a virgin. Said that she hadn't so much as kissed a guy.**"

Jaxson: "**Well, Ezra and Maverick took care of that Friday night. One after the other.**"

The phone shook in my hands. Why was he saying it like that? Making it sound so sleazy.

"**Wow, the Virgin has no shame.**"

"Fucking make up your minds!" I burst out. "Am I a slut or a virgin?!"

Claire: "**Come on, guys, go easy on her...**"

I sat up straighter when my eyes lit upon Claire's name. She hadn't spoken to me at lunch, but she didn't put me down either. Maybe Claire was my ally in this.

I scrolled down some more.

Claire: "They say girls like Val are really just chasing the father that ran out on them."

That one did it. Of all the vile things that had already been said, seeing the girl who came from my hometown, who knew so much of what I had gone through, throw in with these jackals at the sight of a card, was too much.

Tears prickled my eyes, collecting on my lids until the words swam.

Sofia: That would explain it. She said her mother won't even tell her his name, but from the things I've heard about her mom, she might not even know his name."

Another round of LOLs.

Isabella: "Those are some high-priced sugar daddies, if she can drop four thousand dollars on a Bisset dress. How many people have that kind of money in her slum?"

Airi: "Good point. Plus she's not on scholarship. How is she affording the tuition?"

My tears dried up as the conversation took a turn. *Wait, no. Why were they talking about this? Don't go there.*

Isabella: "Exactly. If she is making that kind of money, why hasn't she moved out of the projects? Sofia, what did she tell you about it?"

Sofia: "Nothing. I've always wanted to ask, but she gets really weird when I bring it up."

Isabella: "There is definitely something strange going on with her whether she is turning tricks or not. If we can find out what, we can get rid of her."

The breath left my lungs. *No. No.*

Isabella: "I called Mother and had her hire someone to investigate her. We'll find out how she gets her filthy money."

No!

The phone slipped from my fingers and clattered to the floor. I clutched my head, gasping as the feeling that I couldn't breathe got worse. "No, they c-can't do that. They can't! W-what if they find out?"

I squeezed my eyes shut as more tears threatened to fall.

Scratch, scratch, scratch.

I ached. I ached so deeply I knew I could never reach the pain—never heal it.

No one could find out where that money came from. I said they could never break me, but this was something I wasn't ready for. Bullies with bank accounts. If they put their money toward digging into my past and found out what brought me here... I would do more than break.

I would be destroyed.

What do I do?! How do I stop them?!

Call Mom, a calmer voice spoke up. *She'll help. She'll know what to do.*

I scrambled to pick up my phone. My finger was hovering over the call button when I stopped. I couldn't call her. If I told her how horribly wrong things had gone, she would pull me out of Evergreen so fast it'd make my head spin.

I lowered my phone. *I can't leave. All of this—everything that happened would have been for nothing if I let this chance go. I'm supposed to make a new life for Mom and Adam, I can't let anyone take that from me.*

I stared at my phone, and all the people within it plotting to take me down. *So what was I going to do?*

Call them, the calm voice spoke up once more. *Let them know what's happening. Tell them they have to stop it.*

I hesitated.

Do it.

The next second my fingers were scrolling away from Mom down to one single letter. I opened up my texts.

Me: People are digging. Asking questions. They want to know where I get the money. No one can find out.

I typed the last period and dropped the phone like it burned. How long would they take to get back? What if they didn't re-pl—

My phone buzzed.

I dove for it, tapping it awake, then I deflated. It was just another message from the group chat. I dropped it again.

Buzz.

I took up my phone expecting another notification about the chat, until I saw the single letter. It was S.

S: They can dig. They will find nothing.

That was it—two simple sentences, but they flooded me with relief. No one would know. That's all that mattered.

My phone went off again, and this time it was the chat. I muted it and tossed the phone on my pillow. I wouldn't leave the group. I wouldn't give them the satisfaction of knowing they ran me out, but I also wouldn't spend any more time today consumed by their nastiness.

My chest felt tighter than ever. Every muscle in my body was clenched and I was sure I would crumple in on myself if I didn't release the tension.

My nails dug into my forearms. I needed to do something.

I needed to dance.

I was leaping off my bed before the thought had fully crossed my mind. I flicked my speakers on and music filled the room. A sweet, slow song from my playlist tickled my ears until I hit the next button and cut it off. I kept flipping until I found the right band for the mood I was in: Linkin Park.

I spun the volume as high as it would go, then backed away. The speakers boomed. They throbbed and rattled and dared me to match its intensity. I did my best.

I jumped, swayed, thrusted, and threw myself around the room. There wasn't any coordination to my movements. I gave no thought to looking good. I jerked and headbanged until the ache in my chest was overshadowed by the one in my throat as I screamed.

Chapter Nine

I woke up early the next morning. I don't know why. The nightmare didn't return to haunt my dreams. All I knew was one moment I was asleep, and then the next my eyes were open. I sat there in the dark for a while thinking. Thinking about everything that had happened to get me to this point.

"I knew all I had to do was wait. Soon, you'd screw up and we'd be here. It was fate."

Was it?

The night I walked into those woods and ran into a situation I didn't understand. The night I stepped through the drapes and sat down at Madame Shari's table. Was it all meant to bring me to this point? And what did it really mean to be marked—

Madame Shari's words came roaring through my mind. *"The mark he left on the legacy of Evergreen was wiped out."*

"Walter McMillian," I whispered. Was she turning a phrase, or were the words she chose deliberate? Walter wouldn't fall in line. He was a nail that stuck out. Was he marked too? And when he didn't give in... did they wipe him out?

My skin was crawling. The covers fell to my waist as I pushed myself up. This was crazy. Decades-old murders. Knights, kings, diamonds, and jokers. Students viciously turning on each other because of a stupid playing card. I wasn't in a school; I was in an insane asylum.

How could anyone go along with this? Why weren't people putting a stop to it? How could I put a stop to it? Would they come after me for the next four years? Because that's what they would have to do. Dropping out of Evergreen wasn't an option.

My mind whirled with questions but no answers. Eventually, I dragged myself out of bed and got ready.

I didn't rush my shower. I took my time slathering myself with scented soap and Honey Hair shampoo. I scrubbed my skin until it was pink and raw. The bathroom was clouded with steam when I stepped out. I wrapped myself in a soft towel and padded out into my room. Pushing aside my uniform dresses, I picked out a skirt, top, and blazer. After I dressed, I took care in picking out the diamond necklace that would go with my teardrop ear-rings. When the clock struck seven, I was ready to go.

I grabbed my things and threw open my door. Hands seized me the second I stepped outside.

"Hey!" I screamed as I was yanked to the side.

"Quiet."

Rough hands pinned me to the wall. Airi and Natalie fell in on either side of me, holding tight to my arms. Isabella closed the distance between us as they held me in place.

"Don't put up a fight," she warned. "We don't want to worry Gus."

I glanced over her shoulder at the cameras. "Fuck that," I spat. "I definitely want to worry Gus. Hel—!"

She clapped her hand over my mouth, cutting off my shout. "Shut up. We're not here to hurt you. We need to talk."

I shook her off, but I didn't try to scream again. "Talk about what?" I asked through gritted teeth.

Isabella folded her arms, looking at me steadily. "You've been marked, and I'm guessing by now you know what that means."

"It means the whole school goes psycho!"

Her glacial expression didn't change. "It means you've done something you can't come back from. Something bigger than the Knights can deal with, and now the Spades have to act."

I blinked. "The who? The Spades?"

"There hasn't been a marking in years, but I should have known you'd be the one to break the streak," she scoffed. "Coming into my school and pretending you could take me on, when really you're nothing but a slum trash cliché with no daddy who learned a few moves from a music video."

I bristled. "Watch it, Bruno."

She laughed. "Or you'll what? I told you, Valentina, you've been marked. And now everyone, and I mean everyone, is going to make it their mission to get you out of this school. Professors will look the other way. Your friends will tear you down. You won't last a month of that, let alone four years. But here's the thing." Isabella cocked her head, shooting me a smile.

"I don't have time for these games. You were barely worth my attention before this started, and you're even more insignificant now. I'm the leader of the Diamonds and on track to become the world's youngest principal dancer. I can't have distractions." She stepped back.

"So here's the deal. You go to the headmaster's office right now and tell him you're dropping out at the end of the semester. You do this, and you'll be left alone. You'll get to take your finals and make whatever arrangements to go back to your old school. All we want is to see you gone, so drop out, and we won't have reason to *make* you leave. That's the deal. Take it."

"Such a generous offer," Airi purred. She leaned in and buried her nose in my cheek, breathing deeply. "Do as she says, Virgin." Her lips brushed against me as she spoke. "We don't want to play this game—"

"—but trust us," Natalie continued, "we'll win."

I looked Isabella dead in the eye. "I'm not going anywhere. You can do your worst, but it will be nothing compared to the hell I escaped from."

Isabella's face shuttered closed. "You haven't seen hell yet, bitch. Remember this when you're running from the school, bawling your eyes out. We tried to give you a way out." She snapped her fingers and the hands on me disappeared. "Game on."

The three fell in line and casually walked away without a glance back. The elevator doors closed on Isabella's deceptively lovely face, and I took a minute to gather myself before heading for the stairs. They wanted to rattle me, but it wouldn't work. I meant it when I said nothing could compare to the hell I've experienced—and it wasn't a game then.

Eyes followed me as I stepped out onto the quad and made for the main building. The gagging picked up again when I stepped into the main hall, but this time people followed it up with taunts.

"Are you anorexic too, Moon? It would make things so much easier if you just starved to death."

"Do men really pay to screw a little twig like you?"

"Is that why you came here? To add the Knights to your list of customers?"

"What was it like having Maverick's hand up your dress?"

I flinched. *No, please. Tell me Maverick isn't telling people we did more than kiss. How can I have thought that guy was sweet?*

I picked up the pace amid their snickering and hurried to homeroom. Markham didn't look up when I came in. *Tap, tap, tap* on her keyboard, she wasn't going to help me. A fact that was driven home when I glanced across the classroom and found my desk gone. That's right, gone.

There was an empty space where my seat should have been and more searching told me there wasn't another free desk in the room.

The class was watching me, waiting for my reaction. I schooled my face. I wouldn't let them see that any of this bothered me.

I moved around the desks, walked past my spot, and set my things on the window ledge. I ignored everyone as I took out my homework and went over it. As I kept saying, they would have to do better than this.

Thirty minutes later, the bell rang and I was the first out the door, my head held high. I moved on to Spanish and found myself without a desk again. Senora Fernandez chattered away the whole class, pretending she didn't see me standing in the back. Rossman's class was much the same.

By lunchtime my feet were sore, but my resolve wasn't. I burst into the cafeteria and marched up to the lunch line. The Knights had beaten me to the lunchroom this time. There the four of them sat—coldly cruel and heartbreakingly beautiful. Ryder's fingers drummed on the table as his eyes tracked me. I saw right away that one of them was bandaged and I smirked. That sight had made my day way better.

I turned away and continued on. Their gaze beat on the back of my neck as I headed for the food.

"Why bother, Val?" asked a girl from my math class. "You're just going to throw it up after."

I said nothing, just flipped her the middle finger, and walked past while she sputtered. I grabbed my tray and didn't stick around. There was no point. My friends made it clear I wasn't sitting with them.

I took my tray out and walked with single determination to my new lunch spot. Past the janitor closet, the library, and at the end of a long narrow hall. The door to the Knights' room seemed to peer back at me as I approached it.

I closed my hand on the knob and it opened easily. They didn't think to lock their door. Who would be foolish enough to come in here? Besides me that is.

The lights flicked on at my presence. They shone on a space that was even more spectacular than I imagined. Polished mahogany floors shone with the lights of the hanging lamps. Filling the sunken living room were brown leather couches all displayed around an oak coffee table. There was everything in here from a big screen mounted on the wall, to the grand piano shoved in the corner, to a small kitchenette. Despite the luxury of the space, I could see the individual stamp of the different boys.

The shelf under the television was stuffed to bursting with records and CDs. Scattered all over the coffee table was bits and pieces of machines that Maverick was either taking apart or putting together. There were dry-erase boards on the walls with lists and schedules all in Ezra's handwriting, and then there was Ryder.

I set my tray among the mess on the coffee table and walked up to the piano. Reaching out, I traced my finger along the deep scratch on the cover. How or why Ryder had gotten the school to move this from his home to this room, I didn't know, but just standing here the memory of him sitting before it as he teased the most beautiful sounds from the keys. I remembered the soft expression on his face when he played... and the hideous one that overtook him when he caught me on it. He yelled at me until I ran from his bedroom crying. I hadn't seen it since.

I stepped away from the piano and went back to the couch, picking up my fork and getting down to eating.

Yep, this would do nicely for my new lunch spot.

AFTER LUNCH, I GOT rid of my tray and headed for my next class. I walked a bit taller with the knowledge of my secret. Eating in the lion's den right under their wet noses.

As I got closer to art class, my grin began to fade. Maverick was in this class. What would he do? What was *I* going to do?

We shared a life-altering kiss and then in the space of a few days I find out I was just a bet and he's joining in on the school's mission to make me miserable. Maybe the best question is will I be able to take him by surprise and smash his face in.

I pulled open the door for class and looked toward the window. Our eyes met through the sea of faces. There was no expression on his face as he looked back at me. I waited—for what I wasn't sure.

Maverick stood and turned his back, walking off to the paint station.

Anger spat and boiled in the pit of my stomach. I thought I was getting to know him—that there was more underneath the surface, but I was right the first time. Crack open his chest and you'll find the gears and wires you expect from a heartless robot.

"Valentina?"

"What?" My head snapped around. Scarlett was perched on the edge of her desk, holding a handful of wet brushes. She smiled at me—the first friendly look I had gotten all morning—and it almost did me in. "How are you doing, Val?"

She knew. Everyone knew. "I'm fine," I croaked, looking away.

"Val, I..." She sighed. "I want you to know that even though the project is over you can still come after class. I'll be here if you want to paint... or talk."

I nodded. "Thanks," I whispered. I walked off before the compassion in her voice made me any more emotional. I weaved through the class for my spot. I noticed my stool wasn't missing this time.

Maverick returned moments after I sat down. I tensed as I waited for him to say something, but he didn't so much as glance in my direction.

Scarlett clapped. "Alright, class. The first part of the semester was about bringing to life what we see in others. Now we will be working on what exists in ourselves. What pushes us, drives us, scares us, breaks us apart, and puts us back together again. I want you to get raw, dig deep, as you work on your final project: your worst fears."

I gazed out the window as Scarlett's voice became soft buzzing in the background. I didn't need to dig deep to discover my fears. They were always with me, pulsing beneath the surface.

I DIDN'T GO TO TUTORING after classes ended. I wasn't an idiot. There was no reason to give Ezra the satisfaction of smiling in my face when he announced I was on my own.

Instead, the end of the day saw me viciously jabbing at the screen to get at my crème brûlée Sprite. That was the new flavor Sofia and I had moved on to last week. I squeezed my eyes shut as I thought of us giggling on the roof, sipping creamy soda, and analyzing every word of her texts with Jeremiah.

How could that have been fake?

How could it have been real? a harsh voice said back. *A real friend wouldn't have turned on you for all the cards in the deck. Forget about Sofia Richards.*

A chime signaled my soda was ready so I took it out and put the straw to my lips. Despite my resolution, one sip drowned my mind with thoughts of her... and someone else. How could I drink these things and not think of the first time I met Ezra? Of him stealing my sodas, laughing about all the crazy flavors I tried, or him wrapping his lips around my straw as boldly as he placed them on mine.

I turned away from the machine, marched up to the garbage, and tossed the drink inside. No more soda for me.

Leaving the main building, I walked across the quad to the freshman dorms. The elevator rumbled to my floor and I stepped off, breathing a sigh of relief just seeing my door. What I needed was a warm bed, a hot bath, and some loud music, not necessarily in that order. I would shed this day like snakeskin.

I threw open my door and froze. My backpack slipped through numb fingers and fell to the ground.

It was like a bomb had exploded in here. The remains of my speakers, clock, and laptop were scattered about the floor in a million pieces. Covering the debris were the feathers and cotton from my pillows and sheets. Someone had taken a knife to it and slashed them open.

I slowly came inside. Broken glass scrunched under my feet; the remains of the mirror that used to adorn my vanity. Liquid dripped off the edge of the surface, pouring from spilled perfume bottles. My eyes traveled away from the ruined makeup to the message scrawled in bloodred lipstick on the wall:

Game on, bitch.

IT TOOK ME ALL AFTERNOON and most of the night to clean up my room and take pictures. They had been thorough, destroying almost everything I owned. My Honey Hair products had been dumped out on the bathroom floor. My lipsticks broken, my CDs cracked, and my wardrobe had been reduced to confetti. They even slashed up my underwear. They, like my stereo and laptop, weren't salvageable. I would have to buy everything new.

That wasn't so bad. It was all just stuff. No, what really got to me was what they did to my photos of Mom and Adam. It wasn't enough for them to smash the frames. They had taken out the pictures, ripped them up, and tossed the pieces in my trash can.

My fingers shook as I sat on the ruin of my bed, holding up a corner of Adam's smile. I knew who did this. There was only one person I had told my passcode.

Sofia.

I leaned forward and put the piece in place, carefully re-
assembling my family.

Scratch. Scratch.

My fury was a hot spike in my throat, burning with every
ragged breath I took. I could feel it being scraped and clawed
away along with the hope I had at getting my best friend back.

I WISH I COULD SAY they didn't do better. That my classmates didn't step it up a notch with every blow I withstood. But
I couldn't say that.

By Friday, only five days into my torture, I was starting to unravel.

I had gotten my passcode changed immediately and there
were no more break-ins into my room, but everyone was doing
just fine tormenting me outside of it.

I gritted my teeth as I sped across the quad that morning. I
spotted people huddling together, poring over something, but I
didn't look close to find out what.

"Hey, Val!"

The first person called out to me and I snapped. "Just leave
me alone!"

"Don't be like that," they shouted after me as I yanked open
the door. "That's no way to get business!"

I raced inside and my foot came down on something
smooth. Stumbling, I quickly caught myself and looked down to
see what tripped me up. My own face looked back at me.

I bent down and picked up the paper. My cheeks flamed
when I realized what I was looking at.

My head had been expertly pasted on a butt naked woman putting everything on display. On top of the flyer was the word "Services" and underneath was a list.

Blow jobs: $5
Hand jobs: $2
Fuck: $10
Fuck w/Video: $12

The flyer crumpled in my fists. After days of harassing me about being a virgin and saying no one wanted to fuck a stick, they were back to insinuating I sold my body.

"Do you like it, Val?"

I raised my head. Isabella, Airi, and Natalie were posted up on the opposite wall. This time they weren't alone. The other Diamonds fanned out around them. Cade Trevelyan, top GPA in our year. Axel Leon, record-breaking track star, and Genesis Smith, prize-winning sculptor. I had gotten to know all the kids toting themselves as the best of the freshman class very well the last few days. They were never far behind when I was being tormented. Majority of the time, they were doing the tormenting.

"We thought you could use some help advertising," said Isabella.

Airi nodded. "Yeah, we heard something happened to your stuff and you have to go shopping."

"Now everyone knows you're open for business," Natalie said. "You gotta raise money, girl. New speakers and uniforms aren't cheap."

They weren't even pretending they didn't have a hand in destroying my things. My eyes narrowed on them. "You know, it's amazing how you do that, Isabella."

The tiniest frown appeared on her bow-shaped lips. "Do what?"

"How you get Airi and Natalie to puppet you without sticking your hand up their asses. Being your mindless thugs must be second nature to them by now."

"You—!" Natalie lunged forward and was barely restrained by Cade.

"No fighting," he cried. "You want Jaxson coming down on us?"

"Stop it."

One command from Isabella and Natalie stopped trying to come for me, but it didn't stop her from glaring hot enough to roast my head. I was coming to see that Bella was the cool one, Airi thought this was all amusing, but Natalie was a wild card. The looks she gave me seemed to hold true hatred. I had a feeling if she was allowed to put a hand on me, she would have been coming claws out.

"Speaking of Jaxson," I said as I tossed the flyer over my shoulder. "What do he and his buddies do while you all carry out their dirty work?" I scoffed. "Maybe I was wrong about who's really running the mindless thugs."

Isabella's eyebrow twitched. That was my only hint that I had struck a nerve. "Don't worry about the Knights, slut. They have something planned for you."

My face remained still. I wouldn't give away what I thought of that.

She tsked. "Let's go, guys. Val most likely has someone to suck off in the broom closet. We shouldn't hold her up." The group turned to leave.

"Oh, wait." Airi spun around and gave me that wide smile. "I'd love to take you up on that fuck with video, but your prices are a bit steep." She reached into her pocket and pulled out a nickel. She threw it at my feet. "This should cover it." Airi blew me a kiss as her cronies burst into raucous laughter. "See you tonight."

They walked off and I trudged to my locker. Papering the walls were the Diamonds' flyers. People yelled after me the whole way, going on about the *services* they were interested in.

My throat tightened until it was hard to swallow. *At least they don't know where you truly get your money. I can endure the lies and fake rumors as long as they never know the truth.*

I stepped into homeroom and walked straight to my new seat at the window. My old desk never made a reappearance, and I couldn't bring myself to go begging to administration for one. The class would probably get rid of it again with no consequences.

The rest of the class strolled in and took their seats. Jaxson walked past me on the way to his. He winked as he held up the flyer.

I pointedly turned away from him toward the window. It wasn't a nice day. Heavy clouds filled the sky, blocking out the sun, and they were fit to burst. Any minute now they would open and unleash their rain to wash the earth, but no amount of water could scrub this place clean.

"Class, silence for your announcements."

I faced toward the front as the AV students set up the television. Soon Ezra's smile was blinding the screen.

"Good morning, Evergreen, and welcome to the best day of the week, Friday. As you all know, next week is Parents' Day.

We're all looking forward to seeing our folks again and stashing all the treats they'll be packing under our mattresses. Oops, maybe I shouldn't have admitted that on camera."

The class laughed. I had to hand it to Ezra. He was charming on camera. It was too bad he was an overripe asshole off it.

"We're lucky to attend such a great school with students from every background, status, and different parts of the world, but we must remember we wouldn't be where we are if it weren't for the people supporting us. So, in honor of Parents' Day, a video was put together to celebrate all those who got us where we are now. If anyone would like to add their families to the video, contact the broadcast club during lunch."

Ezra and his co-host faded to black and a title appeared on the screen: Where We Come From.

I blinked at the first face. There was no doubt that was a young Jaxson. Although here he had a full head of blond hair. The sweetest face beamed into the camera while music producer legend Levi Van Zandt held his tiny hands. I was glued. So many people had offered up their photos and videos. Eric with his arms around an older woman that looked like his grandmother. A baby Sofia in the arms of Madeline while she kissed her curls.

They almost look human.

Shaking my head, I turned my eyes back to the window. They weren't those cute, innocent kids anymore, so what did I care?

"Alright, alright, alright!" A loud voice cut through the room. "We are coming at you live from the one and only South Beach, Florida, and I hope you fine people watching are ready for this."

I rested my forehead against the window, letting the coolness chase away my headache.

"Now let's meet our contestants. What's your name, darlings?"

"I'm Sandra."

"Allison."

"Olivia."

My head shot up so fast it knocked me off-balance. I caught a glimpse of Mom's young face as I crashed to the floor. The class howled as the announcer got back in the camera's face. "Those are our contestants, now let's get this wet t-shirt contest started!"

The TV crowd, and everyone watching, cheered and wolf-whistled.

"That's enough!" Markham roared as she leaped from her seat. "Settle down!"

She scrambled for the remote, but I was already up and racing toward the front of the room. One by one, the girls were doused with water until their boobs went from covered by white t-shirts to blurred-out TV censors.

Markham fumbled with the remote, stabbing at the off button, as they turned the water on Olivia.

I didn't think. I didn't pause.

I ran to the television, placed my hand on the screen, and shoved.

The TV cart flew back. Screams echoed from the girls in the front as the television crashed in a shower of sparks and flying glass.

Chest heaving, I stared at the mess in shock. Markham's gaping mouth said it all. I couldn't believe what just happened.

"Shit." A voice broke the silence. "And it was just getting good."

That was the cue. They laughed—loud, piercing laughter that ripped and tore at me. They could do what they wanted to me, but going after my mom—my family was a low I didn't think they could reach. A low that I didn't know *Ezra* could reach, because there was no way he wasn't a part of this.

"Don't worry about the Knights, slut. They have something planned for you."

"Tsk, tsk. Destroying school property." I felt the heat of his body as he moved to my side. "That's a serious offense, mama. You know I can't let that slide."

A hand seized my wrist and dragged me to the door.

"Mr. Van Zandt," Markham cried.

"I'll be right back. Gotta take care of this."

I didn't try to put up a fight as he pulled me out into the hallway. The door slammed shut behind us, cutting off the laughter.

My shoes scuffed the floor as I was led down the hall. Jaxson didn't speak a word, or at least I don't think he did. I could barely hear anything over the roaring in my ears. I may have stopped my class from seeing it, but what about the other class. What about the video itself? How was I going to get it back?

Jaxson suddenly stopped walking. Unprepared, I crashed into his back. "Go in there. Tell them what you did." We were standing in front of the administration office. His voice was hard. I wasn't used to hearing him like this. "And while you're at it..." Jaxson turned his head slightly, peering at me over his shoulder. "Tell them you're withdrawing from this school."

I fought to find my voice. "I— I won't—"

"Do it," he hissed. "It only gets worse from here, and that's a promise."

I said nothing. Jaxson continued on, leaving me standing there. What else was I supposed to do?

I turned the knob and went inside.

"I GOT TWO WEEKS PICKING up trash around campus," I said. "Plus, I'll have to pay for the television."

I held the phone in the crook of my neck as I unfolded my fitted sheet. The bedding I ordered had finally arrived. My room was still bare after I cleaned everything out, but slowly I was reclaiming my space and getting it back to the way it was—taped-up photos and all.

"That's rough, kid," said Mom. "But I still don't understand why you're going around knocking over televisions. I told you to have fun, not turn washed-up rock star."

I clamped down on my lip, thinking of what to say. I couldn't avoid this. Headmaster Evergreen had called my mom and told her what I did, although he left out why.

I sighed. "A couple of bullies posted a mean video to get to this girl. Everyone else was just sitting there, Mom. I had to do something."

"Oh, well, I understand that. I didn't raise you to sit quietly by in the face of those things, and shame on kids for doing nothing."

"You have no idea of their shame," I said under my breath.

"I hope the bullies are punished too."

Doubtful.

"So about next week," I began, shifting the subject. "Are you still coming to Parents' Day?"

"Of course, I am. I haven't seen you in over a month and Adam misses you like crazy."

I cracked a smile. "Does he? I don't think Adam knows me from a jar of applesauce. He just ignores me and plays with his toys when we video chat."

"Cut the boy some slack; he's only seven months old. You wait, he'll be grinning so wide when he sees you, you'll get to see both his teeth."

I chuckled. The thought chased away my gloom which I'm sure was Mom's intent. No one could be sad thinking of Adam's smile.

"Okay, I can't wait to see you two." Part of me knew I should talk her out of coming. I could only imagine what Ezra and the Knights had in store for Parents' Day itself, but I wanted to see them too badly.

"Bye, babe. Love you."

"Love you too, Mom."

I hung up and threw my phone on my freshly made bed. Then I threw myself after it.

Only when my face was buried in my pillow did I let the tears come. I sobbed—heart-wrenching cries that my pillow swallowed.

I didn't take Jaxson's advice to drop out of school. I wouldn't leave, but the thought of things getting worse than they had today was too much to bear.

I cried and cried until darkness took me to where my nightmares awaited.

I DIDN'T LEAVE MY ROOM for the entire weekend. I had food stashed in my mini-fridge that could last me a week. I was sorely tempted to test that theory and not go to classes on Monday, but if my new job picking up trash had taught me anything—I would pay for the things I did even if no one else did.

My alarm clock went off, forcing me out of bed for the start of the new week. It was Parents' Day today. At least I would get to see Mom and Adam.

When I stepped into the hallway, I saw right away that I wasn't the only one gearing up for their arrival. The place was pristine.

The floors were buffed, the windows dusted, and the naked flyers had been taken down. In its place were streamers, banners, and balloons announcing Parents' Day. Clearly the janitors had been hard at work over the weekend. Parents would arrive in an hour. It wouldn't do for them to see the real face of Evergreen Academy.

I walked into homeroom and got my second surprise. My desk was back, sitting whole and neat in its spot like it never left. I approached it cautiously. What was the catch?

Setting my bag on the chair, I carefully sat down as though I feared it would explode. Knowing these sadists, it just might.

The door opened again and a new television was wheeled in. I clenched my jaw as the people around me laughed.

"Settle down," Markham laughed. "I'll let you know right now I won't stand for any more barbaric behavior in this class. Evergreen is an elite school for the best and brightest. Act like it."

That stopped the cackling long enough for Markham to switch on the TV.

I blinked. It wasn't Ezra's face staring back at me; it was the headmaster's. "Good morning, freshman class. As you know, today is Parents' Day and your classes are canceled. I want you to remember that though they are your family, they are also guests of Evergreen and you are the faces of the school. I expect you to conduct yourself in a manner benefiting the emblems you wear." His eyes sharpened. "Anyone who does not do so or dares to embarrass the school, will be punished in the strictest possible manner." He inclined his head. "That is all."

The screen went black and Markham returned to her desk. Apparently, that was the end of the announcements.

Jaxson heaved a sigh, drawing all eyes to him. "You heard the old boy. The Virgin is off-limits. Y'all play nice while Mommy and Daddy are here."

Murmurs of agreement followed his words. I pressed my lips together. I wasn't mad about a day off, but it did piss me off to see how easily they turned their bullying on and off on a single command. Jaxson and the Knights could stop this if they wanted, but with Ryder at the helm... they never would.

The bell rang ending homeroom and I joined the line of students filing out the doors. By a trick of timing, I ended up right behind Sofia but I didn't try to speak to her. Together we tramped out of the courtyard, under the arch, and to the gates of Evergreen where fleets of cars worth more than my whole neighborhood waited for us.

We fanned out as the parents streamed in. Sofia and I ended up side by side as kids peeled off and ran into the arms of their parents. After twenty minutes, there were only three of us left: Me, Sofia, and propped up against the arch, Ryder. I couldn't see his face properly from that distance, but I imagined it was like it always was: chipped from the same stone of the arch.

Ryder's head swung around and our eyes met. I had been caught looking, but I didn't turn away. For a while we just gazed at each other. I was thinking about Caroline locked in her bedroom, standing up her only son for the hundredth time, but what Ryder was thinking I couldn't guess.

Suddenly, Ryder straightened and started walking—right toward me. I stiffened as he closed the gap between us. He got closer and I could see I was wrong about his face being blank. Actually, a grin played at his mouth.

"Where's your mom, Val?" He grinned. "Did she get held up at another wet t-shirt contest?"

I bared my teeth. "Keep talking, Ryder. Next time I will bite it off."

He held up his hands in mock surrender. "Whoa, you can keep your piranha teeth to yourself, Val. It was just a joke." He smiled. Ryder smiled and it was so heartbreakingly beautiful I flinched. His entire face transformed from the lifeless granite to warmth and living perfection. How different things would be if the soul inside matched that smile.

"Jaxson told you that you've got a stay of execution today," he continued. "Everyone, including me, will honor it." He placed his hand over his chest. "Promise."

I studied him for a moment, but the smile didn't flicker. "Fine," I finally stated. "Start now by going away."

He laughed. "I will, but I haven't told you about the party yet."

"Party? What party?"

"There's a gala for the parents tonight. Pretty much another thinly veiled attempt to squeeze our folks for more money. Point is, everyone is going to be focused on that and they won't be worried about us. Even Gus and his staff are taking a break from watching the cameras to patrol the gala." Ryder threw out his hands. "Which means we'll have the perfect opportunity to party down at the cliffs."

"The cliffs?" I cut eyes to Sofia and glimpsed her looking at us before she quickly turned away. "Where's that?"

"Behind campus. Through the woods." He pointed to the side. "Sofia will show you the way."

Sofia jerked. "What? But—"

"Is that a problem?" Ryder cut in.

She snapped her mouth shut, shaking her head.

"Good. See you tonight."

"Hold on," I said, taking my eyes off Sofia. "I didn't say I would come to your party. Do you think I'm an idiot? I'm not walking into your trap."

"It's not a trap." He met my eyes. "My word as a Knight, it's just a party."

I folded my arms. "Even if that's true, the last thing I want to do is party with you people. I'm not going."

Ryder didn't lose his smile. "You'll want to go to this one. I have a present for you."

"A present? A present for me?" I repeated it and it still sounded strange coming out of my mouth.

He nodded. "And you'll like it, I swear."

I edged away from him, eyes narrowing. "What is it? What are you trying to pull?"

"I'm not pulling anything." He smiled again and it tugged at me. "This is something you've always wanted. Come tonight so I can give it to you."

"I—"

"Val! Hey, kid! Get over here."

I pivoted to see Mom waving through the gates. In her arms, was Adam.

I took a step. One. Then I turned back to Ryder. He was already walking away.

Shaking myself, I spun around and ran up to Mom. She threw out a hand to accept my hug.

"Whoa there," she gasped. "Don't break my ribs."

I just squeezed her tighter. Her arm came around me and stroked my back. "Everything okay, baby?"

I nodded from the crook of her neck. "I missed you is all."

"We missed you too."

Pulling back, I beamed into Adam's pudgy face. The baby looked at me curiously as he sucked on his pacifier.

"Hey, baby. You remember me, don't you, Adam?" I held out my hands, holding my breath as he glanced at them. There was a pause where my heart tried to rocket out of my chest. Then he leaned forward, reaching for me.

I snuggled Adam to my chest and felt the knot of worry, pain, and anger that I had been nursing in my chest for the last week begin to loosen.

"So what are we getting up to today?" Olivia asked.

I paused in peppering Adam's face with kisses. "I can show you around campus and let you see my dorm, but really I want to get away for a bit," I said honestly. "We could go into town, get lunch, go shopping. Is that okay?"

"Course it is. I came here to see you, not some dusty old classrooms."

I let out a breath I didn't know I had been holding. "Okay, great. Let's g—"

Slam!

The sound drew our attention across the lane of cars. A limo had pulled up beside us. The driver walked around to the other side, passing by the insignia on the door that let me know who was climbing out before he grabbed the handle.

Caroline Shea extended one pale hand and accepted the help out of the car. She stood to her full height and the wind caught her hair. It whipped and tugged at her glossy locks as she pulled the mirrored shades off her face. When they were gone, I saw she was looking right at us.

"Valentina? Olivia? Is that you?"

Caroline unhurriedly walked over to us. She had a firm grip on the driver's elbow as though she needed the help to stay upright. I was amazed she was here at all. It was constantly talked about in the newsfeeds how she had become all but a recluse.

"How are you?" Her voice was so soft I could barely hear her. "You look well."

I could do nothing but nod. "I am," I replied, matching her tone. "And you?"

She smiled. It looked so odd—so alien to the serene sorrow she had draped herself in, that I wondered if her face would splinter and crack apart from the act. "I cannot complain. Today is a good day. I will get to see my son." Her eyes flicked down to the tiny person snoozing on my chest. "This must be Adam."

"Yes."

"Mom."

Caroline looked over my shoulder. The tiny smile widened at the sight of Ryder. "Hello, my love."

"Mom, come inside. You need to rest." Ryder put his arms around her with a gentleness I didn't know he possessed. He compounded my surprise by pressing a kiss to her cheek. "We'll have breakfast, and then you can take a nap in my room."

"I'm not that hungry, dear," she replied as they walked away. "But a nap would be nice."

Mom threw her arm around my shoulder after the two disappeared. "Ready to go?"

"Yes, absolutely. First stop: my dorm."

TO SAY I WAS HAVING a great day with Mom and Adam was putting it lightly. It was like the last week had never happened. I took her all over campus as she oohed and ahhed over the facilities. After showing off my still-bare dorm and dodging questions about where my things were, we got back in her car and headed to town.

Mom helped me pick out a new laptop and camera, then we ran all over the place taking goofy pictures with Adam. By the time we got to lunch, I had laughed more that morning than I did for the last few days.

We were sitting down to a carb-attack of bread and pasta when Olivia flicked me on the forehead.

"Hey," I moaned. "What's that for?"

"Tell me what I don't know already."

"What do you mean?"

She leveled me with that mom look and I shifted in my seat. "You've been overly peppy all morning and you sounded strange on the phone Friday night."

My eyes fell to my plate. I hated how well she knew me sometimes, but what could I say? Olivia had a right to know about the video, but if she thought I was being bullied, she'd pull me out of school. I came home from Joe Young Middle with a split lip once and she was in the principal's office the next day threatening to beat the ass of the kid who hit me and the *principal* for allowing me to get hurt under his watch. She was almost forcibly removed from school grounds.

Having a mom that would do anything to protect me wasn't something I took for granted, but it was a trait I didn't need right now. I couldn't leave Evergreen.

So she couldn't know the truth.

I cast about for something to say. "Sofia and I got into a fight," I finally said.

"You did? What about?"

My grip tightened on my fork. "She was one of the kids who... just sat there when that girl was being bullied. She even joined in. I can't be friends with someone like that."

Olivia shook her head. "I'm sorry, kid. Situations like this can show you a different side of people. Not everyone is strong enough to face up to a bully." She lifted her hand and stroked my cheek. "But my kid is, and that makes me so proud."

I leaned into her touch. "Thanks, Mom," I whispered.

Her expression changed. "But no one better be coming for you now. Are those bullies harassing you?"

I shook my head without hesitation. "No. I'm fine. No one is messing with me."

She studied me. I held still as she scanned my face, looking for a hint I wasn't telling the truth.

"Okay, but you tell me if anyone does."

"I will."

THAT NIGHT, I KISSED Adam and Olivia goodbye before waving them off in her car. Mom wasn't staying for the parents' gala. She had work in the morning and no money to donate anyway. She wasn't who the school was after.

I tramped back through the school gates for my room. I'd needed today. Seeing them reminded me why I was putting up with everything they threw at me. My family was depending on me, and they were too wonderful to let down.

I went inside the dorms and took a step toward the elevator until I saw the sign. Figures.

Veering off, I headed for the stairs and started my six-flight climb to the top. I was huffing and puffing when I burst through the doors.

Sofia jumped and spun to face me.

"What are you doing?"

"Nothing. I—" She glanced at the lock. "You changed your passcode."

"Of course I changed my passcode." I stomped up to her. "A person I thought was my friend passed it on to a tribe of vicious harpies."

Sofia pressed her lips together, not replying.

"What are you doing here?"

"What do you mean? Ryder told me to take you to the party."

I snorted. "You can't possibly think I would go to that *or* go anywhere with you?"

She frowned. "But you have to go."

"Incorrect."

"If I don't bring you, he'll think I disobeyed him."

"Too bad."

I brushed past her and stepped up to the keypad.

"But no one is going to mess with you today. There's no reason not to go."

"There are a million reasons not to go and all of them start with you all being assholes. I don't want to be around any of you."

The lock chimed and I shoved the door open.

"Don't you want your present?"

I froze.

"Ryder has something for you," she continued. "Don't you want to know what it is?"

"It's a trick is what it is."

"It's not. I'm telling you, if the Knights say you're off-limits, then you're off-limits. Not even Ryder will go against it."

"Ryder is the scorpion on the frog's back that stings him even though they'll both drown. The guy is rotten to his core. He's not keeping any promises when it comes to me."

I took a step inside.

"Fine. Hide in your room like a little bitch."

"What did you just say?" I whipped around, eyes blazing.

"I get it. You're beaten and now you want to cower in your room. But if it were me, I'd show them they hadn't won. That they wouldn't stop me from having fun." She shrugged. "If you're so afraid of Ryder—"

"I'm not afraid of Ryder!"

Then she leaned forward, getting in my face. "Then get dressed and let's go."

I thought about telling her to shove it, but I could picture Ryder strutting about his party laughing about me being too scared to come out. I wouldn't give him—or any of them—the satisfaction of thinking they drove me to hiding in my room. "Wait here."

I slammed the door in her face. I was still rebuilding my wardrobe so it didn't take me long to choose a tight pink sweater and skinny jeans. I finished the look with a pair of cute leather boots I bought that morning with Olivia, and then a light touch of makeup. My hair I let fall around my shoulders in soft waves.

Sofia was waiting in the same spot when I came out. We didn't talk this time as we made for the staircase. The stairwell echoed with our footsteps, the only sound to break our deafening silence. There was a lot I needed to say to her, but the words wouldn't come. It wasn't like they would change anything.

Together we left the building and made for the woods. The grass whispered on our shoes as we passed through the tree line. The chorus of cicadas sounded through the night—unseen but surrounding us.

I had never been to the cliffs although I had heard it mentioned a few times. Through the trees was the very edge of the Evergreen property, and by edge I meant a steep drop to the ground below. But that aside was apparently a gorgeous clearing that was perfect for parties. The upperclassmen had more freedom so they used this spot all the time. Now it was the freshmen's turn.

Sofia and I didn't utter a single word to each other as she led me deeper through the woods, which was fine with me. My thoughts were consumed by the night of the Halloween ball, and the fight that changed everything.

Why was I being punished for what I saw? Why did Ryder want me quiet so badly that he would resort to this?

But it's working, a traitorous voice piped up. *You haven't told anyone about the night of the party.*

Because I don't know what to tell. All students are present and accounted for, no one has been found stabbed in the woods. Neither Ryder nor the mystery person has come forward for the same reason I've been marked. No one was supposed to see anything, and if I say something, it's my word against his.

A low thumping broke through my thoughts. I spotted a soft glow in the distance and knew we were getting close.

Finally, we broke through the trees and the party was laid before me in all its glory. I saw at once the glow was from a roaring fire that was the center of the dance floor. Kids dipped, skipped, and gyrated around it while Jaxson worked the music. My head started bobbing without my permission. I couldn't help it; the guy knew good music.

Sofia broke off and joined a group hanging close to the food table. Paisley, Claire, Eric, and Ciara smiled at her when she joined them. They scowled at me when they saw me over her shoulder.

I turned my back on them and drifted closer to the fire. If I was here to party, then that's what I was going to do.

Jaxson switched up the song to one I didn't know, but I soon picked up the beat. I threw myself into the dance—spinning and tossing my head until the party blurred.

My heart pounded against my chest. My lungs began to ache, but I didn't slow down or ease up. I planted my foot and spun, then I slammed into a hard body.

"Whoa, easy, Moon."

Ezra grabbed me to steady me, but I ripped myself out of his grasp. He chuckled. "Wow, you just got here and you're drunk already?"

"I'm not drunk."

He didn't look like he believed me. "Here." Ezra held out his solo cup. "It's water. Have some."

I eyed it like he scraped it off his shoe. "Why? Did you roofie it?"

Ezra's reply was to put the cup to his lips and take a long sip. He offered it to me again. "Go ahead."

I wrapped my fingers around the cup and tipped its contents onto the ground. The cup followed right after. "Go away."

He sighed. "Let me guess, you're pissed at me for broadcasting your mom's spring break adventures."

I balled my fists. "How could you do something like that, Ezra? Even for you that's low."

"Even for me?" Ezra lifted a brow. "What do you know about me?"

"I know your smile is as fake as your pretty words when you're tricking a girl into liking you. I know you put on a show to prove to Mommy you're worth taking over her empire, but the thing is, Ezra, you're not."

"Is that so?"

"Yes." I stepped closer, leaving only centimeters between us. "Because your mom has class and integrity. She'd never do what you did, and that's how she got to where she is, and why you'll always be hoping she'll pass on her success... because you'll never be able to get it for yourself."

His jaw tightened visibly. The firelight glinted in Ezra's obsidian eyes, belying the tightly controlled anger I sensed simmering beneath the surface.

"The only mistake your mom made," I went on, flinging the last dagger, "was you. She must be ashamed of you every single day. There isn't a part of you that's real."

I knew the instant I went too far. The fire came to life in Ezra's eyes. A growl burst from his chest as he lunged forward and grabbed me. I didn't give him the satisfaction of crying out as he wrapped one hand around the back of my neck and the other around my waist. To anyone watching we were embracing, but they couldn't see the expression on his face.

"Be very careful, Moon," Ezra hissed. "Right now, I'm doing this because I have to. You won't like it if I do it because I *want* to."

"You don't scare me."

"I should." Ezra pressed his forehead against mine. "It's like you said, Moon. Nothing about me is real. From the smile to the charming personality." His grip tightened. "How badly do you want to meet the real me?"

I gritted my teeth. "You shouldn't have gone after my mom."

"It took me two seconds to find that video. If she didn't want anyone to know, she shouldn't have fucking doused herself on camera."

"Get off me, Ezra." I pushed against his chest. "Now. It won't look good for your image if I start screaming." I shoved harder and this time he let me go. The second I was free, I sidestepped him and walked off.

The music didn't sound so great now. It was grating on me, pounding in my skull. There was too much noise. Too many people. I needed a spot to sit and cool off.

I slipped through the party and drifted closer to the cliff. As I freed myself from the crush of bodies, the world opened up to me. The sky was infinite in its darkness and its beauty. A soft breeze blew off the canyon, tickling my cheek as I stepped closer to the edge and looked down. My gaze went down, down, down until pitch-black stopped me from seeing any more. It was amazing that I hadn't known this place existed. It was perfect in its loneliness.

"You're not thinking of jumping, are you?"

I spoke without turning around. "Jumping, no. Pushing, yes."

Chuckling, Ryder stepped to my side. "Anyone in particular?"

"You need to ask?"

He laughed again. "Well, here's your chance."

Suddenly, my view of the cliff was cut off. Ryder stepped in front of me, so close the tip of my nose brushed the button on his shirt. "Go ahead. Do it."

"What?" I breathed.

I jumped when his hands closed over mine. Slowly, he placed them on his chest, resting my palms flat over his heart. I could feel it beating against my fingers—steady, strong, alive within that icy shell.

"Do it." His voice was barely above a whisper. "Push."

Ryder's heart was calm; the same couldn't be said for mine. I swallowed hard as it tried to bang its way up my throat. "What happened to you?" I whispered. "Why are you like this?"

There was no answer.

"What is it you want from me?"

Ryder put his finger under my chin. He tilted my head up until we were looking into each other's eyes. "I want you... to push."

My fingers curled, tangling his shirt in my fists. The words were pulled out of me unbidden. "What happened in the woods that night, Ryder?"

He straightened until his face was covered by shadows.

"I have a right to know. I heard the screams. I thought someone needed help, and then I find you. What happened? What were you fighting about?"

Ryder's hands came up and grabbed mine. He tore them off of him. "Don't pretend you don't know."

"I don't," I cried, lurching back. "I didn't see who the other person was, and I couldn't hear what you were fighting about. All I know is you were there and... the knife."

Ryder sidestepped me and made to walk away.

"No." I darted into his path, pulling him up short. "You don't get to storm off. My fucking life has been turned upside down. My friends all ditched me in seconds and the school has made it their mission to drive me out. All because I thought your stupid, malicious ass was worth saving!"

This time I did push. I lashed out and shoved him. Then I shoved him again.

"How could you do that to me?" I raged. Ryder stood before me—immovable and silent. "How could you mark me?"

"I didn't."

"Then who did? Was it the person you were fighting with? Tell me."

"Out of the way."

He made to get around me again, but I jumped in front of him. "Tell me who it was. Tell me who had the knife. Were they trying to hurt you? Are you afraid of them?"

"Move, Val," he growled.

"Or was it you?" I flung. "Did you have the knife? Were you completing your descent into sociopath and going for murder? Is that why you're so desperate I keep quiet?"

Ryder grabbed my shoulders in a grip like iron. I fought to escape him as he pushed me to the side. "If I was a sociopath," he began, "I wouldn't have gotten you a present. I'm sure you're dying to know what it is. Come with me."

Ryder marched off leaving me no choice but to follow. I ran on his heels. "Ryder, talk to me. Just tell me what happened that night."

"What night?"

"Ryder!" I burst out. "What happened to you in the woods?"

Ryder didn't turn around. He didn't stop walking. "I didn't go into the woods. I was at the masquerade ball all night. Ask anyone."

The breath whooshed out of my chest with the force of a sucker punch. "Ryder, you can't be serious." The music got louder as we approached the clearing. Shrieks of joy and laughter pierced the night, so far removed from the nightmare I was stuck in with Ryder. "You can't pretend this isn't happening."

"I can't pretend what's happening?"

"Ry—"

"Jaxson!" I jumped at his shout. "Cut the music!"

In a beat, the music was off and the clearing was plunged into silence.

"Let's go, Moon."

"Wha— Hey!"

Ryder had snagged my wrist, dragging me after him. He walked us up to the fire and planted us in front of everyone. People drifted away from the food table and their not-so-private make-out spots to form a crowd before us. The Diamonds were right at the front.

Ryder gestured at me. "Everyone knows Val, right?"

Nods and murmurs of agreement went around the clearing.

"Did you also know how we've known each other?" Ryder's voice was smooth, almost pleasant. "Ever since her mom started working for my dad. Val was there for parties, birthdays, and when... my dad disappeared."

I glanced at him. Ryder's face gave nothing away. *Where was this going?*

"It wasn't until then that I understood what Val was going through."

What I was going through?

"Not knowing where your father is. In her case, not knowing *who* he is."

I went rigid. "Ryder, what are you doing?"

He kept going like I hadn't spoken. "We've searched for my dad for over a year, and with every day we don't find him it feels like we never will. There isn't much more I can do to find my father, but I could do something for Val."

Ryder turned to me and leveled me with that smile. I flinched. "What is this? What are you talking about?"

"Val, I found him. I found your father."

"What?" I stumbled away from him. "No, you didn't!"

"Yes, I did." Ryder reached into his pocket and pulled out an envelope folded in half. My eyes latched on to it. "I hired a private investigator and had him tracked down. He doesn't live that far from Wakefield—"

"Stop."

"He's actually doing alright for himself—"

"Stop!" Ryder closed his mouth. The clearing was deadly silent. I couldn't even hear the chirp of cicadas. "You had no right to do that," I whispered. My whole body shook.

"No." He shook his head. "Your mother had no right to keep him from you. He's your father, Val. I would do anything to find out where mine is. Now you can."

Ryder took a step forward, but I backed up, maintaining the distance. I couldn't take my eyes off the envelope, resting innocently between his fingers. "That's different."

"It's not different. All that matters is if you want to see him." He took another step and this time I didn't move. "You do, don't you?"

"No," I croaked. A lump was forming in my throat. I couldn't breathe—couldn't see anything other than that envelope.

Ryder extended his hand. "Take it, Val."

I tried to refuse again, but nothing would come out.

"Val, take the envelope. Find your father."

The world grew hazy around the edges. Only one single thing was in sharp focus. *You could discover who he is. Find him. Speak to him.*

He ran out on us, another voice countered. *He wasn't there for me. Mom was. She has her reasons for keeping us apart.*

I should decide for myself if I want to know him. I should have the choice.

You can't open that envelope. Leave. Walk away.

"Valentina. Take it."

My body moved, responding to commands I didn't feel were my own. I reached for the envelope...

...and then it was gone.

Ryder flicked his wrist and the envelope went soaring into the flames. Time slowed as someone screamed. I dove for the fire; my body was yanked after the letter as though we were connecting by an invisible tie.

Strong hands wrapped around me, pulling me back before the flames could bite my fingers. The fire claimed its prize, crackling and spitting as the envelope blackened and withered away into nothing. Screams echoed through the cliffs.

Ryder's raucous laughter was what finally broke through my haze. I came around to find the person screaming was me.

"Oops." Ryder's body shook with his glee. "To be fair, Val, you should have expected this. I said you were off-limits tonight but... I lied."

The words lashed across my soul. I strained against his hands, fighting to get out. "G-get off!"

"Aww. Don't leave so—"

Smack!

The slap rang out over the noise of the cackling crowd. Ryder dropped me in surprise, his hand flying to his now red cheek.

I picked myself off the ground and ran, knocking people aside as I fled. I didn't care. I had to get out of there.

Branches tore at me, roots tried to trip me up, and the woods blurred through the stinging tears, but I didn't slow down. My sobs echoed through the night.

I EXPECTED THE NIGHTMARE to come, even though I still woke hoarse and dripping with sweat. I had cried until there was nothing left, and then the rage came. I had been right to call Ryder a sociopath. What he had done was cruelty like I had never seen. But what I had done was worse.

I was stupid enough to walk right into his trap, even though I knew he couldn't be trusted. Hope that I would get to talk to him about the night of the party wasn't good enough reason to give him the opportunity to destroy me in front of his gleeful audience.

I threw the covers off and stood. Moving over to my desk, I woke my laptop and plugged in my new camera. My movements were slow and robotic as I pulled up the photos we had taken for Parents' Day. I lingered over our smiles. Despite everything, I didn't want to meet my father. He knew I existed, if he truly cared he would find me, or even more, he would have been there for me my entire life.

Ryder had caught me when I was weak, using the disappearance of his father to make me think he had a heart before he twisted the knife.

I would never give him that chance again.

DAWN BROUGHT ANOTHER school day, and saw me striding through the halls with my head high. I didn't react to dad jokes or crying noises. I was done playing games.

A shadow fell on me as I opened my locker. "Hey, Val. Rough night, huh?"

I riffled through my locker. "No, Natalie. I'm cool."

I sensed the Diamonds falling in around me, blocking my escape.

"You know you can still find him," said Airi. "Use your whore money to hire your own private investigator."

I twisted my head over my shoulder and shot her a beaming smile. "Great idea."

Airi's smirk slipped. "Yeah," she said, a trace of hesitation in her voice. "He only lives an hour away."

Isabella piped up. "Ryder told us all about him after you ran off. Bet you're dying to know his name."

I shrugged. "Nah, not really." I slammed the locker shut on her flicker of surprise. "But it's sweet of you guys to offer. So if we're done here—"

Isabella's hand flashed out and blocked me when I took a step. "You can act tough, Moon, but you're not fooling anyone."

Natalie got in my face. "Why won't you just leave?!"

I threw up my hands. "I'm trying to leave but you won't get out of my way. Wow, make up your minds, people." I shoved past her and Axel, marching off to homeroom.

"Alright, Moon," Isabella called after me. "We get it. We need to step it up a notch."

"You'll need to step it up a thousand notches to get to me," I tossed over my shoulder, "and you still won't get rid of me."

There was no reply as I rounded the corner and walked off.

I walked into homeroom and found my desk had once again disappeared. My day off—if it could be called that—was officially over.

It was easy enough getting through my classes. The students couldn't do much to me but hiss vile things to me while we copied our assignments. Even in PE they didn't try to act out under Coach Panzer's watchful eye. She had a habit of giving out suicides to students who messed around.

I changed out of my uniform and into my gym clothes to the usual comments.

"Look at her. She's disgusting. She's a twig with a pulse."

"Wish we could do something about the pulse part."

I gritted my teeth at Natalie's voice. That girl really had it out for me.

The locker room doors banged open. "Alright, ladies!" Panzer boomed. "I want you changed and out on the track in five minutes." Our coach was as tall as she was wide. The woman was built from hearty stock with broad shoulders and a thick jaw. When she smiled, it transformed her face into a beauty, but she rarely did that.

I hurried out of my skirt and slipped on the drawstring pants. Panzer came down just as hard on people who held her up as she did on those who messed around.

I stuffed my things in my locker and joined the line of girls heading outside. The rest of our classes were split from the front class to the back class but gym class was separated by gender.

Panzer put us in groups and told us to stretch. I ended up with Ciara, Tawnie May from the other class, and of course, Natalie.

Tawnie wandered a bit away and did her warm-ups, leaving the three of us in a silence so thick you could break a nose smacking into it.

I turned my back on the other two and went through my motions. They wouldn't pull anything. Panzer was always watching.

Coach called us back after ten minutes. "Listen up, girls. You'll race your teams and then the winners will go on to race each other. The purpose is to sort you into your final track groups. I want you to pace yourself and do your best. Understood?"

We mumbled back.

"I said, is that understood?!"

"Yes, Coach!"

She gave a sharp nod. "Good. A-group. You're first."

The girls ran over to the starting line while my group followed. We were B-group, going up next. I watched them lap the track, then moved up to the line when it was our turn.

"Ready?"

I took my stance.

One sharp whistle blow and I was off. My feet pounded against the asphalt, carrying me far ahead of the other group. It felt good. The wind in my face, the burning lungs, the way everything faded away as the world blurred. Maybe I should run more often.

"Y-you won't last."

I twisted my head around. Natalie was gaining on me—fast.

"You showed... the whole class how w-weak you were last night." She was straining to keep up with me. "We'll get rid of you. One way or another, the marked always go."

I rolled my eyes. "Whatever, Natalie." I faced forward and fell back into my rhythm. I didn't give a shit about—

A hard blow struck my leg, sweeping it out from under me. There wasn't time to scream as I tripped and went flying across the track. My body skidded along the unforgiving asphalt as it scraped off bits of my skin. I smacked to a stop and lay still, too dazed to move.

A whistle was going off like crazy. I heard the sound of racing footsteps.

"Miss Bard! Ten laps! Now!"

"But, Coach, it was an accident."

"I said now!"

Natalie cursed under her breath. She threw me one last parting shot before jogging off. "Bitch."

Coach skidded to a stop and knelt beside me. Ciara stopped too, standing a few feet away from us. "Miss Moon, are you alright?"

I struggled to push myself up. "I'm f-fine."

"You took quite a fall." She put her hand on my back and helped me sit up. "You're out for the rest of class. Ciara will take you to the nurse to make sure you're alright."

"I don't need to go to the—"

"No arguments." She snapped her fingers at Ciara. "Help her up."

Before I could stop her, Ciara was throwing my arm around her shoulder and hauling me up. We were quiet as we crossed the grounds for the main building. I knew I hadn't broken anything, but my arm and back were stinging from leaving my skin on the pavement. I wouldn't say no to some antiseptic.

"Nobody wants this, you know."

I glanced at her. "What? What did you just say?"

"I said." Ciara kept her gaze firmly ahead. "That no one wants to... do this to you."

"Really?" I scoffed, face twisting. "Because Natalie doesn't seem too bothered."

She didn't say anything to that. We had skirted the sports complex when she tried again.

"You're marked, Val. We don't have a choice."

"Everyone has a choice." I pulled out of her grasp. "I don't need your help. I'm fine."

"But, Val—"

I ignored her. A quick trip to the nurse's office got me doused in antiseptic and given a bandage for my arm. She finished ten minutes after the bell rang, and I had to hurry back to the gym. Lunch was only served at designated times and I wasn't missing out on eating, or spending time in my new lunchroom, because of Natalie.

Girls were already drying off and getting dressed when I burst in. I stripped off my gym clothes, grabbed a towel, and headed for the showers. I rinsed off as best I could. It was a little tricky trying not to wet my bandage. Despite my rushing, the hot water felt amazing. I stuck my head under the spray and let it wash every trace of that gym class from hell from my skin.

Blindly, I shut the water off and stumbled toward my hook. I grabbed for my towel and closed on empty air. My eyes sprang open.

There was nothing there.

No. No, no, no!

I raced out of the showers into the empty locker room. I beat it to my locker, and yanked it open.

Gone. My uniform. My gym clothes. Even my scrunchie. It had been emptied out.

I stood there dripping onto the tile as the panic set in. *What am I going to do?! I can't leave and after lunch is the boy's class!*

Calm down. I bit my lip so hard it sang with pain. *They won't get to me. They won't get to me. Think of something.*

Taking a deep breath, I walked away from my empty locker and started searching. There has to be something here that I can cover—

My eyes lit on the dirty laundry hamper. I rushed up and threw it open. My nose wrinkled at having to wrap myself in a towel from someone else's dirty, sweaty body, but desperate times.

I knotted the terry cloth tight around me and marched up to the door. I braced myself as I placed my hand on the metal. I wasn't hiding out in here until Coach Panzer came and took pity on me.

They can mess with me, but they will find out I can play this game better.

With that thought in my head, I threw open the door to a round of guffaws. A group led by the Diamonds were waiting just outside the doors, no doubt hoping to get the full view of me streaking away with my face burning.

Instead, I flashed them a smile. "Hello, everyone. Were you waiting for me?"

The laughs faltered. They exchanged confused looks, but the best sight of all was Natalie's snarl. She was not pleased to see me so unruffled.

Isabella peeled herself from the pack. "Missing something, Valentina?"

I made a show of looking around, up, and down. "Nope," I replied. "Don't think so."

A flicker of anger crossed her face. "What is wrong with you?" she snapped.

"Me?" I grinned. "The real question is what is wrong with you? I thought you 'never lose' and 'rise to every challenge.' So far, this is pretty pathetic."

"I'm just getting started."

I shrugged. "Or you could just give it up. You have better things to do, minions to boss around, titles to chase. Stop wasting time on things you're clearly not good at." I twisted my hand in my hair and wrung it out, splattering the floor between us with water. "Now if you'll excuse me, I'm starved."

I marched off.

Airi sputtered. "You're not actually going to—?"

"Why wouldn't I?"

I didn't slow down. I didn't think. I strolled right up to the cafeteria and threw open the doors. The lunchroom was a riot of noise. Students laughing, joking, and goofing around. That all came to an abrupt halt after the first—

"Oh, shit!"

I lifted my chin higher as every eye in the room turned to me. The towel reached mid-thigh. On display for everyone to see were my smooth, creamy legs and blue toes. I let the smirk show on my face when Jaxson's mouth fell open and his fork slipped through his fingers.

To complete silence, I walked up to the lunch line, bypassed everyone waiting, accepted a tray from an astounded lunch lady, and swept through the doors like nothing happened.

Chaos erupted the moment it swung shut.

Chapter Ten

"Miss Moon, walk me through what happened this afternoon."

Headmaster Evergreen's eyebrow was twitching something fierce. It was very distracting. I guess I didn't expect to get away with what I did.

I walked out of the cafeteria, went straight to my room to get dressed, and ate on my bed. After I walked back into the main building to go to my next class, I found the headmaster and Professor Markham waiting for me.

"Miss Moon?" he pressed. The effort he was making to stay calm was obvious, but what did he have to be mad about? It wasn't like his clothes were stolen.

"Headmaster," Markham piped up from my other side. "I would just like to say Miss Moon is a good student and this behavior is most out of character. I'm sure there is a reasonable explanation."

His twitchy eyebrow shot up his forehead. "A reasonable explanation for parading around the lunchroom naked. Evergreen is an elite institution. I will not have this nonsense in my school."

I met his gaze head-on. "Really? That's interesting. So what will you have in your school, Headmaster?"

He blinked. "Excuse me?"

"Is bullying allowed in your school? Theft? Destruction of property? How about breaking and entering?"

"What on earth are you talking about?"

"I'm talking about all the nonsense that *I've* put up with in your school."

"Miss Moon," Professor Markham warned under her breath.

I plowed on. "I wonder why your eyebrow isn't twitching over that, Headmaster."

"You watch your tone." Evergreen rose up and leaned over his desk. My eyes crossed looking at the finger he put in my face. "The circumstances by which I let you into this school will not sway me should I decide it's time for you to leave."

The threat came through loud and clear. Wincing, I swallowed my anger. "My clothes and towel were taken while I was in the shower," I said in a politer voice. "Not long ago, my room was broken into and everything destroyed, ripped, broken, or shredded."

Evergreen slowly reclaimed his seat. The eyebrow stopped twitching. "Why wasn't I made aware of this earlier?"

I looked him in the eyes. "I didn't believe anything would be done to help the marked." I studied his face for a reaction but there was none.

"Marked?" he repeated. "I am not aware of that term. Miss Moon, if your room was broken into and your things were destroyed, then you should have reported it immediately. There is not much we can do after the fact."

"I took pictures of the damage."

He inclined his head. "And can you name the culprit?"

Sofia.

"No," I said aloud. "But that's what cameras are for. Check the security tapes."

"The recordings remain on the server for one week, then they are wiped. I'm sorry but there is little I can do in that regard except to reimburse you for the cost of replacing your items. Now, if we can return to the issue of today."

I gritted my teeth. I expected him to do nothing, but still this was irritating. "What issue? My clothes were stolen. It's not my fault."

"You could have waited for Coach to return and help you find your clothes."

"Help me find them?" I was really struggling to keep my tone respectful. "They weren't lost; they were taken. My classmates stole my things and tried to humiliate me, but once again, I am the one sitting in your office facing punishment." The words were tumbling out of my mouth with no sign of stopping. "Between my room, the Parents' Day video, and now this, it's becoming clear that this school doesn't value the safety of its students."

Red splotches rose to his cheeks. "That's preposterous. Safety is our number one priority and—"

"And I'm sure from here on out," I finished, "you will do everything in your power to ensure *my* safety. If there are any more break-ins or disappearing clothes, the world will find out what it's really like in Evergreen Academy."

"Miss Moon," Markham hissed.

"Is that a threat?" asked the headmaster.

"No, sir."

Evergreen leaned back in his chair. He gazed at me over steepled fingers for so long the silence grew uncomfortable.

After five solid minutes had passed, he inclined his head. "There will be no more incidents. As I said, safety is our first priority and I will take steps to ensure you feel safe. I hope that will put your mind at ease."

"Thank you, sir." I rose to leave.

"Hold on, Miss Moon. There is still the matter of your walking around in a towel. Despite the circumstances, I can't ignore something like that. Two more weeks will be added to your trash duty, and be thankful that is all."

"Yes, sir," I forced out. "Thank you."

He waved us on. "You may go."

I left without another word. No part of me believed that he would do anything to help me. Just like I didn't believe he wasn't aware of the markings. So far, I could see that this wasn't the first time it has happened. There was no way the headmaster of the last couple decades hadn't heard the same whispers I did.

He's just like the rest of the staff. Burying their heads in the sand and letting the Knights run the school. I'm on my own.

"GOOD MORNING, MISS Moon."

"Ahh!" I jumped almost a foot in the air. My heart pounded as I took in the giant lying in wait when I opened the door. "Who are you?" I demanded.

She stuck out a hand. "My name is Noemi Kennedy. I've been assigned to escort you around campus."

I goggled at her. "You've been what to what? By who?"

"Headmaster Evergreen." Her hand was still hanging in the air between us. "He expressed concerns for your safety following a few incidents. Your safety is our—"

"First priority. Yeah, I've heard that before." I stepped out in the hall and finally shook her hand. "But it's only been a day. I didn't think anything would be done so fast."

I didn't think anything would be done full stop.

"I will be by your side every moment you're outside of this dorm."

"Every moment?" I held up a hand. "Hold on. I appreciate that the school is trying to step up, but I don't want a bodyguard."

Noemi didn't lose her smile. "Miss Moon, if I'm understanding, are you refusing these security measures?"

"I wouldn't put it like that, but yes."

"I see." Noemi reached into her jacket pocket and pulled out a pen and folded paper. "If you could sign this form acknowledging that, I will be on my way."

I eyed it. "What is it?"

"This states that efforts were made to increase your security and you refused them, thus waiving any right to sue or defame the school if there is another incident."

"Are you serious? You're saying I either let you follow me around, or I suck it up and take it if someone comes after me again?"

Noemi didn't reply.

I was tempted to choose the latter option. I had been taking care of myself just fine, I didn't need them to protect me.

But you also don't need the school getting off scot-free if someone does strike. This whole thing reeks of Evergreen fighting to protect the school's ass more than he is trying to protect mine. Lesson Number One: Evergreen values its reputation above all.

"I'm not signing that," I announced. "So I guess you and I are going to be spending a lot of time together. Tell me more about yourself, Ms. Kennedy."

Noemi pocketed the form. "Gladly. I've worked here for three years and..."

I OBJECTED TO HER PRESENCE at first, but there was no denying Noemi brought results. Like she promised, she was on my tail from the moment I stepped out of my dorm to the time I went back inside. She posted up in the back when I had class. She followed me around while I did trash duty. She sat at my table with a book while I studied in the library. With her around, my classmates were reduced to hissing cruel comments at me when she was out of earshot, but that was all they pulled. Between her and finals, life had almost returned to normal... if it wasn't for the fact that I had zero friends and the people that used to be, promised to run me out of school the moment my little body-guard was gone.

I couldn't think about that now though. There was only one week left until winter break which meant a whole three weeks away from this place. But before that, I had to get through fi-nals. Bodyguard or no, no one in this school would study with or tutor me. I was cramming twice as hard and staying up way too late—whatever it took. I hadn't gone through everything I had just to be kicked out for letting my grades slip.

"We're going to the library now," I told Noemi after classes let out.

"How much can one person study Shakespeare before his words get even more nonsensical."

I snorted. "Don't let Professor Strange hear you say that."

We shared a laugh. How sad was it that my bodyguard was the closest thing I had to a friend?

Together, we walked into the library and were welcomed by its dim lights and serene quiet. The only noises that broke the silence were the whisper of pages. Noemi went off to claim our usual table in the back while I veered off to the modern art section. I had crammed as much Shakespeare in my head as could fit. Now I was moving onto art class. Scarlett wanted a five-page paper on a neo-Expressionist artist on top of the painting of our fears. Even my laid-back teacher was piling it on.

I weaved through the stacks, scanning the titles looking for the name Jean-Michel Basquiat. "It should be here some—"

I rounded the corner and stopped. Standing in front of me, taking down the very book I was after, was Maverick Beaumont.

Just turn around and go. It's been weeks of almost peace. I don't want to deal with him today.

I took a step back the moment his eyes snapped up and met mine. We stared at each other across the row.

Maverick said nothing. Of course, he said nothing. That was his go-to move. He hadn't uttered one single word to me since the night of the masquerade ball. The night we kissed.

He would go entire class periods without looking in my direction. I don't know what hurt worse: Ryder, Jaxson, and Ezra's attacks and taunts or Maverick acting as though I wasn't worth his time.

But the way he kissed me was so—

I shook the thought away. It was a trick. A bet. The sooner I accept that the Knights were all liars, the better.

I jerked my chin at the book in his hand. "I need that one, Maverick. I was coming to get it."

Maverick looked down at the book in his hand, looked at me, then turned his back and walked off.

"Hey!" I hissed. I darted out in front of him, blocking his path. Although I say blocking. The guy was a two-ton truck and I was the furry bunny hopping out into the street. I didn't have a chance if he came bearing down on me. Maverick pulled up to a stop, gazing down at me with a blank look.

"I said I need that book, Maverick. Hand it over." He didn't even twitch. "Maverick, come on."

I lunged for it, and in one smooth move, he lifted it over his head and effectively out of my reach. "Maverick," I cried. I shoved his chest but it didn't move him an inch. I jumped up, straining to reach the book, but my fingers didn't rise higher than his elbows. He just kept standing there with all the emotion of a mannequin.

Growing angry, I grabbed the collar of his blazer and leaped. Maverick grunted when he suddenly found me wrapped around him like a spider monkey, climbing his body to get at that book. I pressed down on his head for balance as I took hold of the spine and yanked.

I felt a second of victory before Maverick seized me around the waist. The book fell to the floor as he roughly pulled me off and deposited me on the floor. I stumbled back, and the asshole took the chance to bend and retrieve the book.

That's when the dam broke. "What is wrong with you?" I asked as I straightened. "All of you. How can anyone be so dead inside that they would do the things you guys have done?"

Maverick stepped to the side.

"Oh, no." I jumped back in front of him. "You're not fucking running away. You don't want to speak, then fine, you'll listen." I jabbed his pecs. "I thought that we were friends. I thought that underneath that strong, silent type cliché was an actual person. A smart, funny guy who got me. I thought you were different, Maverick. I thought you thought I was different."

I was running off into weird babbling now but it was too late to stop the tide. "The worst part is I liked you. At the beginning, I thought Jaxson was an ass; Ezra too intense; and Ryder the devil, but you..." My throat tightened, threatening to choke me, but I forced the rest out. "Like I said, I thought you were different."

I moved closer to him. I could see the hard line of his jaw. He was tense, possibly upset, but his face was impossible to read. "Just tell me one thing," I whispered. "The video of my mom. Tracking down my father. Were you a part of that too?"

He didn't move. I wasn't entirely sure he was breathing.

"This is the part where you speak, Maverick." I was shaking so hard I had to ball my fists to keep them still. "Answer me," I demanded as a tear slid down my cheek. "Answer me!"

I sucked in a sharp breath. Maverick had lifted his hand. I held still as he cupped my cheek, and with a touch so featherlight it was barely there, he brushed the tear away.

"Maverick..."

His hand traveled down my body, ghosting along my neck and then continuing its journey over the mounds of my breast. My heart pounded so furiously I was certain the entire library could hear it. My eyes fluttered shut as Maverick's fingers skimmed over the thin fabric covering my stomach, then his hand closed over mine. I felt something heavy on my palm and then the hand was gone.

Maverick was walking away by the time I opened my eyes. I peered down and found the autobiography of Jean-Michel Basquiat in my hand.

It took me a minute to collect myself and step out of the stacks. I walked out and my eyes fell on Noemi gesturing for me. I slid past her and saw Maverick sitting down next to Jaxson, Ryder, and Ezra. As if they sensed me, all four looked up. I hadn't spoken to Ryder or Ezra since the party. I hadn't spoken to Jaxson either, but that didn't stop him from talking to me. He regularly offered to pay me for sex even in front of Noemi.

I held their gaze until Ryder smirked. I had no clue what just happened with Maverick, but if the look in Ryder's eyes said one thing, it was that this wasn't over.

FINALS WEEK WAS WRECKING me even more thoroughly than I knew it would. Wednesday morning, I staggered out of Rossman's class in a fog. I could honestly say I had no clue if I did well or not. At one point, the numbers had started to look like meaningless squiggles so I was leaning toward not.

I threw my books in my locker and turned to Noemi. "You can go have your lunch now. I'll be fine."

"Are you sure?"

I sighed. "We do this every day. I'll be okay. Go ahead and eat."

"You're right; we do this every day, and every day I wonder where it is you go to have your lunch."

"Somewhere that no one will bother me, which is why I don't need an escort and you can enjoy your lunch in peace."

Shaking her head, she replied, "Okay. I'll meet you back here in an hour."

She took off and I went in the opposite direction for the cafeteria. No way I was letting her in on my secret. Noemi still worked for the school and it was no mystery that Evergreen values its Knights more than a marked girl who kept making trouble.

I pushed through into the lunchroom. It started up as soon as I was noticed.

"Whoo, baby. Why are you wearing clothes today? Where's the towel?"

I didn't react as I made for the lunch line.

"Forget the towel *and* the clothes," shouted Axel. "I wanna see if she's as stacked as her mother."

I pivoted, teeth bared, to flip him the finger. So focused was I on the asshole that I collided into someone else.

Crash!

"Hey, watch it!" I twisted around at her voice. Sofia's lunch was all over the cafeteria floor. She glared at me, face splotchy, as the orange juice stain darkened her blue dress.

"Oh, be quiet," I snapped. "It was an accident. Get another tray."

Isabella's chair screeched across the floor. "You're not going to let her talk to you like that, are you, Sofia?"

"Yeah," echoed Natalie. "Her little bodyguard isn't here. Nothing to stop you from teaching her a lesson."

Sofia's eyes swept the room. The artificial lights shone harshly on her, revealing the sweat collecting on her forehead.

"No, that's okay." Sofia stopped glancing around and pinned me with a look. "I don't want to hold her up from going off to wherever she hides. She's probably off to meet up with a customer." She planted her hands on her hips. "I heard your blow jobs are amazing, Val."

"And what are you off to go do?!" I shouted over the laughter. "Beg Mommy and Daddy to let you come home for winter break?"

Sofia's smile melted away. "What?"

"You heard me." I stepped forward, kicked the tray out of my way, and bore down on her. "Because it's obvious they don't want to see you. Your mom lives twenty minutes away and couldn't be bothered to come to Parents' Day. How sad is that? Why doesn't she want to be with you, Sofia?"

Hands falling off her hips, Sofia tried to step back. "At least my mom doesn't flash drunk college boys in South Beach."

Scratch, scratch.

I was so angry—so hurt. The tide of emotions was pulling me down and drowning me. I clutched my chest as I followed her, not letting her get away.

"At least my mom... loves me."

Sofia flinched like I had slapped her. She held my gaze for all of five seconds before her face crumpled and she ran from the room in tears.

I held out for one more minute before I was running too. My heart pounded in my ears so loud it almost covered the sound of my gasps.

I didn't slow down until I was in the elevator rising to my dorm room. The lock chimed and I threw myself on my bed, clutching my pillow as I tried to remember how to breathe.

"DID YOU HAVE A GOOD lunch?"

I shrugged.

"Everything okay?"

"Yep," I replied with a little pop on the "p." Thankfully, Noemi seemed to pick up on my mood and didn't ask any more questions.

I barely got through the rest of the day. My class had moved on from calling me "Whore" and "Virgin," and took up "Heartless Bitch." The worst part was that I agreed with them. What I said to Sofia was awful. No matter how mad I was at her, it was no good for me to be brought down to that level. If that happens, then I truly will have lost.

Noemi escorted me to the library to study, but I had to call it quits thirty minutes in when I realized I had read the same paragraph three times.

"I'm going back to the dorm. I need this day to be over already."

"Alright." Noemi heaved her bulk out of the chair. "Let's go."

We left the library and headed out for the doors. Noemi rode with me up the elevator and waved goodbye instead of stepping out.

"Bye."

I need food and sleep. I tapped in my passcode and pushed open the door. *After that, things won't seem so bad. I have a—*

"Hi, Val."

"Ahh!" I spun around as my bathroom door opened the rest of the way. Sofia wiped her red nose with the edge of her sleeves. Puffy eyes gazed at me as I flipped out.

"How did you get in here?! I changed the passcode."

"I know." She stepped out of the bathroom, padding across the carpet. "To Adam's birthday. It wasn't hard to guess."

She sounded funny. Why was she here? What was she going to do now?

"Sofia..."

"I knew what you would pick, Val," she continued, "because you're my best friend, and I— I—" Tears sprang to her eyes. That was all the warning I got before she launched herself at me. My hands came up quickly to defend myself, and were immediately crushed to my chest as Sofia seized me in a strangling hug.

I could barely hear her through the wailing and my own shock.

"I—I'm so s-sorry!"

"*Oomphf!*" I cried when her hold tightened.

"I missed you so much. I never wanted any of this, Val. Please believe me."

"Sofia—"

"I can't do this anymore. I hate fighting with you."

What was she saying?

"I've cried like every day for the past month. This has been such a nightmare."

"Sofia," I wheezed.

"I don't want to do awful things to each other anymore. I don't—"

"Sofia!" I finally shook her off and backed away. "Stop. You can't just break in here and say sorry like that's going to fix everything. How do I know this isn't another trick?" I balled my fists. "Like the party."

Sofia sniffled. "I didn't know what Ryder was going to do. I wouldn't have brought you if I did."

"I'm supposed to believe that?"

"It's true," she insisted. "Val, no one wants to do this. *I* don't want this. But you were marked, I didn't have a choice."

"Everyone keeps saying that to me, but you do have a choice. You all had a choice, and you chose to turn on me and make my life hell. You were supposed to be my best friend, and you let them into my room."

"I didn't have a choice—"

"Stop saying that!"

Sofia pressed her lips together. We gazed at each other from opposite ends of the room. She was the first one to break.

Sofia walked over to the bed and perched herself on the edge. She patted the spot next to her, and the silence was tense as I decided what I was going to do.

"Val, please."

Despite myself, my feet carried me over to the bed. I sat down. "Is this the part where you give me excuses?" I asked.

"Yes." Her voice shook. "It is."

I sighed. "Sofia, I don't want to hear—"

"You need to hear this." She shifted around to face me. "Val, you know better than anyone what happens when you're marked, but you don't know why."

I didn't reply, so she continued.

"A lot of us grew up in this world. We live in the town the Evergreens founded. Our parents and grandparents went to school here. We go to the junior prep school. We've all heard the stories, and by the time we get to the academy, we know to be afraid."

"Afraid?"

She nodded. "The Knights were meant to keep the students in line, but some became problems. Problems that needed to be gotten rid of."

"So to do that the school devolves into savages? That's insane."

"Marks didn't start that way. At first, they were like eviction notices. You got one and you packed your bags and left. It's when people refused to leave that things got... bad."

My head was spinning. "I'm sorry. What? Why couldn't they just be expelled like a normal school?"

"These aren't things you could get expelled over, but still reasons enough that they'll want you gone."

I nodded slowly. "The Knights."

"No."

"No? What do you mean no?"

"The Knights don't choose who gets marked any more than they choose themselves." Sofia's eyes were starting to clear. She was red-faced and shaky, but her tears had slowed. "That's done by a person or people that no one knows. We only know that he/she/they calls themselves the Black Spades."

"Excuse me?" I shook my head in disbelief. "Now I know you're making all of this up. Sofia, that's ridiculous. There isn't some secret society running around beneath the nose of the entire school."

She pinned me with a look that chilled. "There's also no way four fifteen-year-old boys rule an academy and have even professors bowing at their feet. There's no way an entire school would turn on their friend because of a playing card."

I looked away. "Okay, you've made your point."

A hand on my arm drew me back. "Evergreen is like nowhere else. This school churns out world leaders, kings, and king-makers, captains of industry. People would sell their second-born to get their firstborn in, and they do that because Evergreen is, without a doubt, the best, and everything from the professor and diets to the Knights and Spades makes sure we stay that way."

"You're being serious," I whispered. "You really believe these Spades exist."

"The Spades exist, Val. That's not even a question. They chose the Knights, and then they chose you to be marked. Do you still have the card?"

I shook my head. "Why?"

"Because it's their signature. One-of-a-kind cardstock, color-shifting ink, and the joker is dressed in the colors of the school. They can't be replicated. That's how you know it's from them."

"And no one knows who they are?" I asked, desperation lacing my voice. "Someone has to know. How can this be allowed to go on?"

"It's been going on for decades, and that's because no one knows who they are, or even how many." She lowered her voice even though we were the only ones in the room. "Why do you think people are so afraid? They could be anywhere—any-one—watching you and ready to mark you if you make the wrong move.

"When people tried to ignore the marks, the Spades decided it was on the rest of the school to support the Knights and get them out by any means. It didn't matter; they couldn't be al-lowed to ruin our reputation."

I lurched to my feet. "And people didn't fight back? They didn't say hell no to doing their dirty work. They didn't think for a minute that bullying and harassment is wrong!"

"Of course, they did, Val. People fought back... and every single one of them regretted it."

I sank back down. "What happened to them?"

"What didn't happen? Deep secrets came out, family businesses were put under, futures were sabotaged, and, for one guy, a life was lost."

In that moment, I knew. As I had the answer all along and was waiting for someone to tell me the question. "Walter McMillian."

"Wal—" Sofia blinked. "Yes, how did you know?"

"Good guess. Are you telling me the Spades murdered him?"

"I don't know the whole story. Just the bits my mom would tell me."

"Your mom?" Goodness, it *was* like another world. I had stepped into a separate reality when I passed through the gates.

"She said it was like a scary story they liked to tell the freshmen. Walter McMillian: off-the-charts genius but boy from the wrong side of the tracks. Scholarship student and rebel."

"He was marked?"

"He was friends with a person who was marked." She gave me a sad smile. "And he was a much better friend than I was because he tried to protect them. The thing was people liked Walter. They liked his friend who got marked and they didn't know why they were chosen in the first place. So when Walter decided all of this needed to stop and the Spades brought down, people began to listen. He wanted to root out the Spades, end their rule, and change Evergreen forever."

"So he was killed," I said through numb lips. "But how can people be sure it was the Spades who..." I trailed off at Sofia's look.

"They murdered him, Val, and no one has questioned the rule of the Spades since. You were marked, you wouldn't drop out, and rather than risk the same fate, we've all worked to drive you out." Sniffling, her face crumpled. "And I'm so sorry. I don't expect you to ever forgive me, but I want you to know it's over for me—"

I shook my head. "No."

"Val, I mean it. I'm on your side. I don't care what happens to me."

"No, Sofia." The weight of this situation was settling heavy on me. I felt so many conflicting emotions I couldn't keep track of them all, but one that stood out in sharp focus was relief. Now, I understood.

I understood why I lost my friends.

I understood why the school turned on me.

I understood how witnessing a fight in the woods had changed my life.

"You may not care what happens, Sof, but I do. I don't want anyone to come after you the way they have me."

Her tears were flowing freely now. "How can you do that? Be worried about me after everything I've done?"

My eyes slid off her face, growing unfocused as I gazed over her shoulder. "I know what it's like to be scared, and the awful things it can make you do." I looked back at her. "If this isn't a horrible trick—"

She lunged forward and pulled me in for a hug as strangling as the first. "No. No way. I'll never hurt you again. I missed you so much."

"I... missed you too." And then I was hugging her back. We held each other so tight I was sure we'd wake up with bruised ribs in the morning. I didn't care. I needed Sofia. The pain of her betrayal had been another lash on my soul. It ate away at me until I was forced to numb myself to survive the pain. It all disappeared as we spent the night crying, laughing, and talking like we used to.

I didn't know what the next semester was going to have in store for me, but I could face it with Sofia on my side.

Year one, final semester: bring it on.

Chapter Eleven

"We'll have a limit for presents this year."

"You can't put a limit on presents." The pan popped and sizzled as I flipped the bacon. The end of the semester had seen me with six As and two Bs. It was a bit strange having my grades posted for the entire class to see, but it did feel good to know I was holding my own among my classmates.

The end of the year also saw me on a bus home to Wakefield. I never thought I would miss our shoebox apartment with its puke-green walls, and single bathroom, but it was paradise compared to bodyguards, bullies, and secret societies.

I stood barefoot in the kitchen over the stove, cooking up breakfast while Adam babbled in his high chair and smeared avocado on his face. We were gearing up for a Christmas decorating marathon. Tree, lights, the whole works. If there was one thing the Moon women loved, it was Christmas, and we weren't holding back for Adam's first one.

"The whole point is giving and being generous," I continued.

"Well, I don't want you getting too generous, so we'll have a fifty-dollar spending limit. Deal?"

I sighed. "Okay, deal."

"Good." Mom walked up to the sink and rescued a washcloth. She advanced on Adam. "Your first present comes today, it's awesome, and I didn't spend a dime."

"Have you ruined the brag by saying it was free?"

"Nope."

I laughed. Flicking off the stove, I got busy plating our breakfast. We were sitting down to eat when the doorbell rang. Olivia popped up with a grin. "Right on time. Wait here."

I shrugged and speared a bit of egg. I overheard Mom opening the door. "Glad you're here. Come in and make yourself at home."

"Thank you." The fork slipped from my fingers. "It's so nice of you to let me stay."

I got out of my seat and poked my head into the hall. No, I wasn't dreaming. Sofia Richards was truly standing in my entranceway. She waved.

"Hi, Val. Surprise."

Olivia was looking pretty pleased with herself. "Sofia called and said you two made up. She asked what our address was so she could send a present, and I told her to bring herself instead. Isn't this great, baby?"

"Yeah, it is." I meant it. Sofia and I patched things up, even though the rest of Evergreen didn't know. The fact was that I needed my best friend. I had to trust her. I held out my hands and she rushed into my hug.

"Turns out you were right about my parents not wanting me for the holidays," she said into my ear. "Madame Madeline is off to Spain to visit Dad, and they want alone time after being so long apart. I'd rather spend Christmas with you than in that empty house."

I squeezed her tight. "I hope you're still saying that after sleeping in a tiny room with me and an infant."

She laughed and we went straight to my room to unpack her things.

It was the best Christmas in fifteen years' worth of Christmases. The three of us stuffed our faces in front of the television watching Christmas movies. Mom took us to Santa's village where we loaded up on eggnog and got dozens of pictures of a screaming Adam on Santa's lap. On Christmas Day, we opened presents before having an impromptu dance party to the holiday radio station.

I was bordering on depressed when the sun dawned on January third. The new semester began today. Sofia had left the day before to get ready for school and now Mom was piling me in the car to drop me off to bodyguards, vicious classmates, and ruthless Knights.

As we got closer and closer to Evergreen, I got quieter.

It doesn't matter what they throw at me, I can survive it. I've been through hell worse than anyone can imagine. Nothing will break me.

"Alright, kid." Olivia pulled up to the gates and killed the engine. There was a long line of sport and luxury cars waiting to unload their own students. The air was filled with shouts and shrieks as friends met up with each other and parents said goodbye. "Have a good time. Call me if you need me."

"I will."

I kissed her cheek, told Adam I loved him, and climbed out of the car. I popped the trunk and reached in for my suitcase.

"Let me get that for you." A hand shot past my vision and closed around my handle.

"Hey!"

Ryder heaved my case out and slammed the trunk. I barely had time to leap out of the way to avoid getting brained. "Ryder, give it back!"

I lunged for the case and he moved quickly. He twisted it out of my reach and caught me around the waist in one smooth move. I was crushed to his chest, nose buried in his blue lapel, as he put his mouth to my ear.

"Uh uh," he whispered. "We wouldn't want Mommy Dearest to think something is wrong."

"Val?" On cue, Olivia spoke up. "Is everything okay?"

"What do we say?" Ryder hissed. His arm tightened.

I clenched my jaw. I hated him. I hated him with every fiber of my being, but Olivia was driving off, and I would be staying here... with him. It was better not to rile the psycho up even more.

"Everything's cool, Olivia," I called. "Ryder's just helping me with my stuff."

"Alright, love. I'm going to head out. See ya."

"Bye."

The car rumbled to life and Mom pulled away from the curb, leaving me with him.

At least there are witnesses.

The moment Olivia's car disappeared down the hill; I smacked my hands on his chest and shoved. "Get off me, Ryder!"

Winter break had been good for Ryder. His hair was growing in. The inch of new growth didn't yet match the look of his formerly long raven locks, but it still looked good on him. Everything looked good on him. From the large watch digging painfully in my side to the new silver stud in his ear. It was against the rules for boys to wear earrings, but he wasn't letting that stop him.

His silver orbs gazed down at me, completely uncaring about my struggling. "You and I need to have a talk about the way things are going to go."

"You need to let me go," I shot back, "before you get smacked."

He smirked. "Biting. Hitting. You're barely a step above an animal."

I was reeling my hand back to show him what I thought of that when he abruptly dropped me. "Calm down, Moon. We're just talking."

"I don't have any interest"—I dove for my bag—"in talking to you!"

Ryder stepped to the side and I flew through the space he was standing in. "Shut up. Let's go." He took off, forcing me to run to keep up with him.

"You think you're real smart," he began, "getting a bodyguard to watch your ass." Ryder passed through the gates of the school. His long legs strode over the cobblestone path, gliding through the crush of students. "But you don't think that's going to stop us. You're marked, Moon. That's never going away."

"I didn't ask them to assign me a bodyguard. I didn't need one then or now." I darted out in front of him and planted myself in his path. "I'm not afraid of you."

Ryder looked me up and down in a way a farmer checked out a fatted calf to be slaughtered. "No, you're not. But you should be."

Folding my arms, I stood my ground. "You think I don't know why you're doing this. I heard about the Spades, Walter

McMillian, and the history of cowards that went along with this school's barbaric traditions instead of fighting them."

Ryder laughed. It was a sound without mirth. "What can you do? Quae sequenda traditio."

"But I didn't think you were so pathetic, Ryder."

The smile melted off his face. "Excuse me?"

"The tough Ryder Shea—running so scared from the Spades that he jumps whenever a card appears in a locker. I understand why everyone else is too pathetic to stand up to them, but I thought you had backbone." I treated him to the same dissecting look he gave me. "Just one of the many ways you disappoint."

Ryder's face could have been chipped from granite for all the expression he showed, the same couldn't be said for the look in his eyes. I always felt deep down that Ryder wanted to hurt me. That he wanted me broken and bleeding at his feet. This was the same look he gave me when he threw me in the pool. The look in his eyes when he promised to get my mother arrested.

His free hand rose—slowly, unhurriedly—and wrapped around my neck. I swallowed against his palm as cool fingers pressed on my throat.

"This is what you don't seem to understand, Valentina." His grip wasn't tight enough to choke, but a thread of fear wrapped around my spine. I didn't fight him when he drew me to himself. "I'm not hurting you because you're marked." His thumb traced a lazy pattern on my neck, enticing goose bumps to break out on my body. "I'm doing this because I want to. Because there is nothing I enjoy more than seeing you cry."

My lower lip began to tremble and I bit down on it hard. He wouldn't see me react.

Ryder bent his head until his face was hovering millimeters from my own. "I'm not afraid of the Spades," he said, his breath ghosting over my mouth. "They've given me everything I've ever wanted: to be a Knight and to see you broken."

"You won't break me," I whispered.

"I will," he replied like he was stating a simple fact. "Marked or not, it was always going to end this way." Ryder's silver orbs swept over my face, unease filled me when the look of them began to change. "It's a shame though. You've gotten so beautiful."

I gasped when the pressure on my neck increased ever so slightly. Fear competed with my shock. *Beautiful? What was he saying?*

"Ryder," I croaked. "Let me go."

He cocked his head. "Do you remember our kiss, Val?"

"No."

He laughed. "Liar, but that's okay. Maverick and Ezra tell me that's another way you've gotten better with age."

A flush crept up my neck. "I said let me go."

Ryder didn't appear to have heard me. He was still stroking my neck—an intimate gesture so out of tune with the secret promise to throttle me. My heart was rocketing out of my chest and beating against his. My palms felt slick with sweat. I needed to stop this. Smack him. Throw him off. Run. *Something!*

My brain screamed at my frozen body as Ryder closed the distance between us and pressed his lips to my mouth. "Maybe before this is all over... I'll steal another one."

"You won't." My lips puckered on the last word and caressed his in a way that could have been a kiss. But it wasn't. This—like everything with Ryder—was a game. "Because if you try... I'll bite them off."

He chuckled, his laughter rolling out of his chest and transforming into warm air on my lips. "I'd be worried about that"—his hand tightened—"if I couldn't feel your pulse."

"Excuse me? What is going on here?"

Just like that the hand disappeared.

"Valentina," Noemi's voice broke through. "Are you okay?"

Words were too difficult at that moment so I nodded. My bodyguard stepped up to me and pointedly put herself between us, forcing Ryder back. "Is there something you need, Mr. Shea?"

"I've got everything I need." Ryder held up his hand and released my bag. "See you around, Val."

I rescued my stuff off the floor once Ryder was well and truly away. Together, Noemi and I walked past hostile faces on the way to my room, and I looked around and sighed.

"Welcome to another semester at Evergreen."

SOFIA SNUCK INTO MY dorm that night after curfew. I had never met Gus or the rest of the security team, but we were trusting them not to reveal we were hanging out again.

"I can be like your spy," she said as we flicked through our movie choices. The two of us were lounging on my bed getting ready to queue up Netflix like we did over winter break. "I'll warn you whenever I overhear someone plotting some shit. We can have a code word like we did when Ryder was around."

I pulled out the pack of Oreos I had snuck in my bag from home. I tossed them to her. "I love it. It can't be too weird though. Something people would believe you'd randomly say to me."

She hummed around a mouthful of chocolate and cream. "How about... virgin?" She clapped, falling for her own idea. "That's perfect. Everyone is calling you that anyway. If I say it, no one will think twice."

I tapped my nose. "Pretty and smart. You'll go far in this world, Sofia Richards." Laughing, I ducked when she sent a pillow flying at my head. "I'm lucky I have you on the inside." A bit of unease pushed through my amusement. "Ryder is saying they're going to get more creative this semester—bodyguard be damned."

Sofia's fingers stilled on the keyboard. She gave me a look that would have been reflected in my eyes if I would allow myself to give in to fear. No matter what Ryder believed, he wouldn't break me.

"But he won't— They won't touch you," she reminded. "No one is allowed to hurt you."

Visions of crackling fires and ripped photos flashed through my mind. "There are other ways to hurt someone," I said simply. "Plus, not everyone is as obedient to the Knights as you think. Natalie had no problem sending me skidding along the track."

"That won't happen again. Noemi has your back, and Ryder is just trying to get in your head. I'll bet he'll be too busy to invent new ways to torture you. This last semester is the most important. Our grades are weighted heavier and if we don't pass, we're out."

I groaned. "You know, normal high schools don't have a GPA cutoff. Especially as high as 3.5."

Sofia patted my arm. "You haven't figured out yet that this isn't a normal high school?"

Now it was my turn to whack her with a pillow. She screeched and set off the pillow fight of the century, but even while I laughed, part of me knew she was wrong about him.

Ryder would never be too busy to torment me.

"BREAK WAS AWESOME."

I put my phone in its slot and closed the wooden door. Jaxson's voice floated to me as I walked to my desk. A bunch of students surrounded him, all obsessed with hearing about his vacation.

"Dad had The Undisturbed in for a few recording sessions and I heard their entire new album."

One of the girls, Michaela, gasped. "Jaxson, that's amazing. I love that band." She scooted her seat closer and slipped her hand under his blazer. "I'm so jealous," she purred.

I barely restrained myself from rolling my eyes. It was incredibly cool and I'd sell my teeth for a chance to look at The Undisturbed, let alone listen to their recording sessions, but still it rankled seeing that smug look on his face.

"Course you are," the ass replied. "But if you're good, I'll let you listen to a few tracks. Dad would flip shit if he found out, but I snuck my phone in and recorded a few tracks."

Michaela giggled. "Oh, I'll be good."

It couldn't be helped. I kissed my teeth loud enough for their eyes to fly to me.

Jaxson lifted a brow. "Got something you wanna say, baby?"

I put my books on my desk and folded my arms. "Nope. Nothing except to remind you I'm not your baby. Why don't you *record* that and play it whenever you forget."

A smile curled his lips. "You won't believe this, but I missed you over the break."

"You did?"

He nodded, his smirk growing wider. "But whenever I wanted you too badly, I pulled up the sight of you in that towel—strutting that ass for everyone to see." He winked. "That got me through the cold nights."

Michaela glanced from me to Jaxson. From her glower, she didn't like his not-so-subtle implication.

"You're disgusting, Jaxson."

"Come on, Val. When are you going to stop playing hard to get?"

I smiled at him. "The second you stop playing impossible to want."

"Ooh." He flinched theatrically. "She comes back with a good one. But you shouldn't have told me that. Now I know I've got a chance."

If things had been different, I would be hiding a smile at falling into this familiar dance. But things weren't different. There would be no finding a stairwell and banging it out. I'd never forget that Ryder and his buddies had made me a bet.

"You have no chance," I said honestly. "But the sad thing is, you might have if you hadn't been such a... you."

Jaxson's good-humored expression disappeared, and I knew my strike landed. He clicked his tongue. "Whatever. I don't have time to waste on you anyway." Jaxson turned back to Michaela who lit up at having his attention again. I was dismissed.

It was a relief when homeroom was over. I couldn't stand to hear Jaxson's bragging or Michaela's giggling. It had gotten to the point where their flirting had gotten pornographically detailed and I wondered how everyone in their vicinity wasn't blushing.

I stomped out of class with Noemi on my heels. "You okay?"

"I'm fine."

"That guy your ex?"

I almost tripped. "No, he's not! What guy?"

She gave me a knowing look. "Why'd you say no if you don't know what guy I'm talking about."

I huffed. "He's just a flirty jerk who I used to think had a good side. I was wrong."

"Everyone has a good side."

My eyes were drawn over her shoulder. Across the marble floors, Ryder sauntered down the hall alongside Ezra. Ezra must have said something funny because he threw his head back and laughed—infusing his glacial features with warmth. As I looked at him, I could feel his soft lips on mine.

I could feel his fingers on my throat.

"Not everyone," I replied. I picked up my feet and continued to English class.

Professor Strange was up and standing behind her desk as we filed in. I walked past Sofia on the way to my desk and she tossed me a wink.

"Good morning, class," Strange began after the bell rang. "Welcome to another semester at Evergreen."

There was a polite applause.

"As I'm sure you're not surprised to hear," she continued. "Your workload will only get more rigorous as you pursue your journey to graduation. My job is to prepare you for that."

I do not like where this is going.

"This semester you will be undertaking a special writing assignment. You will choose one famous writer in history and craft a detailed paper analyzing their body of work, characters, setting, prose, imagery, etc. You will couple this with a biography of their life." Strange's wrinkled face shone with excitement. It was the only one. "Both papers will be due at midterms and presented to the class. This will comprise a quarter of your grade. Any questions?"

A boy in front of me raised his hand.

"Yes, Mr. Myles?"

"Will we have partners?"

She shook her head. "This is a solo project and no two students will share the same author. Today you will choose your writer and tell me by the end of class. First come, first served."

That set off a chorus of paper ruffling and unzipped bags. No one wanted to be stuck with some obscure random guy, or worse, one that wrote a thousand novels they'd have to compare. But I didn't reach for my laptop.

I stood and approached Strange's desk. She peered curiously at me over her glasses. "Yes, Miss Moon?"

"I'd like Aldous Huxley."

"I see, and are you familiar with him?"

The class fell hushed behind me. "Yes. Aldous Leonard Huxley. English writer born 1894."

She hummed, looking pleasantly surprised. She was already reaching for her pen when she asked, "Why Aldous Huxley?"

"Because he saw the world around him for what it was and wasn't afraid to call it out. He knew the society he lived in needed to change—to be better." I turned slightly, letting my voice carry. "And he reminds us that we need to challenge the problems in our society, not blindly go along with them." I shifted back to face her. "Plus, he's got a great quote about the power of music that I've loved since I was little."

Strange clapped. "Very well said, Miss Moon. I look forward to your presentation."

I returned to my desk, passing Natalie and Airi's table on the way. "Go back to sucking dicks," Natalie scoffed. "Your mouth is a lot better at that than preaching."

Half the class burst into laughter.

I sighed. *It begins.*

ONE THING SOFIA WAS right about was that this semester would keep us busy. For the next few weeks, I practically lived in the library. With all the projects, assignments, tests, and homework, I didn't have time to worry about whispered insults, the threats, or the website the Diamonds had created for me listing all the sex acts I'd perform. The assholes topped it off by linking my school email to the site and now every day I opened it to at least a half dozen messages from pedophilic old men.

Sofia had to talk me down after I read the first few messages and what those men wanted to do to a fifteen-year-old girl. In the end, we decided to forward all the emails to the police, but I still had nightmares for a week.

The fact is the Diamonds operated on a whole other level of vicious, proving their desire to be the best. They were almost as bad as the Knights, but those guys were awful in a different way. At least the Diamonds came at me head-on. The Knights were being worryingly quiet.

There had been nothing from them since the start of school. Maverick continued to not say a word to me. Ezra plastered his bland smile on his face when he passed me in the halls. Jaxson had seemed to grow tired of propositioning me for sex, and Ryder...

I sunk onto the couch and balanced my spicy carrot and hummus sandwich in my lap. The Knights' room was even messier than usual. Apart from their usual gears, gadgets, records, and schedules, the place was loaded up with textbooks and library borrows. Midterm exams and presentations began the next day and they were clearly feeling the pressure like the rest of us.

I kicked a funny-looking robot thing aside and propped my feet on the coffee table. I quite liked eating in here. I liked the peace, the quiet, listening to Jaxson's music collection and, every now and then, moving things slightly out of place to get the boys scratching their heads. It wasn't much in the way of revenge, but I couldn't bring myself to sink to their level. The only thing that would truly piss them off is withstanding everything they threw at me.

Sighing contentedly, I got comfy on their couch and polished off my crunchy sandwich.

After classes I'll have to redo my section on Brave New World. Probably should have picked an author that wrote pulpy entertainment but I had to make a point.

I reached for my banana bread. *Good thing I'm almost done writing the—*

Click.

My eyes snapped to the doorknob. Time slowed as the knob turned and the bread slipped through my fingers. In the seconds it took to bounce onto my plate, the door had swung open to reveal Maverick.

Our eyes locked—surprise mirrored on our faces. I opened my mouth to say something, anything, but only a croak came out.

In a blink, Maverick's face smoothed out. He stepped inside. "So this is where you go."

The tray clattered to the ground as I lurched to my feet. "Maverick, I—"

"We wondered where you disappeared to every day and the whole time you were hiding out here." He inclined his head. "Smart." Maverick let the door swing shut and then positioned himself in front of it.

"Yes, it was." I stepped over my mess. "And now I'm leaving so if you could move—"

Maverick reached behind him and I heard a soft click. "No."

I blinked. "No? What do you mean no?" Advancing on him, I grabbed his arm and tugged. "Get out of the way. I won't come into your stupid clubhouse again, so—"

"No, I didn't know."

I tugged harder. The guy was a block of stone. Honestly, they shouldn't be allowed to make fifteen-year-olds this big. "What are you talking about?! Just move!" I wouldn't lie, I was starting to panic. I knew the boys wouldn't take it kindly if they ever found me in here, but I wasn't expecting to be locked in with no one around to help. "Maverick, I swear, if you—"

"About the video or the private investigator."

I stopped as his calm words penetrated. "What?" I breathed.

"I didn't know about it, Val. That Ezra was going to broadcast that video or that Ryder found your father."

I gazed at him; eyes wide. Maverick didn't look blank now. His face was tight, forehead scrunched up as though saying this pained him. "I didn't know about any of it, Valentina."

"But... you wouldn't have stopped it if you did."

He pressed his lips together, but didn't deny it. I dropped my hands and stepped back. "I don't know what to do with that, Maverick. I don't know why I asked you at all because it doesn't change anything. It doesn't change the fact that you guys made a bet over me. It doesn't change that you've done nothing but lie to me since we've first met."

"No."

"What do you mean no?" I cried, throwing up my hands. "You can't tell me it didn't happen. I was there."

"I didn't lie about everything."

"Really? Then what were you honest about, Maverick? Tell me."

"This."

That was all the warning I got before Maverick seized me and crushed me against his body. My cry was quickly swallowed by his lips. Despite the almost feverish way he kissed me, his hands were gentle as he curled them around my waist.

What the fuck does he think he's doing?!

Rage swelled within me, hot and pulsing as it beat out the shock. He can't just—

Maverick slipped his hand under the fabric of my shirt and brushed his thumb along the tender, sensitive skin of my stomach. Electricity surged through my body and swept me under. A soft moan escaped my lips, parting enough for Maverick to deepen the kiss. My anger fled like a bat exposed to light, and the hands meant to push him away, traveled over the ridges and dips of his muscles and settled on his neck.

Kissing Maverick was like being plunged into a roaring fire. My body sizzled with heat that promised to overwhelm and burn me away. His fingers skimmed the top of my skirt and the feel of him on my skin made me quiver. He didn't try to head higher or lower, but I could only guess at the effect it would have on me if he did.

The thought no sooner crossed my mind than the hands disappeared. Before I could miss the loss, Maverick was grabbing my thighs and lifting me up. He carried me to the couch and sat us down without breaking our kiss. I was straddling him, rocking against his lap, as his hands moved up my thighs and slipped under my skirt. I didn't know if I was thankful or regretful that I had put on a thong that morning.

Maverick cupped my cheeks.

Definitely thankful, I thought as another moan escaped my lips.

We broke apart, our breaths ragged as he gazed at me through hooded eyes.

"So beautiful," he whispered.

"You've gotten so beautiful."

Ryder's words slid through my mind and brought me crashing back to reality. What the hell was I doing?

I yanked Maverick's hands off my ass and scrambled off of him.

"Val, wait!"

I didn't stop. I tore out of the Knights' room and didn't look back. I'd have to find another place to eat lunch.

"I'M SORRY, I MUST HAVE hallucinated. There's no way I heard you right."

I paced up and down the carpet. My body was brimming with too much nervous energy to stay still. "You definitely heard right."

Sofia gaped at me from among my sheets. "You and Maverick Beaumont kissed. Again?!"

I winced. Flashes of seeking fingers and soft moans plagued my mind. "Kiss is too small a word for what we did."

"What? You had sex?!"

"No!" Heat flooded my cheeks at the thought. "I only meant we got carried away."

"What are you going to do now?"

I groaned. Veering off, I flopped down face-first on the bed, narrowly missing Sofia. She patted my head.

"It'll be okay."

"I have no idea what came over me," I moaned into the comforter.

"I do. You were alone in a room with a hot guy who clearly knows what he's doing. It's no wonder you can't keep your hands off of him. You two had chemistry before all this started."

"You mean when he was playing me for a bet," I shot back. I pushed myself up and sat cross-legged. "All of this is new to me, Sof."

"Making out?"

"Making out, chemistry, dating, crushes, getting felt up, being betrayed by smirking assholes. People hated me at my old school and guys avoided the weird girl with holes in her clothes like the plague. I don't know what I'm doing here, but I do know I can't do it with him. I can't be with a guy I don't trust."

She hummed. "You should probably stop kissing him then."

I promptly shoved her into the pillows. Sofia went down laughing, but she was right. I needed to channel all of my energy into surviving the semester and the students so desperate to get me out—the Knights among them.

"ARE YOU EATING IN YOUR secret spot again?"

"I'll be in my room. It's taking longer than I thought to finish my Huxley paper and it's due tomorrow. I'll be working on it all day so get ready for another trip to the library."

Noemi shrugged. "Alright. Then I'll walk you and then head back to the security office."

Morning classes had just let out and we were on our way to the lunchroom. My run-in with Maverick the day before had seen to it that I was back to eating in my room. The result of getting discovered by Maverick was... interesting. I didn't want to guess what would happen if Ezra or Ryder had found me.

As expected, my paper demanded my attention all through lunch. I had one hand on my tuna wrap and the other on my laptop, and I still wasn't done by the time Noemi came to get me.

"Haven't you been working on this for weeks?" she asked as the elevator dropped to the ground floor. "What else is there to say?"

"I have to write about his life on top of fourteen different novels. I'm on my last one, *Brave New World,* but that's his most famous novel so I have to knock it out. Strange has given me nothing but Bs all year. This time I'm getting that A."

"You deserve it for the work you've put in."

I got through the rest of my classes and took off for the library the moment they let out. I went to my spot in the back and pulled out my book and laptop. Consumed by my work, I didn't look up from my screen until a voice broke the silence.

"This project is stupid as shit. Who has ever even heard of James Joyce? Let alone cares enough about the guy to want twenty pages on him?"

I peeked over my screen and watched the Knights file in.

"Why are you complaining?" asked Ezra. "Maverick's got Agatha Christie and the woman wrote sixty novels. He's been writing that paper since five minutes after she assigned it."

"Ricky likes reading and all that smart shit." Jaxson was ignoring the dress code once again. His shirt was open to the waist and his blazer nowhere to be seen. He ran his hand over his growing blond spikes and shot Maverick a grin. "Don't let that football thing fool you; the guy's a nerd."

Grinning, Maverick shoved Jaxson and almost sent him to the floor.

"Seriously, man," Ezra deadpanned. "How did you get into this school?"

Jaxson dropped his bag and did a little spin. "Charm. Good looks. Dad's an insanely rich and famous record producer. You pick."

Ryder threw himself into a chair and laced his fingers behind his head. "Well, it's definitely not the first two, so I'll go with number three."

"Haha. The boy's got jokes. But I've got this." Jaxson flipped him off and the boys burst out laughing.

Seeing them like that I couldn't deny how close they were. A friendship that made no sense to me but here they were.

I must have stared for too long because Maverick's eyes flicked up and found me across the room. Heat spread through my body. I didn't know how to be around him before the Knights' room incident; now I definitely didn't know what to do.

Despise him. Ignore him. That's what you do.

I sighed at my internal voice. It was right. It was the only choice.

Maverick smiled. A small smile that was just for me, then he sat down with his boys.

I gripped my book tighter than necessary. It was the only choice, but that didn't mean it was an easy one.

After a minute, I returned to my paper and the library was quiet again. The Knights had taken up studying. Ezra, Ryder, and Jaxson either didn't know I was in the room or they didn't care. Jaxson and Maverick were busy typing away on their laptops while Ryder and Ezra bent over the same textbook studying for their own midterms.

The clock ticked down and every second brought me closer to being done with this paper. I beamed when I hit my final paragraph. This was going to get me that A; I had no doubt.

"Maverick." Ryder's voice broke the silence. "Get it done and let's go."

"Right. One minute."

The boys were tossing their books in their bags and gathering their stuff. Maverick bent over his laptop, his fingers a blur as they flew across his keyboard.

I bent my head and went back to my project. *How to sum up fourteen books and the impact he made—*

A notification popped up on the bottom of my screen. I was going to ignore it until I noticed the name.

Email Notification: mbeaumont@evergreen.edu.

Maverick.

I stilled. Why would he be emailing me?

You know why. You devoured his face like he was a triple cheeseburger and you were a vegetarian looking to binge.

I hesitated for a few more seconds before navigating to my email. His subject line stood stark on the screen.

Give me a chance to explain...

Was there any point in this? There was no explanation that he could give me that would make yesterday anything other than a mistake. I should delete it unread. Forget about that kiss and keep in mind the awful things he had done.

I clicked the email.

Val,

You have every right to be pissed at me, but you need to know that not everything was fake...

That simple line was followed by a link. I did have every right to be pissed at him, but if Maverick had something to prove to me, then I wanted to know. I deserved an explanation. I clicked the link and a small window appeared at the bottom of my screen.

I squinted. *What the hell was this?*

A stream of random words and numbers flooded the window, scrolling so fast I couldn't make it out. I leaned in closer for a look when the screen winked out. I gazed uncomprehendingly at the blackness. The soft hum of the laptop faded under the slowing fan.

No.

I tapped the on button as the laptop stopped humming. Nothing happened.

I tried again. Then again. Then I held it down so hard my finger turned white.

No. No, no, no!

I leaped out of my chair, startling Noemi into dropping her book.

"Valentina? What's wrong?"

I couldn't speak for the lump that had lodged in my throat. I took a step toward the door and wobbled. I fell down hard in my seat and caught only a glimpse of Maverick's blazer as it closed behind him.

"VALENTINA, ARE YOU okay? You've been acting strange since you ran out of the library last night."

Everything went dark as I pressed the heel of my palms to my eyes. I was dull and achy all over, and not only physically. "I'm fine, Noemi."

"Okay, but if something is wrong—"

I tuned her out. Well-dressed, polished students streamed past me in blue blurs. I couldn't make sense of their noise; it devolved from words to a meaningless *whomp, whomp, whomp.* My feet carried me to Professor Markham's door but didn't stop. I walked past and kept going until I was standing outside of the English classroom. There was no point in putting it off.

"Miss Moon." Strange looked up from her computer with a smile on her face. "What can I do for you? I hope you're all set for today. I'm eagerly looking forward to reading your report."

I fisted the hem of my skirt to still shaky fingers. "Professor, that's what I wanted to speak to you about—"

"I'll wait outside." Noemi patted my shoulder. I waited for the soft click of the lock before I tried again.

"What is going on, Miss Moon?"

"Professor..."

Why drag it out? Just get it over with.

"Professor, my computer was infected with a virus and I lost e-everything." My voice caught, but I pushed on. "The paper and... everything. I stayed up all night trying to retype what I lost, but it's not finished."

Strange's normally pleasant smile disappeared. "What have you completed?"

"I have the biography, but I don't have the novel comparisons."

"I see."

How could two simple words make me flinch, but I did all the same. "But if you give me more time, I can give you the rest. I swear it was all done. If it wasn't for my computer—"

Strange held up a hand and stemmed my rush of words. "Miss Moon, you are well aware that I do not accept late or incomplete work."

"But, Professor, it wasn't my fault. The virus—"

She shook her head. "You should have backed up your work. I'm sorry, Miss Moon, but it is your responsibility to be prepared for class, and mine to hold all students to the same standards.

Giving you more time is unfair to the students who worked hard to have their presentations ready on time."

"But it wasn't me!" I burst out. "My laptop was infected on purpose."

"On purpose?" A frown formed in the corner of her mouth. "Do you have proof of this?"

"Well, no, but—"

"Then how am I to know you didn't procrastinate and are now using sabotage as an excuse."

"Because I can show you the piece of junk that used to be my laptop!"

Her frown deepened. "I'm sorry, but that wouldn't change anything. You will receive a zero on this assignment."

The words pierced through me, sticking in like pushpins until my lungs popped under the assault. I couldn't breathe.

This wasn't happening. Please don't let this happen.

"With a zero on this project, your grade will drop to a D," she relentlessly plowed on. "Even if you get a hundred on the final exam, it won't bring you to the required seventy-five percent. I'm sorry, Miss Moon, but you will fail the year."

"But if I still have a 3.5—"

"It won't matter." Strange rose from her desk and stepped around to my side. Her expression softened into what could only be pity. "English is a core class. You cannot fail English I and expect advance to English II."

I cast about for anything that could save me. "What if I retake the class?"

"You can do that—"

Hope unfurled in my chest.

"—at another school."

"What?" I croaked, stepping back.

"Evergreen is an elite academic institution. Students do not retake classes here. I'm afraid there is nothing I can do, Miss Moon. In all likelihood, you will not be returning to Evergreen next year. I suggest you call your mother and begin making arrangements."

I staggered, falling against the desk like she had punched me. "But, Professor Strange—"

"The matter is closed." She stepped aside and pointed to the door. "Now I suggest you go. You're late to homeroom."

A thousand pleas sprang to my lips, but one look at Strange told me it was no use. After a minute, I unglued my feet and walked toward the door. Her voice reached me when I eased it open.

"—out of here. You should all be in class!"

"Watch yourself, bodyguard, or your next job will be chasing sticky brats in the mall."

There was no mistaking the owner of that voice. I stepped around Noemi and there they were. Jaxson, Ezra, Maverick, and Ryder took up the entire hallway with their presence. I knew they had been waiting for me.

Ryder forgot about Noemi and focused all his attention on me. His smile was terrible to see. "So that's it then. You're out."

I didn't speak.

"I promised I had plans for you, Moon." Ryder grasped Maverick's shoulder. The taller boy was expressionless. I barely recognized him from the guy in the Knights' room who held me and told me I was beautiful. "Something that not even your pet could protect you from."

"Now just a minute—"

I seized Noemi's arm and held her back. "Noemi, can you leave us alone, please?"

She spun on me. "What? No. I won't—"

"Please. I'll be fine."

She hesitated, looking from me to the boys. "Val—"

"Just go."

She looked like she wanted to argue some more, but the look in my eyes must have swayed her. "If that's what you want." She turned and left. It wasn't until the sound of her footsteps faded that Ryder spoke again.

"Say it, Moon."

I swallowed hard.

"Say it."

"I'm out. I'm going to fail the class and the year. Just like you wanted." The pressure was building behind my eyes, in my throat, throughout my whole body.

Don't cry. Do not let them see you cry.

"*Exactly* like I wanted," Ryder taunted.

"It had to be this way, Valentina," Jaxson spoke up from Ryder's other side. "You know how it works now. There was no way you could stay."

"Not when the Spades decided you had to go." Ezra picked up the line. "I don't know what you did that they chose you, but they would have made sure you left one way or the other."

My eyes cut to Ryder. *Don't know what I did to make them choose me? So he never told them about that night in the woods.*

I thought I saw something flicker in his eyes, but it was gone so fast I could have imagined it.

"It's right that it was us who got rid of you." Ryder broke away from the group and moved toward me. "I would have been disappointed if you had fallen to anyone else."

The pressure was swelling, rising, becoming unbearable. I bit my lip so hard it hurt. *I couldn't cry. Please, don't cry!*

Ryder didn't stop until we were only inches apart. He filled my vision—blocking out the other Knights and making himself the center of my crashing world.

"You never belonged here, Valentina." His voice was soft, almost gentle if it weren't for the words falling from his lips. "Where you belong is that disease-ridden slum with your whore mother and her second fatherless mistake."

I felt it well up and collect on my eyelids. I blinked and the tear dripped down my cheek and onto my mouth. That's when the pressure broke. I couldn't hold it in anymore and a sob choked me as tears rushed from my eyes.

"It's going to be okay," said Ryder. "Everything is going to go back to the way it should have been. There's only one more thing."

I didn't see it coming through the blur of my tears. In a breath, Ryder's lips were on mine, tasting the salty pain of what he had done to me and claiming his final prize. It was the barest of kisses—over before it even began.

Ryder turned and walked away without another word. The other boys followed him, not sparing me another glance as I sank to the floor and let the sobs come.

Chapter Twelve

What am I going to do?
        The cold seeped from the floor into my bare legs. They began to feel as numb as the rest of me.

After everything that's happened. Everything I've gone through; I'm going to pack my bags and go back to Wakefield.

My mind spun. *I'll lose everything graduating from here would have given me and... I'll never find out who took it from me.*

That thought lodged in my mind. My tears slowed as the full weight of that hit me. If I leave, I'll never discover why all this happened. Never know what I stumbled on in the woods or why the Spades wanted to make sure I never did.

If you leave... Ryder will have won.

My stomach heaved at the realization, and once that feeling broke through, a wave of emotions followed. I wasn't letting that happen.

Bang!

Strange jumped in her seat when the door flew open. "Miss Moon! What on earth do you—"

"I know you know." I marched up to her and planted myself in front of her desk. "I know you *all* know that I've been marked."

She visibly stiffened. "Now listen—"

"No, you listen." I leaned over and looked her dead in the eyes. "One night, I saw something I shouldn't have and everything changed. My friends and class turned on me, and my teachers abandoned me.

"I can accept that this is the way things will be, but I wonder if you can." Her eyes were huge behind her wire-framed glasses. "This is an elite school. One of the best in the world. I know you're proud to teach here. You love your job and care about your students, so unless you're a sadist, you can't be okay with what's going on.

"It must be bothering you deep down that your students have been hurt and there was nothing you could do, but this time you can."

"B-but I can't." She lowered her head. "I'm sorry, but no matter how I feel, I cannot give a grade for work I don't receive."

"Then don't," I announced. "Give me the zero. Just allow me the chance to make it up. Give me another assignment and I'll do it, whatever it is."

"It's not that simple."

"Yes, it is. It's not against any rules to give me a makeup assignment, especially when you didn't get the first one due to sabotage." I peered into her eyes, my desperation leaking through. "Please, Professor. I worked so hard to be here, and now a few bullies are going to take it away. You don't have to let that happen."

I fell silent after my speech and held my breath as a mix of emotions flashed across her face. With every second that passed, the vision of Ryder smirking his victory grew sharper in my mind.

She really won't change her mind? She's going to turn her back and let this stand when we both know it's wrong. She—

"Did you tell anyone else you didn't finish the assignment?"

I blinked. "What? No."

Strange's gaze sharpened. "Alright. Here's what we'll do." She lurched to her feet and my head swiveled to follow her as she hurried to the door and locked it. "You're sick today. Horrible bug that hit you suddenly and forced you back to bed. It couldn't be helped; you had to miss class."

I bobbed my head, barely believing what was happening. "Right. Awful. I've been throwing up for hours."

She nodded curtly. "Final midterm grades aren't due until the end of spring break. If you get me that paper by then, you'll get whatever grade you deserve."

Happiness swelled like a balloon inside me. "Thank you, Professor. Thank you so much."

"Miss Moon, I must impress on you the seriousness of the situation." She advanced on me and grabbed my shoulders in a grip that made me wince. "*You were sick.* That is what you tell everyone."

"I will. I promise."

"And you must give me the paper by next Friday morning. If there are any more problems, I will have no choice but to give you that zero."

"I understand."

"Good." She released me and stepped back. "Now get to your dorm before classes let out."

She didn't need to tell me twice. I darted out of English and beat it back to my dorm. I didn't waste a second on texting Sofia and telling her I needed her laptop. My tears were gone. The encroaching darkness that descended when Ryder claimed his kiss was pushed back. I was not leaving this school. Ryder, the Knights, and the Spades had met their match.

THE CAMPUS WAS A GHOST town over spring break. Ninety percent of the freshmen evacuated the dorms including the Knights. Only Sofia and I remained, but this break was not nearly as fun as the first. After getting through the rest of midterms—and enduring the shit-eating grin on Ryder's face—I threw myself into the paper. Sunup to after sundown, I rewrote every line, comparison, thought, and conclusion on Aldous Huxley's sixteen novels. I typed my last period at four a.m. Friday morning, three hours before my deadline.

"I'm done."

Sofia jerked awake. "Huh? What?" She blinked blearily at me from my bed. "Val, you finished?"

"Done." I pulled up my email and attached the paper for Professor Strange. I hit send riding a wave of triumph that made the last week of sleepless nights and sore typing fingers worth it. "I can't wait to see that fucker's face when they announce the grades."

"I'd love to see that too... but I'm not eager to see what comes after it. Val, you know he's not just going to give up. No one is."

"That's okay." I rose from my desk and slipped under the covers. I was long overdue for some sleep and I planned on spending the weekend doing only that. "He may not give up," I continued, "but neither will I."

MONDAY MORNING DAWNED early but not bright. The sky was heavy with dark clouds and the damp in the air seeped into my hair as I stepped out of the dorm. I kissed my teeth as my efforts with the flat iron immediately went to waste and tried to smooth down the frizz.

"Don't you have bigger things to worry about?"

I twisted around. I hadn't noticed the group of people posted up beside the entrance.

Isabella peeled herself off the wall. "I hear you're not coming back next year. We're finally going to be rid of you."

"But it would be nice if you didn't draw it out," Natalie chimed in. "Don't wait until the end of the year. Leave now."

I gave them my back and walked off. I had nothing to say to them. However, they weren't done with me.

"I'll help you pack your bags," Airi said as the three of them trailed me. "While we do, we can take care of that fuck you owe me. I've already paid you."

Their laughter rolled over me like smoke. Honestly, their vileness would make it that much more satisfying when they found out I wasn't going anywhere.

I crossed the quad and walked into the main building. I didn't miss the looks on passing faces as I went to my locker. I may not have said anything, but word had spread the Knights had succeeded: the heartless virgin whore bitch, or whatever they were calling me these days, was on her way out.

I stopped in front of my locker and spun the dial.

"Move!"

The shout was accompanied by a cry, a thud, and then the thunder of oncoming footsteps. I got my locker open only for it to be slammed in my face. I stared at the olive hand covering my locker number. "Good morning, Ryder. Something I can do for you?"

He leaned in, putting his mouth to my ear. "How the fuck did you do it?" he growled.

"Do what? You'll have to be more specific."

A hand grabbed me and spun me around. Ryder was blocked by the paper he shoved in my face. "How did you pass?"

I found my name on the list and went down the line.

A. A. B. B. B. A. A.

And then right under English I: **B.**

"How did I pass?" I repeated. "I studied my butt off same as you."

The paper crumbled in his fist and I got my first look at him. Ryder couldn't be described as cold or lifeless now. Over his shoulder, Jaxson, Ezra, and Maverick watched, each with different expressions. Jaxson looked annoyed, Ezra politely indifferent, and Maverick confused.

"You lost your paper. You said you were out!"

I shrugged. "Turned out I didn't lose it after all. It's amazing what a call to tech support can do. Now if that's all..." I made to go around him and his hand flashed out.

Ryder shoved me back, slamming me against the locker. My head bounced against the metal and I cried out.

"Ryder!" Maverick surged forward and grabbed his shoulder. He violently threw him off. "Fuck off, Rick!"

The stars didn't have a chance to clear before his hand was on my throat. I gasped, hands flying to my neck and clawing at him as he squeezed.

"I tried to do it the nice way," he hissed. Fire burned in his eyes—twin pools of molten silver that struck true fear in me.

There was no hint of mercy in those eyes, and there was no bit of surrender in mine. Black spots danced in my vision as his grip got tighter.

His hand was a steel band wrapped around my throat. I gave up trying to pull him off and lashed out, raking my nails across his face.

"Argh!"

I sucked in deep lungfuls of air as Ryder's hands flew to his face. He staggered back into Maverick's grip.

"Hold him," Jaxson ordered.

Maverick didn't need to be told. He wrestled Ryder's arms down and pinned them to his side. Ryder struggled viciously to get to me. The angry, bleeding marks on his face only served to make him more frightening. I didn't want to know what he would have done if Maverick let him go.

"Get him the fuck out of here," said Jaxson.

Maverick hauled Ryder up and dragged him away while he shouted awful things at me.

Ezra swept his eyes over the people watching; his face was deeply pale. "None of you saw a thing. You got it?"

Fervent murmurs of agreement echoed through the crowd as my shaky legs quit their efforts to hold me up. I collapsed to the ground in a heap, still clutching my throat.

"Get out of here. Now."

Our audience dispersed, racing off in a dozen directions like they couldn't get away fast enough.

"I'll go after Ryder," said Ezra. "You take care of this."

"Okay."

I jerked when a hand touched my back. "No," I rasped. Tears leaked from my eyes as I tried to crawl away. "Stop!"

"Relax." Jaxson put himself in front of my path and took my face in his hands. "I'm not going to hurt you." His thumbs swiped across my cheeks, wiping away my tears. "Come on. I'll take you to the nurse."

I didn't have a chance to protest before he was scooping me up in his arms. He cradled me to his chest and took off. If I wasn't so weak I might have fought to get away but as it stood, all I managed to do was bury my head in his blazer and cry.

Jaxson didn't say a word as he carried me to the nurse's office. Nurse Runyon leaped to her feet when we came in, demanding to know what happened, but he ignored her and set me down on a cot. Jaxson swept out of the room and it was just the two of us.

"What happened, dear?" She fluttered around me feeling my head, then pulling a blanket over me, then finally running to get me tissues. "Are you hurt? Did that boy do something to you?"

I couldn't respond. I hadn't stopped gasping since Ryder let me go.

Scratch, scratch.

My chest wouldn't stretch enough for the air to get in, or at least that was what it felt like. A stabbing ache, worse than my throat could ever feel, gnawed inside of me. I knew one thing for sure now. The pain that I had been trying to run away from would never go away. I would never truly be free.

THE KNIFE GLINTED IN the scant amount of light.

"Ryder!"

I raced through the woods. My bare feet trampled twigs and rocks that broke the tender skin but I ignored the pain.

Ryder struggled with the shadowed person, yelling things I couldn't hear. He threw them off and then lifted the knife. He turned and looked at me before he struck...

...and then I was looking at me.

The sight of myself running at me, face contorted with fear, confused me until the feel of something in my hand drew my attention.

I was holding the knife... and there was someone at my feet.

"Val?" A hand shook me, jarring me awake. "Val, wake up."

I shot up and threw the hand off. I scrambled across the bed until light flooded the room.

"Val, it's me."

"Sofia?" I looked from her to the clock as my racing heart slowed. It read one in the morning. "What are you doing here?"

"I came to check on you." Sofia pulled back the covers and crawled into bed. I didn't hesitate to fall into her hug. "Are you okay? It sounded like you were having a bad dream."

"Yeah," I whispered. "I have a lot of those."

She rubbed my back. "I heard what happened today."

What happened is that after Ryder choked me out, the nurse spent so much time trying to calm me down she eventually had to notify the rest of my professors that I wasn't going to class. She called in the doctor on staff and sat with me while she checked me out. Noemi found me in there, demanding to know why I had left her standing in front of my dorm.

What was I supposed to say? I left early so I would have the pleasure of seeing Ryder's face when he saw my grades. That turned out not to be such a pleasure.

"How did you find out?" I asked. "Ezra said no one was allowed to speak."

"Isabella told me. She showed up at my dorm after class demanding to know how you got around being kicked out. She's still on that money thing and won't believe that I don't know how you can afford the things you do."

If Sofia felt me stiffen, she gave no sign.

"Her idea now is that you have a rich benefactor who stepped in and saved you at the last minute, so she wants the names of literally everyone you've ever mentioned to me. I only just got rid of her so I could come here."

I laughed mirthlessly. "You'd think she'd give taking me down one day off considering what happened, but I guess that's why the girl doesn't lose. She never lets up."

She squeezed me tight. "Val, tell me you reported him. He can't get away with doing something like that."

"There's no point. It would be my word against his because I'm not stupid enough to think anyone is going to back me up."

"But he—!"

"Sofia, no. This thing with Ryder can't be settled by anyone else. It will always be between me and him. I'm the one who has to handle it." I pulled out of her arms and burrowed into the pillows. Between the nightmare and the day's events, I had invented a new level of exhaustion. "Let's just get some sleep."

She didn't argue with me any more. Sofia flicked off the lights and snuggled into my side. Despite my words, I stayed awake looking at the darkened ceiling long after she fell asleep.

I BRACED MYSELF FOR hell, but the days that followed weren't so bad. Noemi stuck to my side like glue, but even when she wasn't in earshot no one whispered their usual taunts or tried to pull anything. Regardless of Ezra's warning, the whole class seemed to know what happened with Ryder, and instead of shooting me nasty looks, they gave me uncomfortable ones.

Bullying me, sure. Almost killing me was apparently where they drew the line.

I didn't question it. If they were willing to back off, then I would enjoy it for as long as it would last. As for Ryder, I hadn't run into him since it happened, and during my daily trips to the lunchroom, I was careful not to look toward the dais.

I woke early that Friday and took my usual care in getting dressed. I was smoothing down my blue plaid skirt when Noemi knocked. I picked up my backpack and we headed out for homeroom. I was about to sit in my seat when Sofia brushed past me, knocking into my shoulder.

"Watch it, Virgin."

I watched her go with wide eyes. That was our code. *Someone was going to strike? Who? When? Damn this school and locking up our phones!*

I thought fast. "Professor Markham, I need to use the bathroom."

"Go ahead."

I hurried out of class and locked myself in the stall. *How long should I wait? What if she doesn't come?*

The door swung open. "Hello? You in here?"

"Sofia." I stepped out of the stall and went behind her to lock the door. "What's going on?"

"I don't know." She grabbed my hand and sat us down on the chaise. "I heard from Eric at breakfast that there was talk of hitting you again while you were down. He doesn't know who," she said quickly, no doubt seeing the look on my face. "That's all he heard from someone else who heard it from someone else—that you need to watch your back."

"But I can't do anything with that. Can Eric go back and find out more?"

"I'll ask him." She cursed. "It would be so much easier if Eric, Paisley, and Claire were on our side, but I'm too afraid to ask."

"They don't matter as long as you're on my side." I gave her a hug. "We should go before someone finds the door locked and wonders what we were doing in here."

"Be careful."

"I will."

"SECRET SPOT TODAY?"

Noemi strolled next to me on the way to the cafeteria.

"No more secret spot. I eat in my room from now on." That sounded especially appealing today. I had been fretting through all of my classes wondering what was coming next. I had already been humiliated, sabotaged, undressed, and choked. What more could they do to me?

At least in my dorm with the security system I once thought was too much, I would be safe.

I ran into the lunchroom, got my food, and practically ran out. Noemi walked me back to the dorm and said goodbye at the door. "I'll meet you back here after lunch."

"Alright. See ya."

I only fully relaxed when the lock clicked shut behind me. Setting my tray on the desk, I woke up my new laptop and resumed one of the movies Sofia and I had been watching.

I didn't want to go back, but soon the clock showed one o'clock, rudely telling me I had ten minutes to get to class. I closed my laptop, grabbed my things, and stepped outside.

I sighed. Noemi wasn't here yet.

She must have gotten caught up. I'll meet her on the way.

I trekked down the hallway to the elevator and groaned.

Out of Order.

Spinning on my heels, I jogged over to the stairwell. If I didn't hurry, I would be late. I burst through the doors and crossed the landing. *I'll have to finish that movie when I come back. It was just getting—*

Something unseen grabbed hold of my foot... and I was falling.

I screamed as the stairs rushed up to meet me. I tumbled head over heels, hitting every part of my body on the way down.

Chapter Thirteen

"Miss Moon? Valentina? Valentina, can you hear me?"

I peeled my eyes open and immediately regretted it. Light assaulted my eyes like two hot spikes. "Wha...?"

"Miss Moon, it's Doctor Miller. Speak to me if you can." I tried again to open my eyes. The white blur above me slowly came into focus. "Good morning, Miss Moon."

"Morning?" I cringed. My head was pounding.

"Yes, you've been asleep since yesterday."

"What happened?" My fuzzy, aching mind thought back. *I was in my room, then I left for class and—*

I gasped.

"Yes, it seems you remember what happened. You took a nasty spill, Miss Moon. Broke your wrist, dislocated your knee, and you got a concussion."

"But how?"

"It was an accident." Dr. Miller reached behind her and pulled up a stool. We were in the nurse's office in the room I had been in only days ago. It was a mark of how rich this school was that they could outfit a place for Band-Aids and boo-boos with a proper patient room and licensed doctor on staff. "Now, if you're up to it, I'd like to ask you some questions. If we get this out of the way, you can go back to resting."

It took me a minute to make sense of what she was saying. "Can I have... something for this headache first?"

"I can give you some ibuprofen, but for something stronger, I'll need more information first." She held up a folder I only now noticed she was holding. "This is quite an oversight, but your medical forms aren't completely filled out."

"Oh." I tried to push myself up and promptly gave up when my body screamed at me. "My mom was supposed to do all of that."

"It's no problem. We can do it now. First, I need to know if you have any allergies."

"Just one," I replied as I carefully eased myself back onto the pillow. "I'm allergic to azithromycin."

She hummed. "Okay, good to know. Next, have you ever...?"

Dr. Miller quickly went through the list. "Alright, that's it. Let me get you something for that headache."

"Wait, what about my mom? Is she here? Is she coming?"

Miller flashed me a smile. "Your mother hasn't been contacted."

"What?"

"When it was determined you didn't need outside care, we held off on calling your mother. We didn't want to alarm her."

My eyes narrowed. Who was "we"?

"You're free to tell her once you leave, of course," she finished. Miller patted my good wrist. "I'll get those painkillers. Your head must be splitting."

Miller slipped out of the door and I sunk back onto my pillow. Splitting was a nice word for what my head was doing. I heard the door open again and breathed an audible sigh of relief. I was taking those painkillers and going back to sleep, maybe pain wouldn't follow me in there.

"You look like hell, baby."

I might have snapped my head up if self-preservation didn't keep me still. I tensed as Jaxson stepped into my line of vision.

"What are you doing here?"

He grinned. "Came to make sure you're alright of course."

"Get out."

"Don't be like that." Jaxson plopped down on the stool. "If I wanted to see you like this, I wouldn't have made the no-physical-harm rule."

"You also made the rule that everything else was fair game. I made the mistake of letting one of you get close once." My hookup with Maverick and that stupid email roared through my mind. "I'm not doing that again."

He put up his hands. "Fine, I'll leave, but there's something I need to know first. Knight business so I'm not going until you tell me." Jaxson's grin faded, morphing into the serious face I rarely got to see. "Valentina... was this an accident?"

My fist curled underneath the sheets. I was shaking and was sure he could tell. "Would it matter to you if it was?"

Jaxson reached out and brushed the hair behind my ear. His fingers lingered, caressing my cheek before he pulled back. I wanted to say my treacherous body didn't respond—shivering the way it always did—but if that was the case it wouldn't be treacherous.

"Yes," he said softly. "It would."

"It was an accident," I said after a minute. "So your Knightly duties are over."

Thankfully, Jaxson didn't say any more. He backed out of the room, passing Dr. Miller on the way.

"Goodness. When did you get here?" she asked after him, but got no reply. She shook her head and handed me my painkillers. "Get some rest. You'll be sticking around for a while."

She didn't need to tell me twice. I swallowed the pills then shut my eyes to the world while I waited for the headache to subside.

I needed to have a clear head... because that fall was no accident.

I SPENT THE ENTIRE weekend in that bed before Dr. Miller sent me off with a knee brace and my wrist in a cast.

Sofia was waiting for me when I stepped into my room. She hugged me so hard I squeaked. "You know," I wheezed, "I didn't break a rib, but you seem to want to change that."

She laughed, but it sounded partly like a sob. "Shut up. I'm so glad you're okay. If they would just get those stupid elevators fixed!" she burst out.

I pulled back. "About that—"

"But there is good news," she plowed on. "At breakfast this morning, Jaxson announced that it's over." Sofia's eyes shone brightly with a mix of relief and unshed tears. "He said that if anyone touches you, they'll deal with him personally. Val, you're not marked anymore."

"Sofia, are you— Are you serious?" Of all the things I thought she would say that hadn't made the list. I could barely conceive of that. I had been living under the axe of that joker card for months, and now it was just gone.

"It's true. This means things can go back to the way they were."

Sofia pulled me into another hug.

"Wow," I breathed. I was happy too, of course I was, but I wondered if what this really meant was that Jaxson didn't believe this was an accident either.

IN SPITE OF SOFIA'S hope, things couldn't go back to the way they were—not for me. In the weeks that followed, I hobbled around on my bum knee to apologies, offers to make up and hang out, and tear-filled speeches about how they didn't want to treat me that way; they were scared.

Eric, Paisley, and Claire welcomed me back into the group, but it wasn't the same. Sofia came to me and apologized *before* the Knights gave her permission to act like a decent human being. They didn't.

As for the Knights, Ezra offered to tutor me again, but I walked away from him mid-sentence. I wasn't there yet. I didn't know if I would ever be. Maverick made no attempt to approach me. We kept up our regular routine of pretending we didn't see each other in the halls or during art class.

Jaxson was a whole other animal. The guy went back to flirting with me like the last few months never happened, but him I tolerated more than the others. Offering to sleep with me for money was awful, but still way down the list of broadcasting my mom to the whole school, using my deadbeat dad against me, destroying my work, choking me, or sending me tumbling down the stairs. I was at the point where I had to prioritize my enemies, and the person or people responsible for the last one were top of the list.

Even though I kept my eyes and ears open, the days ticked down to finals without me finding out who it was.

"I still think it was the Diamonds," Sofia said as we chilled in our favorite spot on the roof. "Lots of people were just following along, but those three went out of their way with bullying you. I think Natalie even enjoyed it."

My head was tilted back as I looked up at the stars. "You noticed that too."

"Yep. She freaked me out with the things she would say about you. Then there's..."

"Ryder," I finished.

"I mean, it happened the same week he tried to choke you."

I shook my head. "I've thought about it a hundred times, but I believe that if Ryder wanted to kill me, that's not how he would do it." I brushed my fingers along my throat. "He's a bare hands kind of guy."

"But he's also not a stupid kind of guy. Making it look like an accident keeps him out of prison."

"I don't know how we'll prove it was him or anyone else. The line that tripped me up was gone when I came back, and there are no cameras in the stairwells. I may never know who it was."

She leaned over and rested her head on my shoulder. "At least that psycho hasn't come after you again, and the Knights did the right thing. Tomorrow is our last day of finals and then two months away from this place." She looked up at me. "You'll come visit over the summer, right?"

"I'll try, and you can come stay with us too."

"I'd love that. Your mom is way cooler than Madame Madeline—something you'll find out when you stay."

We laughed and shifted to talking about our summers. The knowledge of what someone tried to do to me would always lurk at the back of my mind, but at least I would soon be home.

THERE WAS CHEERING—ACTUAL cheers when the final bell rang the next day. Sofia tackled me outside of class sporting two strawberry root beers.

"To celebrate," she announced.

I laughed and linked arms with her. We had one more thing on the agenda and then everyone was heading back to the dorms to pack.

Together the freshman class piled into the auditorium and filled in the rows. Sofia and I snagged seats in the middle, ignoring a wave from Paisley to join her, Eric, and Claire. She was still friends with them, but she respected that I needed time.

Headmaster Evergreen tapped the microphone and quickly got silence. "Hello, freshman class. I would just like to say congratulations on completing your first year at Evergreen Academy."

Whoops and cheers rang out again.

"We won't keep you long as I know you're all eager to get ready for your summer vacation. So let's begin the awards ceremony. Mr. Van Zandt?"

Jaxson jogged out from the back of the stage, waving his hands as he yukked up the applause. "Alright, everyone. Let's get this thing started because the limo is already running and I've got a year's worth of shitty junk food to devour. First, top GPA goes to...."

I tuned it out as the Diamonds got their accolades. It wasn't enough that they fancied themselves the best, but then the school had to go and confirm it too.

It's been so long since I've been home, I mused. *Adam turned a year old and I had to celebrate it over video chat. Maybe we could go somewhere this summer. It would be nice to—*

"And student of the year goes to... Valentina Moon!"

Wait. What?!

"Val, that's you!" Sofia grabbed me and hauled me up. She propelled me over the feet of my classmates and I stumbled up the steps of the stage in disbelief.

"We award student of the year to the person who exemplifies dignity, honor, integrity, and class." Jaxson rattled this off from his cards. I had no idea why the school kept choosing him as an MC but the headmaster was smart enough to give him a script.

I passed the line of students who had already been awarded. Isabella met my eyes and gave me a bland smile. Natalie didn't look at me at all.

I walked up to Jaxson and plastered a smile on my face. *This is probably the administration's way of apologizing after looking the other way when I was marked.*

The rest of the Knights sat in the front row with their eyes fixed on me. I looked away from them and sought Sofia. She had her phone out like the rest of the class, filming my big moment. She waved when she caught me looking.

"The student of the year is someone who we should all look up to as an example of the best of Evergreen Academy." Jaxson turned and beamed at me. I held out my hand for my award. "Which is why I can't give her this award."

My smile slipped. There was a lull as his final sentence penetrated the audience.

Headmaster Evergreen half rose out of his seat. "Mr. Van Zandt?"

Jaxson peered at him over his shoulder. "I'm sorry, man, but I can't do it." He tossed the cards aside and they fluttered to the floor. "How am I supposed to give her an award for dignity, honor, and class when she's got none of those things?"

A sick feeling churned my stomach. *No, not again. Don't do this.*

"For one thing, my girl's a liar."

I need to get out of here now. I backed away from Jaxson and hit a wall. I spun around and found the Diamonds were at my back. The smirk on Natalie's face curdled my insides. Six pairs of hands grabbed me and made me face Jaxson. They held me still while I struggled.

"She's not a virgin."

"What?!" I shouted. "Yes, I—"

Jaxson reached inside the podium and pulled out a folder. I froze. My denials lodged in my throat at the sight of my medical file. Why did he have that? How?

"Not only that," he continued, "but we called it on the slut thing. She had chlamydia."

The auditorium erupted into chaos—screaming, shouting, gagging, laughing, and chanting.

"Dis-eased Slut!" "Dis-eased Slut!" "Dis-eased Slut!"

With strength I didn't know I possessed, I ripped myself out of their hold and ran. A few of them gave chase, but once I escaped out of the back doors into the courtyard, they gave up. Tears blinded me as I bolted across the quad and tore into the dorms.

Sofia was not far behind me. She burst into my room minutes after I threw myself on my bed.

"Val?! Val?!" The bed dipped as she clambered up. I felt a hand on the back of my head. "Holy fuck, Val. I can't believe that piece of shit," she spat. "Please, don't cry. You didn't do anything wrong."

I sobbed and sobbed. Crushing, body-wracking cries that I was certain would never stop. Sofia spent almost an hour trying to console me. When my tears slowed, she guided me up and gently wiped my face with a blanket.

"It's going to be okay, Val. There's no way Jaxson is going to get away with breaking into your medical records."

I put my head in my hands. "The damage is already done. Whatever slap on the wrist he gets won't take it back."

"I... guess that's true." She put her arms around my shoulders and drew me in. "But still, you don't have to be ashamed. There's nothing wrong with not being a virgin—"

"I *am* a virgin!" My shoulders shook as my tears returned—hot and furious leaking down my cheeks. "I a-am! Rape doesn't count."

"R-rape?" Sofia's arms slackened and fell off my body. "Please tell me that this didn't..."

I lifted my head and looked her in the eyes. She went deathly pale.

I cried for hours. For a while, Sofia cried too. Eventually, we fell into an exhausted sleep. I would have welcomed the darkness, but mine brought me no comfort. The nightmare returned, and when it woke me in the middle of the night as it always did, I sat up in bed and stared through the darkness.

I didn't cry or shake or sweat. My body was still, but my mind wasn't.

That auditorium had been waiting for Jaxson's big reveal. It had been a setup from start to finish. Maybe even as far back as when I fell down the stairs and he declared the marking was over.

This was always coming.

A buzzing drew my attention to the nightstand. I answered Mom on the second buzz.

"Hello?"

"Hey, baby." A lusty wail came through the speakers. "Did I wake you?"

"No." I pushed back the covers and stood. "I was up."

My feet carried me into the bathroom. I flicked on the lights and got the full look of my puffy face, red nose, and ratty hair. I looked horrible, but it stirred no emotion in me. My green eyes were clear.

"It's Adam," Mom sounded in my ear. "He won't stop crying no matter what I do."

I placed my hand on my chest. No tightness. No gasping breaths. No deep ache like my soul was being scraped away.

"Can you talk to him? It might help if he hears your voice."

"Sure, Mom," I said easily. I reached out and opened my medicine cabinet. When my reflection reappeared, she was holding the scissors. "Put him on."

Adam's wails reached deafening. They battered against my ear as I placed the phone in the crook of my neck. "Shh, baby. It's okay."

Snip, snip, snip.

My long chestnut hair fell in clumps around me. "Don't cry, Adam. Mommy is here." My son's hiccupping sobs continued. "It's alright, baby boy. Listen to my voice. I'm right here."

I continued my crooning until the baby was down to soft sniffles. "Everything is going to be okay, son. Mommy is going to make it okay." I gazed at my reflection in the mirror. I didn't recognize her. That was good. I would need to be someone else to do what was going to happen next. "I'm going to make everything right again, Adam. I promise."

Broken

They broke me.

Ryder, Maverick, Ezra, and Jaxson didn't think I would come back for my second year.

The coldly cruel Knights of Evergreen believed the mark would be all it took to get rid of me... to keep me quiet.

But now I've got a whole new reason to stay. Those four will know a pain far worse than what I've endured.

They tore me apart until there was nothing left... and now I'm going to return the favor.

Mailing List

Join Ruby's Mailing list for news, teasers, and more:
https://www.subscribepage.com/rubyvincentpage

ABOUT THE AUTHOR

Ruby Vincent is a published author with many novels under her belt but now she's taking a fun foray into contemporary romance. She loves saucy heroines, bold alpha males, and weaving a tale where both get their happy ever after.

Made in the USA
Coppell, TX
05 April 2021

53139574R10166